# Exceptional Emma

## MARIE SOLEIL

To my Caleb,

I hope you know how exceptional I think you are.

# Contents

# Chapter 1

Today is a good day for a promotion.

I nervously bounce my leg, catching a glimpse of my newest pair of Christian Louboutin high heels—tan patent leather with the signature red sole. It must be a good sign, right? The day I wear my new shoes is the same day we have this impromptu company meeting. Which only means one thing: they're announcing a promotion.

I've been working my butt off for six years at this company. They hired me fresh out of college, a wide-eyed twenty-two-year-old with a degree in structural engineering and a mission to become a self-made woman.

Structural engineers work with architects to make sure buildings don't fall down. That's probably the easiest way to explain what I do. Here in Southern California, where the threat of earthquakes is always looming over our heads, it's a pretty big deal. After completing my four-year degree in structural engineering, which included a ton of math and physics classes, I started working here as a junior engineer. Then I got my professional engineers license two years later.

And now, at twenty-eight, I'm about to become an associate. I'll get more managerial responsibilities, a voice in running the company, and not to mention a few shares of stock. This has been my goal for the last six years, spending endless nights in the office, working until 2:00 a.m. to meet deadlines and please clients. Everyone loves me.

I've got this in the bag.

Jeff, the principal engineer in charge, stands in front of the small conference room full of employees. He waves his hands at everyone to get them to settle down, since his casual demeanor doesn't really intimidate anyone into silence. His blond surfer hair is longer than the typical business executive's, but he fits in here at Harbor Sands, Southern California.

"All right, everyone, let's make this quick so we can all go to lunch," he calls over the chatter. But, as expected, no one quiets down.

*Stop talking!* I want to shout. But I hold myself back, just as an associate would. Eventually, the predominantly male voices were quiet enough for everyone to hear him.

"Thanks everyone for being here on such short notice," he says. "I'll keep this brief, since we have lunch coming up soon. We have some very exciting news to share with you all."

I sit up a tiny bit straighter in my chair, pulling my long brown hair over my shoulder. Any minute now, everyone will look over at me, and I need to look my best.

"We're pleased to announce that we have a new associate in the company. Everyone please join me in congratulating..." I suck in a breath. "Samuel!"

Samuel.

Not Emma.

Not me.

A moment passes before the announcement registers. The sound of twenty people applauding echoes around me, taking an extra second to travel from my ears to my brain. Another second passes before I realize I should paste a smile on my face and clap, too.

Samuel looks genuinely shocked, as if he had no clue this was coming. It wouldn't surprise me if he didn't. He doesn't stay here until 2:00 a.m.

But I do.

His clients don't call the principals, raving about his commitment to their project and how much they appreciate the relationship he has with them.

But mine do.

I notice a few glances heading my direction, but I ignore them and smile at Samuel. Because I know what they're thinking.

*Hasn't she been here longer than him?*

*Doesn't she seem jealous?*

*Why didn't Emma get promoted?*

Or maybe they're not wondering.

Maybe they know something I don't.

"Thanks, everyone," Samuel says. "This was so unexpected. I look forward to representing the company and making you all proud."

Gag. I had such a beautiful speech prepared. I've been planning it for the last three years. How grateful I am to be at such an incredible company that leads the way in design, known in the community for fostering talent. How I can't wait to represent the company on a higher level, taking everyone's thoughts and feelings into consideration.

What a waste.

"We know you will," Jeff says, beaming. "All right, we'll see you all after lunch!"

Everyone stands and encircles Samuel, but I want nothing more than to get out of here. I stand, but my heel gets caught on a snag in the carpet, and I go down.

Flat on my face.

"Emma, are you okay?" I hear Jeff's voice above me.

*Don't think about how gross this carpet is. Don't. Think. About. It.*

"Yep. Just fine." I push myself up, which is especially difficult in my fitted dress. I was so proud of my red pencil dress and gorgeous new shoes when I got dressed this morning. Now I wish I had just worn slacks so I could get up from the floor without worrying about flashing everyone.

So much for escaping unnoticed.

"I'll see you later!" I squeak, and with a wave of my fingers, I scurry out of the room. The only thing I need right now is to get out of here.

I text my best friend Sharleen Ito, who should be done with her cosmetology classes for the day. Hopefully, she isn't in the middle of cutting someone's hair. *I got passed for the promotion.*

It doesn't take long for her response to come through. *Say WHAT?!?!*

I type back as fast as I can, willing the tears to stay behind my eyeballs. *Samuel got it instead. I feel like an idiot.*

I grab my purse from my cubicle, taking a moment to make sure everything at my desk is in place. My computer is logged out, my picture frames are angled perfectly, and Herbert, the hardy little green plant that sits on my desk in his smiling pot, has been freshly watered. All of my design plans from the architect are neatly stacked in a corner.

Sharleen sends another message: *Want me to come and teach him a lesson?*

I snort a laugh. Leave it to Sharleen to make me smile right now. *Nah, I think I can take him. But maybe we can do dinner tonight.*

I grab my keys and head out to get lunch. Even though I packed something to eat today, I need to get out of here. I slide into my car, the cute silver Audi I bought last year. At least that's the one perk of having a full-time job. Despite spending most of my life here, I have a few nice things for myself.

As I'm pulling out of the parking lot, my phone rings with a call from Sharleen.

"Hey," I say, answering the call.

"Hey. You okay?"

"Not really." I grip the steering wheel a little tighter. "But I need to get out tonight and forget about this awful day. I don't want to sit alone at home and wallow in my misery. Let's get dinner after work so I can unwind."

"I have a better idea," she says.

When Sharleen says she has a good idea, that usually spells trouble.

"I don't know," I say. "I'm not in the mood for something outrageous."

"Hear me out. Remember what Elle Woods said in Legally Blonde? About how exercise makes endorphins, and happy people don't kill their husbands?"

"Uh-huh," I say slowly.

"Well, I think you should come to hip hop with me tonight."

I don't even have to think about it. "Absolutely not."

"Come on!" she whines. "You'll have so much fun."

"Nope. Remember your cousin Hannah's wedding? I tripped over that little girl and couldn't walk for a week."

"There were other factors at play. I told you that was one too many glasses of champagne." She pauses a moment. "Look. I'll stand in the back with you the whole time. You'll be able to listen to some music, move your body, get all of that frustration out."

As crazy as it sounds, I can't deny that it might be *kind* of fun. Who *am* I?

"Plus," she adds, "I hear the new teacher is totally gorgeous. He was a backup dancer for Nova Sky."

That's pretty impressive. Nova Sky is basically the biggest pop star around right now. But I'm still not convinced. "You know I'm not interested in dating right now."

"But you could be..." she says, singing the last syllable.

I sigh. She's not going to let this go. "Fine. Okay? Fine. I'll meet you there."

She squeals out loud. "Yay! The class is at eight thirty, and I'll text you the address. Byeee!"

She hangs up before I can tell her I'm already in bed by eight-thirty, wrapped up in my fuzzy blanket with a pint of Ben & Jerry's and Planet Earth on the TV. I sigh again, wondering if I should call her back and tell her I've changed my mind. But in the end, I decide to stick to the plan.

How bad could one hip hop class be?

# Chapter 2

I am a starfish.

Well, not literally.

But I'm currently lying on my back, in the middle of a dance class, sprawled like a starfish. And no, this is not some cool new dance move. On the contrary, I tripped over my own two feet and landed on my butt, then flat on my back.

I'm talented like that.

I guess I shouldn't be so hard on myself. This is my first hip hop class—scratch that, my first dance class—*ever*, and I was doing okay. Until I tripped.

Besides, after getting passed for the promotion, there isn't much room for improvement on this terrible day.

But that's cool.

"Are you okay?" The (unfortunately) ridiculously good-looking instructor, Jacob, rushes over to my side and places a gentle hand on my arm.

I turn my head to look at him, his striking green eyes filled with concern. I swear I've seen him before, but I can't place him anywhere. My fingers itch with the desire to touch his hair. His dark curls are cropped short on the sides but longer on top, and they look super soft. From this close, I can see the stubble on his tanned cheeks, and I want to touch his face, too.

Yikes. Maybe I have a concussion.

"No. I mean, yes. I'm fine. I'm good." I push myself up on my elbows, finally realizing that I'm on the floor with twenty people watching me, and my cheeks flush with embarrassment.

He reaches his hand out to help me up, and the second our hands touch, I'm filled with warmth. Holy smokes. This guy is *literally* made of fire.

Once I'm standing, he holds onto my hand for an extra second, his eyes never leaving mine. "Are you sure you're okay, Emma?"

I swallow hard. I swear I'm normally more put together than this, but I'm having trouble forming a sentence around him. "Yes. I'm fine. Thank you."

He nods once, then turns his attention to the class. "While that was an impressive fall, let's try not to imitate that one. I don't have liability insurance, after all."

Giggles flitter around us, made up of all the women who are trying to capture his attention. Whispers have been flying all night, wondering why he's back home so suddenly after his successful career. Not that it matters when he's so good-looking. Everyone wants a piece of him.

I haul over to Sharleen, wincing a bit as I realize there's some pain in my tush from my fall.

"Seriously, are you okay? That looked rough." Her black hair with pink tips is gathered up in a ponytail, and it shakes around her face as she looks me over. Sharleen is in cosmetology school and loves experimenting with her hair.

"I'm fine," I insist, swatting at her. "We can't all be talented dancers, like you."

"Psh." She straightens and looks me in the eye. "You're doing great for your first time. I've just been taking classes forever."

"True." I observe the next group dancing the routine, studying their movements and trying to remember the steps, while Jacob watches and joins in occasionally. "This is pretty fun."

"It's *awesome*," Sharleen confirms. "You'll have to come back again."

"I don't know about that. It was kind of a spur-of-the-moment decision."

Sharleen rubs my arm reassuringly and makes a sympathetic noise.

It's her turn next, and I marvel as I watch my friend perform the moves. She's not professional level, since she just started taking dance classes for exercise a few years ago, but she's definitely better than me.

A thought hits me as I watch them dance.

*Emma.*

He said my name.

He didn't take roll, so there's no reason for him to know my name. Unless...*do* we know each other? I swear, I would have remembered this gorgeous man. I'll be on my deathbed, croaking out to anyone who will listen about the gorgeous dance instructor I met when I was twenty-eight.

Sharleen's group finishes, and thankfully, it's almost the end of class, so Jacob has the entire group perform one last time. I stick to the back row, not wanting to cause a scene, and dance with a little less energy. Better safe than sorry. After the music ends, Jacob leads a quick cool down and applauds to signal the end of class.

"Don't you feel better?" Sharleen asks as she skips over to me. "Nothing like a dance class to make you forget a horrible day."

"Yeah, I *was* feeling better," I say, poking her shoulder. "Thanks for reminding me about the promotion."

Sharleen winces. "Sorry. Wanna grab a drink?"

"Girl, it is *way* past my bedtime." I pull my bag over my shoulder. We walk past Jacob on our way out the door, who's being mobbed by the girls in class, either trying to get his number or get hired as backup dancers. I feel like I should thank him for the class, but I'm half-embarrassed, half-exhausted, and I don't want to communicate with anyone more than I have to.

"Emma! Wait!" Jacob calls out to me.

Sharleen furrows her brow at me. "How does he know your name?"

"I was wondering the same thing," I mutter, as Jacob breaks out of the circle of women and approaches us.

"I'm fine," I say quickly. "It wasn't that bad of a fall. But thank you for—"

"No, Emma, that's not…I mean, I'm glad you're fine…it's me, Jacob. Jacob Perez." He pauses for a moment. "Jakey?"

*Jakey.* Just that one word brings back a flood of memories and warms my heart. "Jakey!" I repeat, and I see the ten-year-old boy, my best friend in fourth grade, all grown up in front of me. How did I miss it before?

Well, he's definitely grown up, and looks like a man now. Back when we were ten, he was all knobby arms and legs. Now, he looks like he should be an action star in the latest superhero movie. His chest and arms fill out his long sleeve green shirt, and his navy sweatpants... Let's just say I didn't know sweatpants could look so good on a guy.

But I still should have put the connection together. My childhood best friend is back, the one who moved away to Los Angeles after fourth grade to pursue his career in dance.

His face lights in a huge smile, and *wow*. Did not expect my Jakey to grow up and be so...perfect. "I'd hug you, but I'm all sweaty and gross."

"Yeah, same." I don't say that I wouldn't mind a hug, even with him all sweaty, because that would be creepy, right?

Sharleen nudges my arm.

"Oh, this is Sharleen Ito," I say.

She sticks her hand out to meet his. "Emma's best friend."

I raise a brow at her, telepathically saying *Jealous, much?* She rolls her eyes, and Jacob shakes her hand.

"Jacob Perez. Emma's former friend." He lets go and looks me in the eye. "But hoping to make that current."

My heart races in my chest, and I know it's not just because we're done with the most intense cardio workout I've done in years.

"What are you up to these days?" Jacob asks.

I shrug. "Just working."

"Something with math, I'm guessing."

I smile. "Yep. I'm a structural engineer."

His face takes on the same blank expression as most people do when I tell them my job title.

"I make sure buildings don't fall down," I explain.

"Gotcha." He smiles. "I'd love to catch up sometime. I just moved back home after being on tour for a few years." He clears his throat. "Can I get your number?"

Dang. So forward. I kind of love it. "Um, sure." He pulls his phone out of his pocket, and I rattle off my digits.

"Emma...still Nazarian, right?" he asks, not looking up at me. I know what he's asking. He wants to know if I'm married.

"Yep. Still Nazarian."

I don't miss the small grin that teases his lips upward. He schools his face back to a friendly expression. "I just texted you, so you'll have my number too. I'd love to talk, but I have to get closed out here."

"Sounds good." I give a little wave of my fingers, then whirl around before I can say anything stupid.

"Oh. Em. Gee," Sharleen hisses at me once we're out of earshot. The lobby is filled with dancers gathering their bags and saying goodbye. "How have I never heard about this extremely handsome, famous dancer friend of yours?"

"Because I haven't heard from him in...eighteen years?" I push the entrance door open into the warm summer night air. "He moved to LA with his dad after fourth grade to pursue his dance career and never really wrote me or anything. I guess he did well for himself, though."

"Clearly." She looks at me with a mischievous glint in her eye. "So...are you going to go out with him?"

"Don't say it like that. He didn't mean that he wants to 'go out' with me. He just wants to catch up."

"Uh-huh," she says, unconvinced. "So, are you going to 'catch up' with him?"

I grimace. "I don't know. It seems too weird."

She sighs. "Well, while you decide, let's hang out this weekend. Just me and you on Saturday."

"Can't. I have a family dinner."

"Ah, the Mathletes and their cheerleader." Sharleen always gets a kick out of how my mom, siblings, and I are super math nerds, but my dad is...not so much. He's a nerd in his own right, with a private office no one can enter unless invited that is lined with incredible bookshelves. He's a huge history buff and has a ton of books on the Revolutionary War.

I pull my keys out of my bag. "But honestly, now that I got passed for the promotion, I don't have time for anything outside of work. You probably won't even see me much."

"You're kidding, right?" Sharleen stops dead in her tracks and turns me to face her. "I hardly see you as it is. I couldn't believe you agreed to come tonight. Planning a hangout during the week with you is like pulling teeth. You're *always* at work."

"Well, apparently it isn't enough." I cross my arms over my chest, keys jangling in my hands. "If I had been good enough, then I would have gotten the promotion, not Samuel."

"I don't know what they're thinking." She pulls me into a hug, and fight it as much as I try, I lean into her comfort. I haven't really expressed to anyone how I'm feeling. But she knows, even without me needing to say anything.

"You're amazing, Emma. I'm so proud of you and everything you've accomplished. You'll figure this out."

"Thank you," I say into her shoulder, then straighten and paste a smile back on my face. "I'm going to talk to Jeff tomorrow and see if he can tell me what I need to work on."

She purses her lips. "Well, let me know how that goes."

I unlock my car. "Thanks, girl. And thank you for inviting me tonight. I'm glad I came."

"Me, too." She hugs me one more time. "And I really think you should 'catch up' with Jacob."

"We'll see." I climb in my car, legs shaking like Jell-O. With a wave, I pull my car out of the parking lot and onto the road. As I drive home, I finally let all my feelings catch up to my thoughts. Disappointment in myself, knowledge that I wasn't good enough for the job. A touch of anxiety at the thought of asking my boss where I went wrong.

And, if I'm being honest, a little flutter of butterflies in my stomach, knowing that Jakey is back home.

# Chapter 3

My alarm buzzes at six thirty the next morning, just like it does every morning. But this time, I'm beyond *exhausted*. It's partly because I fell asleep with my phone in my hand, staring at Jacob's text and debating if I should write him back. I didn't come up with a solution. But beyond that, my body aches. That's what I get for going hard at a dance class when I haven't worked out in *years*. But exercise hasn't been a priority. Work has been.

Work.

I roll gingerly out of bed, trying not to aggravate my sore backside. While getting dressed and doing my makeup, I mentally prep for my conversation with Jeff. He's been my boss for the whole six years that I've been with AGT Engineers, and I feel comfortable enough to talk to him about the promotion.

We have a pretty decent relationship. He's about fifteen years older than me, and he's a great boss. He keeps things professional, but we chat about our lives outside of work and what we're interested in. And he always says we can come to him with concerns about the company. I've kept my minor complaints to myself.

Until now.

As soon as I get into the office, I walk in with a determination to find an answer. I *need* to know what I did wrong. Or, at the very least, what I can do to improve my chances of being promoted in the future.

I knock on Jeff's door and tell my racing heart to slow down. *Don't be overly emotional. Be logical and present the facts.*

"Hey, Emma," he greets. "Come on in."

"Thanks." I step over to the seat across from his desk. His office has enormous windows behind him, overlooking the business center below. He decorates in a modern style, all shiny with sharp edges. He even has a set of those clacky-balls on the edge of his desk. I fight the urge to bounce one and get the rhythm going.

"How can I help you?" he asks.

"I have a kind of sensitive topic I need to discuss with you."

His face sobers. He gets up and shuts the door behind me. "Sure, of course. What do you want to talk about?"

I smooth my skirt down and brace myself. "I want to know why I didn't get the promotion."

Jeff blows out a low breath. "I guess I can't say this is an unexpected conversation."

So he knew I was going for the promotion. At least I wasn't completely off his radar.

"There isn't a single explanation," he says. "Just a lot of little things all piled up."

"Is this because I didn't pass the SE exam?" I ask. "I told you I'm going to try again next year. I just have to save up enough money to pay the fee."

Last April, Samuel and I both took the Structural Engineer exam through the state of California, the final license for our type of engineers. Along with credibility, it allows you to design schools and hospitals without oversight. The fee just to take the exam is $1000.

Samuel passed; I didn't.

But I didn't think that would hold me back from a promotion. There are a couple of associates who don't have their SE yet, and I thought being a good worker was more important than my book knowledge.

"No. I mean...in a way, yes." Jeff rakes a hand through his hair. I know I'm making him uncomfortable, but after sacrificing six years of my life for this company, I deserve an explanation.

"You're doing well, Emma," he finally says. "But Samuel is...exceptional."

"Exceptional." I repeat. "How so?"

"He always does his work perfectly and on time. He's solid, dependable...exactly what we need in an associate."

I nod, feeling a lump forming in my throat. "And what does that make me?"

His eyes widen as he realizes what comparison he just made. "You're great. Truly." He puts his hands on the table. What isn't he saying? "But, overall, your work is...average."

"Average." I can't stop repeating what he says.

Average.

He nods and looks down at the table, unable to hold my eye contact.

"But...I've been here longer than Samuel," I say. "And I've been working just as hard as him, if not harder."

Jeff nods. "You're an incredible asset, Emma. We're so thankful to have you."

"But I'm...average." I spit out the word.

"You have potential!" he says quickly. "You're extremely person-able. All of your clients love you. But your work is…"

"Average."

His eyes are sad as they meet mine, and my stomach sinks lower than I ever thought possible.

There's nothing else really to say, so I stand and put out my hand for a shake. "I appreciate your honesty. And I'll keep working to improve your opinion of me."

"You're a wonderful person, Emma. Like I said, we're so thankful to have you."

I just nod as he puts his hand in mine for a quick shake. My eyes fill with tears, but I spin around quickly before they can fall.

Is this what everyone else sees when they look at me?

If I'm only average, then what am I doing here?

Two days later, I step into my parents' house through the garage, greeted by Sparky's overly aggressive barks.

"Sparky, it's just me," I say. The thirty-five pound mutt stands two feet away from me and keeps barking until I put out my hand for him to sniff. He relaxes and lets me pet him, but I notice the gleam in his eye that means he's about to snap, and I carefully pull my hand back.

"You're psychotic," I say to him, and I swear he gives me a doggy smile.

Sparky is insane. We rescued him when I was fifteen. He's half Pomeranian, half Miniature Pinscher, and should not have grown over ten pounds. For some reason, he turned into a giant. Not only does he look like an overgrown Chihuahua, but he has issues. He hates all people, except the five of us in our immediate family. He'll snap at any chance—not an actual bite, but he'll give little scratches on everyone's hands—even his favorite people. We don't know exactly why he acts this way, if it's just his breed or something that happened before we rescued him, but he's literally the craziest dog I've ever met.

"Hush, Sparky," my mom calls, and he rushes to her side. If there's anyone he loves the most, it's her. After my younger sister Mariam and I begged for a puppy, my parents agreed under one condition: they would never help with him. That lasted about two weeks. Now Sparky sleeps in bed with my parents, and they love him more than I ever did.

"Hi, Mama," I say, wrapping her in a hug.

She's petite and gorgeous; her short, wavy brown hair is styled above her shoulders, and she always holds herself with grace. But she's intimidating. Just ask her calculus students.

She got her degrees in math when I was little, taking classes while I was in school. I have many memories of her doing homework at the kitchen table late at night, even after making dinner and cleaning. My dad helped a lot, especially because he was home for days at a time as a firefighter, and she was able to reach her goal of becoming a math professor. Which explains why all three of her kids are great at math.

We walk into the living room, Sparky trailing behind us, and see my dad outside at the grill. Tall and lanky with his signature mustache, he holds up a hand in greeting to me.

"Everything smells amazing," I comment to Mom.

"Thank you!" Mariam calls out. "I'm making cookies for dessert."

"Is this your latest hobby? Baking?"

"Not just baking," she says, turning to face me. Her clothes are covered in flour, and her golden brown hair is piled on top of her head in a messy bun, but she still looks like a fairy princess. "Cookie decorating. The TikTok videos are amazing."

"What happened to calligraphy? I thought that was going well."

She wrinkles her nose. "It got boring. On to the next!" She sticks her finger up in the air with a dramatic flair, then turns back to her work.

I roll my eyes. That's Mariam in a nutshell. She can never stick with one hobby. So far this past year, it's been painting, ballet, calligraphy, and now, baking—excuse me, cookie decorating. She's always hopping from one thing to the other, following her passions. It drives me completely bonkers, and partly because she's *so good* at everything she tries. The one thing she's stuck with is playing the violin, and she's nearly professional level.

The craziest part about her is that she's a genius. I'm not exaggerating. She's been tested. Her grades in school beat all of mine, but she didn't even have to try. After high school, she got her degree in *astrophysics*. As in rocket science. She could have been a literal *rocket scientist*. She even had a job lined up at Jet Propulsion Laboratories.

But instead, one week after graduation, she decided to completely change course. She got her early childhood education certificate and is a preschool teacher.

She spends her days with kids who don't know how to blow their noses and can't read.

She's gorgeous, too. While we both have the pronounced Armenian nose, hers looks dainty and delicate. On the other hand, mine looks...let's call it distinguished. I definitely take after our dad. Her hair is beautifully wavy, and she keeps it a light golden brown with highlights that look like she spent a week at the beach.

She's...exceptional.

There's that word again.

I don't hang out with her much, because she's the most frustrating human alive. Add to her lack of ambition the fact that she's super emotional. She calls it being "highly sensitive," like it's a good thing, but she's always crying. A commercial with a dog and a horse? Crying. A beautiful piece of music? Sobs. A sunset at the beach? Tears everywhere. I can only handle so much of her overflow of emotion.

"Where's Garen?" I ask my mom, shifting my focus to my nineteen-year-old brother.

She sighs dramatically. "I never know for sure. I think he's playing video games with Aaron again."

Dad comes in with the meat from the grill. "Dinner's ready!" he says, giving me a quick kiss on the head. We all head into the dining room and take our usual seats. After a quick prayer, we pass dishes.

"Emma-jan, can you pass the pilaf?" Mariam asks in her adorably obnoxious voice. She adds the Armenian "jan" suffix, which means "dear" or "sweetheart."

"Absolutely, sister dearest," I tease in a similar tone. Good natured as ever, she laughs and sticks her tongue out at me.

Mom and Dad are both second generation Armenians, born here in the United States from parents who emigrated. We're mostly Americanized at this point, but Armenian words occasionally slip through the cracks, and our favorite foods are all traditional Armenian dishes. Tonight, for example, my dad barbecued some lamb shish kebab (don't knock it 'til you've tried it), and my mom made incredible, buttery rice pilaf with tabouleh salad.

"How's work going, Emma?" my dad asks.

"Oh, you know, the same," I reply, my mouth full of pilaf.

"Any news about the promotion?" he continues.

Ugh. The question I've been dreading. "Nope."

"Dating anyone?" my mom asks. She's an Armenian Mrs. Bennet. Even though she raised us to be independent, strong women, she wants nothing more than for us to fall in love and live happily ever after.

A vision of Jacob flashes through my mind. Jakey. *My* Jakey. I wondered how he was doing for a few years after he left, especially when I saw him on a few commercials and TV shows. But once I hit high school, my movie-star crushes on Henry Cavill and Chris Hemsworth took over that part of my brain. Maybe if I'd done a little social media stalking, I would have known that Jacob turned out more gorgeous and suave than any of the men in my dreams.

My mom would probably love to hear about Jacob. When we were kids, he was here *all* the time, soaking in the functional family relationships. At least, that's what I realized as I got older. His dad and mom fought constantly over his potential dance career: his dad wanted him to pursue fame, and his mom thought it was too much for him. In the end, his dad won. Jacob's parents divorced, and Jacob left Harbor Sands with his dad, leaving his older sister and mom back home alone.

But I'm not ready to share that he's here, especially not to get my mom's hopes up. "Nope," I say, effectively shutting down that conversation. My mom frowns, but the conversation continues around me.

We finish dinner, and I stay back with my dad, quietly falling into a rhythm of picking up dishes. Mariam and my mom go in the kitchen to prepare dessert and Armenian coffee, aka *soorj*, for everyone. *Soorj* is a super specific type of coffee—the beans are ground down to the consistency of powdered sugar, and then they're cooked in water over the stove and served in tiny cups. It's incredible.

"You okay, kiddo?" Dad asks.

"Yeah, why?"

"I can tell something's got you down. Is it work?"

I set the dishes back down on the table. "I didn't want to tell Mom, but I got passed for the promotion. They gave it to Samuel instead."

He nods and sets the plates down, his big brown eyes full of sympathy. "I'm sorry. I know you were hoping for that."

I shrug. "It's fine. I'll just keep working. I'll get it someday."

"There's more to life than just promotions." He observes me, examining my expression and searching for what's *really* bothering me. "What else happened?"

My face fills with heat. "Jeff said I was 'average.'"

"Average," my dad repeats.

I nod, watching him for a reaction.

He lets out a breath. "Is that such a bad thing?"

I huff a laugh. "You're not going to tell me I'm not average? Wow, Dad."

"That's not what I mean. Your generation is so obsessed with being incredible and spectacular, you don't sit and think about being content. Maybe being average is all you need."

I roll my eyes, and he puts a gentle hand on my arm. "Emma-jan, you're beautiful, kind, and intelligent. You don't have to be a world class pianist or CEO of a Fortune 500 company to be important and valuable. You're special just the way you are."

I twist my lips to the side. "Thanks, Dad."

While I appreciate his Mr. Rogers-esque attempt to build me up, he just validated that I'm nothing special. And he thinks that's fine.

If he thought that would make me feel better, he was wrong.

"Be careful," he warns. "You can get very single-minded."

I roll my eyes. It's not the first time he's said that. "Yes, I know."

"I don't think you do. First it was school, then college, then getting a job. Right now, your only focus is that promotion. Don't let it crowd out the most important things in your life."

"Like what?" I ask. Because right now, the promotion *does* feel like the most important thing.

"Family. And dessert." He winks at me and resumes clearing the table. We finish our task in silence and take the plates to the kitchen sink.

"Where's Garen?" Mariam asks my mom.

As if on cue, the front door bangs open. "Hey, everyone!" my brother Garen calls through the hallway.

I rush to the front door and squeeze my baby brother in a hug.

"Jeez, sis, what's the big deal?" he asks.

At nineteen, he finally enjoys big sister hugs. He also towers over me, but he's still all angles and bones. I can see the man starting to peek through his baby face, though. He's looking more and more like Dad, with his matching brown hair and big, brown eyes framed with eyelashes I'd die for.

My mom rushes to the front door with pita bread and a piece of kebab. "Here, Garen, eat."

"Ma, I just had a ton of pizza at Aaron's house."

Never to be deterred, my mom literally shoves the food in his mouth. He nods and chews. "Mmm, thank you."

She pats his cheek, then pinches his arm. "You were supposed to eat dinner here, with your family."

"Sorry, sorry. We got caught up playing video games and lost track of time."

My mom rolls her eyes and walks back to the kitchen, her hands in the air. "Again with the games."

"At least I'm not doing drugs," he mutters.

"You're just in time for cookies!" Mariam exclaims. She decorated them as Xbox controllers, which makes my mom scoff and Garen smile.

We stroll back to the dining table, and he tells us about his upcoming video game competition. Garen is an incredible prodigy. Mom never let him play the violent games, so he found this really cartoony game called Heroes of the Kingdom that has a huge following online, and he and his friend Aaron are killing it in tournaments. Mom's not a big fan of the esports scene, but as long as he keeps up his grades, she tolerates it.

Me? I'm insanely proud of him.

Besides, he's a track star and plays classical piano. What more could you ask for?

But now, I look around the table at my sister and my little brother, eating these incredible pieces of art that my sister just threw together. Where do I fit in with them? What makes me special?

I have no idea.

When I finally get home, my body screams to climb under the covers and go to sleep. Instead, I sit up in bed and pull my journal from my nightstand onto my lap.

It might seem embarrassing, but I use a kindergarten journal as my personal diary. You know, the ones with the big space to draw a picture and the huge guided lines for practicing proper letter formation. The listing online says they're for ages 6-8. I double up on the lines for writing, but I love doodling little pictures to match my day.

For tonight, I draw a picture of my family sitting at the dinner table. I write a few sentences about my family and how I feel around my incredible brother and sister.

While I wouldn't want to *be* my sister—I still don't know how she handles her job of herding children—it must be nice to know that you're admired for something, right? Even though she doesn't use her violin or painting talents, people *know* that she's incredibly skilled.

I've never experienced that. The more I think about it, the more I realize Jeff was right. I'm always in the middle of the pack.

Average.

Mediocre Emma.

Ouch.

I flip back a couple pages to my entry on the day I got passed for the promotion. But my drawing wasn't of the meeting; it was the dance class with Jacob. Sure, I drew the most embarrassing moment, when I was flat on my back, but it was a good visual. Apparently, my smooth moves didn't deter Jacob from wanting to catch up, though.

I don't know what his intentions were in asking to catch up. He was just being friendly, right? I haven't responded to his message, and texting him now will seem desperate. He must know how gorgeous he is, right? And if I text him now, wouldn't it seem like I'm trying to pursue something with him?

Clearly, I'm not good at this.

I pull out my phone and reread his text. *Hey Emma! It's Jakey *winky face* Let me know when you're free to hang out.*

Maybe it's time to do something out of the ordinary. A break from mediocrity.

Instead of thinking about it, like ordinary Emma, I type out a text. *Hey Jakey! I'm free whenever. I'd love to catch up.*

Not necessarily true, since I'm always working, but I don't want to spell out my exact schedule. I lock the phone and take in a few deep breaths. There we go. Putting myself out there.

Oh, no.

Did that sound like a booty call? I check the time: 9:00 p.m. That *definitely* sounds like a booty call.

The three scrolling dots appear, disappear, and reappear. I hold my breath.

*Can you meet up right now?*

# Chapter 4

C ue panic attack.

Because now I'm *definitely* sure he thinks I'm asking for a booty call.

I stare at the phone, trying to decide how exactly I should respond. I am *not* that kind of girl. Is he that kind of guy? I wouldn't have expected him to be, but eighteen years of fame may have changed him.

But then another text comes through from him. *I'm out at a salsa dancing party with my not-so-big sister, Sara. We'd love for you to come.*

A wave of relief rushes through me. Thank goodness.

Should I go? It's *very* out of character for me, but so was sending the message in the first place. I should stop thinking and start saying yes.

I start typing a response, asking for the address, then realize this still seems pretty shady. Salsa dancing party? Really? Maybe he's just trying to cover for something.

I delete the message and try again, writing a response that I'm too tired and it's late.

But that's the type of thing Average Emma would do.

I delete that message, too, then decide to call Sharleen. She picks up after two rings.

"Emma? What are you doing up so late?"

"SOS! I need you!"

"What? What's wrong?" Her voice sounds panicked.

"I sent Jacob a text saying I wanted to get together, and he asked me to come hang out *tonight*. He said it's some salsa dancing party but it sounds suspicious. Will you come with me?"

"Heck, yes!" She laughs. "I've been waiting for this day to arrive! Come pick me up."

I sigh with relief. "You're the best ever. And I promise, if it's weird, we'll leave right away and do whatever you want."

"I'm holding you to that."

I hang up with a smile, then send Jacob a text. *Sure, sounds fun! I'd like to bring Sharleen with me.*

Rifling through my closet, I settle on a loose red blouse, fitted jeans, and my new tan Louboutins. I can't let the memory of being passed for the promotion ruin my opinion of these gorgeous shoes.

Jacob responds back with the address, and I finish getting myself ready, a little flutter in my chest with the anticipation of tonight.

"So, I guess 'salsa dancing party' wasn't code for something else," I say loudly to Jacob with a mischievous grin. The salsa music echoes through the abandoned warehouse, packed with bodies dancing to the rhythm. I'm intimidated for sure, but the energy here is contagious. I feel like I'm buzzing.

And, of course, Jacob looks like he should be on TV, dancing in one of those competition shows. Hair perfectly styled, messy curls that don't look *too* messy. A fitted dark green tee, and deep blue jeans. He doesn't have to do anything to his piercing green eyes to make them stand out.

Next to Sara, they look like the model brother and sister pair. I notice all the eyes watching them. Sara's long, dark brown curls are almost to her waist, and her brown eyes remind me of their mom. She's petite, adorable, curvy, and I'm sure the envy of every girl here.

"Are you disappointed?" Jacob asks.

I glance around the room. "In a way, yes. I doubt my salsa skills will be any better than my hip hop skills."

He laughs out loud. "You weren't bad. It was a minor mistake."

"That's what I said!" Sharleen agrees, squeezing my shoulder. "I thought she did really well. She's too hard on herself."

The current song ends, and I hear one I recognize: "Despacito." Something about that song just makes me want to move, even if I'm not very talented.

"Ooh, I love this song," I say.

Jacob holds out his hand to me. "Want to dance?"

I look over at Sharleen, unsure if I should be ditching her this early in the night.

She pushes my shoulder. "I'll be fine. Go have fun."

I slip my hand in his, and his warm, strong hand does funny things to my stomach. He leads me through the crowd of people until he stops in a tiny pocket of space for us. "Okay, put your left hand on my shoulder, and your right hand in mine."

I can do this. Left hand on shoulder, right hand in his. And then he slides a hand around my waist.

My entire body tenses, halfway between feeling ticklish and fighting the urge to press myself right up against his body.

"Relax," he says. Apparently he's not feeling the same urges I am. "We're going to do a step and then a little rock step."

He steps to one side then the other, gently pressing on my waist to lead me in the right direction. I catch on quickly, and we repeat the motion over and over for a minute. I'm determined not to make a fool of myself tonight, so I concentrate fully on my feet and don't let his nearness distract me.

"Am I doing okay?" I ask.

"Great!" He dances a few more steps with me. "Just try to bounce with it a little. And feel free to move your hips."

Uh, no thank you. I glance at the dancers around us. "There's a lot of hip action going on."

He shrugs. "No more than in hip hop."

He's got me there. I remember doing some hip isolations at the beginning of class and laugh. "True, true."

"Ready for a turn?" he asks.

"Okay!"

He lifts his arm and guides me under. I feel so fancy doing a turn, and the grin on my face hurts my cheeks.

"Having fun?" he asks.

"Yes!" He pulls me in to our original position, and being so close to him distracts me. I lose my footing and stomp on his foot. "Oh, shoot! I'm so sorry!"

"It's all good." He laughs. "My toes have seen worse days."

Even still, I'm super embarrassed, and I duck my head down to avoid his gaze. His chest is *right there*, and I rest my head against it for just a moment before I realize that's *way* too close for comfort. I pop my head back up and smile at him. That didn't mean anything. Not at all.

The song finishes, and a new one begins. I watch the dancers around us transition into some other kind of dance—slower, more sensual, and *definitely* beyond my skill level.

"That's...a little more advanced," I comment.

He smirks. "It's not so bad. But we don't have to add another dance to your repertoire. I think hip hop and samba are enough for one week. If that's what you want."

That's a relief. I nod. "We can try another samba later. That was fun."

Jacob doesn't let go of my hand, and he pulls me through the crowd back to Sara and Sharleen.

"Look at you go!" Sharleen cheers. "I'm so proud of you."

I glance over at Jacob, a little embarrassed that Sharleen has such an obvious reaction. Am I *that* lame, that just a little dance deserves a cheer?

He doesn't look phased. "Should we go outside and talk a little? Catch up?"

He sounds so hopeful, but I'm a ball of nerves. "Sure." I look over at Sharleen. "Are you okay without me?"

"Psh." Sharleen waves her hand at me. "I'm gonna dance." Typical Sharleen goes straight into the crowd and taps a man on the shoulder, and they begin to dance.

"She's bold." Jacob says, awed.

"You have no idea."

Jacob waves at Sara, who has a grin on her face, and he leads me out into the warm summer air. We stand on a curb, and I wrap my arms around myself. Is he waiting for me to say something?

I figure I'll try to break the ice. "So…"

"So…" he echoes.

I titter a laugh. "I don't know. This is kind of awkward, don't you think? It's been almost twenty years since we've seen each other. That's basically a lifetime, at least for us."

He nods in agreement.

I continue. "So, tell me what you've been up to for the last twenty years. And why you're back home."

A muscle in his jaw twitches. Interesting. "Well, after I left here, my dad took me to LA and got me really involved in the modeling and acting scene."

I smile. "I remember seeing you in a couple of commercials on the Disney Channel."

He relaxes and nods. "That was a lot of fun. And then I had a stint on Broadway, which was great but exhausting. I had a few small gigs when that was done, but when I was twenty-two, I got hired as a backup dancer for Nova Sky. It was a great job. But I missed having a sense of home and family. I'd been on the road and away from a home base for…well, forever. Ever since I left here."

He still hasn't answered my second question. I push a little bit. "What made you come back here?"

"Sara."

I tilt my head, urging him on.

"She has a daughter, Cami. She's four years old." His face lights with a huge smile, and I can see exactly how much he loves her. "She's got me wrapped around her finger. But her dad isn't in the picture at all. Sara needed help with her, so I came back home."

I nod, but I can tell that's not the whole story. It's clear that was hard enough for him to share, though, so I'm not going to pry.

"How about you?" he asks. "What's your life been like for the last twenty years?"

My feet are starting to ache in my heels, so I sit down on the curb. Jacob mirrors my action.

What *has* my life been like? I can't think of a worse question for him to ask right now.

"Oh, you know," I say, waving my hand around. "Average."

He furrows his brow. "Average? What does that mean?"

"Exactly that. Middle of the road. Not exceptional, not awful. Average."

He opens then shuts his mouth. I guess I rendered him speechless, so I continue. "I got my degree in structural engineering, and I've been working at the same firm for the last six years. I was sure I'd become an associate, but I just got passed up."

"I'm so sorry." He's silent for a moment. I see the wheels turning in his head, trying to spin this in a positive direction. "How about outside of work?"

I laugh. "Honestly, I don't have much else going on besides boring work and a boring life. I have my own apartment, and I spend the evenings eating ice cream and watching nature documentaries." I can't hold his gaze anymore. The pity in his eyes is killing me, so I look down at my shoes.

"Hey, I recognize those," he says brightly. "Louboutin?"

I huff a laugh. "Yeah, I kind of have a shoe obsession. Did you learn about those from your sister?"

"No way. She'd never be able to afford those. But Nova had a closet full of them."

My heart drops in my chest. He's seen *Nova Sky's* shoe closet... Meaning he's been in her bedroom? I try to play it off. "Ah, you and Nova Sky are on a first name basis."

"It's not like that. But she is a pretty cool person."

Unfortunately, I know that's true. "That's what I've heard." I rub my shoe, wiping away an imaginary smudge.

The silence seems to stretch forever. Great. I've unloaded all my issues on him, and now he's freaked out.

But he interrupts my inner scolding. "What about...dating?"

*Dating?* What made him ask that? I shake my head. "No time for that. Not when I'm at work until two in the morning finishing projects." I sigh and lean back on my hands, gazing up at the moon and the two or three stars that are visible from all the light pollution. Millions of stars are hiding back there, and I feel like those invisible stars. I'm here, but no one sees me. "Seriously, everything in my life is just average."

"Life isn't about the things you do. It's about who you are as a person. That's what makes you more than average."

I snap my head to face him, eyes narrow.

Before I can speak, he tries again. "And is being average all that bad?"

I fold over my legs, resting my chin on my forearms and looking out at the parking lot. "You sound like my dad," I mutter. "Besides, how would you understand? You've been dancing professionally with *Nova Sky* for the last three years. That's literally the *opposite* of average."

He shakes his head. "It's not all it's cracked up to be."

"But you know what it's like to be exceptional. For once, I'd love to know how that feels." My voice shakes, and my eyes fill with tears, and I hate that I'm so vulnerable in front of him. But for some reason, being with Jacob feels comfortable. I'm sharing things with him that I haven't shared with anyone else, not even Sharleen.

So I wait patiently for his response. And he doesn't look like he's judging me. He's thoughtful, processing my words.

His eyes soften, and instead of giving me an answer, he lifts his hand and starts to rub slow circles on my back. A shiver runs down my spine, but it's comforting at the same time. I turn my head to look at him and rest my cheek on my arm. His green eyes look deep in mine, and I feel the moment turning into something heated and intense.

As much as I want to sit here with him longer, I feel like sneaking off and ditching Sharleen isn't fair. I clear my throat and turn back to the building. "Hey, is that another samba?"

Jacob blinks, as if shaking off a dream. "Uh, yes. It is."

I smile brightly and stand, wiping the dirt off my jeans. "Shall we dance?"

# Chapter 5

"Okay, that was the most fun I've had in a *long* time," Sharleen says from the passenger seat on the drive home. It's one in the morning, but the buzz of adrenaline still pulses through my veins. "I can't believe you wanted to do this."

"Me, neither," I agree, keeping my focus on the road.

"Seriously, when's the last time you went out after 8:00 p.m.? Well, other than taking hip hop with me on Wednesday." I see her shake her head out of the corner of my eye. "What's gotten into you?"

I glance over at her, then turn my head back to the road. "I don't know. I guess I just need a change."

"From being 'average?'" She uses her fingers in air-quotes, far out enough that I can see them without looking at her.

I shrug. "Maybe."

"Come on. Average, how? You're gorgeous, kind, and genuinely a good person. You're killing it at your job. I don't know how many people like you exist in this world."

"That's not what I mean."

She huffs and crosses her arms. "In that case, I'm not better than average, either."

"You're not average!" I protest.

"And neither are you!" She lays a hand on my arm, careful not to disrupt my driving. "I'm happy, Emma. That's what matters most. Being content with my life." She gives my arm a little squeeze before pulling her hand back. "Aren't you happy?"

Am I? My lips twist to the side of my mouth as I consider the answer to that question. "I don't know," I murmur.

Sharleen makes a sympathetic murmur but doesn't expand on the topic. "So, you and Jacob seemed to have a lot of fun," she says, a teasing tone in her voice.

"Mm-hmm," I murmur, noncommittally.

"How come I never heard about this fourth-grade best friend?"

"Is that *jealousy* I hear?"

"No!" she protests, then pauses. "Well, maybe a little. There's something sweet about you two together. I haven't seen you loosen up like that in a while."

I think back on my childhood experiences with Jacob and the same rush I felt dancing with him tonight. "He always pushed me to try new things. I wasn't the most outgoing, but when he was by my side, I could be brave."

"And with me?" she asks, a hesitant tone in her voice. "Do I hold you back?"

"Sharleen, no!" I reach one hand over to squeeze hers, trying not to crash the car. "Other than my parents, you've been my biggest cheerleader. But I've been happy watching you from the sidelines. And maybe...maybe I need to live a little."

She squeezes my hand back. "I'm happy to cheer you on, whatever you decide."

I pull my hand back to the steering wheel, but glance over at her with a smile. "And that's why you're my best friend."

"Good. Don't forget it. I'm not giving up my place to Jacob, even if he is super hot."

A flush rises in my cheeks, but I try not to let it show.

Because there's no way a guy like him feels butterflies about me, right?

For the next week, I have a hard time concentrating at work. After being passed for the promotion, it feels like everything doesn't matter as much anymore. I try my best to put on a brave face and act like I'm unaffected, but I can tell by everyone's stares that they're waiting for me to break down. The whispers float around me, but I pretend not to notice.

I don't blame them. I feel like I'm at a breaking point right now. What's the point of staying late anymore? I'd rather be in bed, eating Ben & Jerry's and watching animals in their natural habitats.

I get the fundamentals done. I work on calculations, talk on the phone with clients, attend the meetings I'm supposed to. No buildings will fall down on my watch.

But I can't help feeling like there's something missing.

After feeling that fire burning in my soul over the last week, taking Jacob's hip hop class and going dancing with him again on Sunday night, I can't sit still. Now it's Thursday afternoon, and I'm wondering what else I'm missing out on, spending all day and all night here. That heart-to-heart with Jacob, breaking down and telling him I feel *average*, is weighing on me, too.

So instead, I'm finding that hiding in my cubicle and stalking Jacob on Photogram is a lot more fun than working. Holy smokes. I got a brief glimpse of his moves in the hip hop class, but when you add in his performance quality, my heart can't stop racing. I feel an extra little twinge of jealousy every time he dances near Nova Sky, and she teasingly runs her hand down his arm or puts a finger on his chest.

*He's mine!* I want to scream.

Yikes. I think I need a break from my stalking.

I grab my latest calculation packet and head over to the copy machine, where Rita and Greg are taking a break. They're both pretty cool, a little older than me, with a few kids of their own. I've maintained friendships with everyone in the office, thinking that would make me seem like an asset to the company and help with my promotion. That got me nowhere. So now I don't really feel like talking, but I don't mind overhearing their conversations.

"What are you doing this weekend?" Rita asks Greg.

Greg sighs. "My daughter has a dance competition."

"*Another* one?" Rita shakes her head. "How many competitions does she have a year?"

"I can never keep track." Greg grabs a little paper cup and fills it with water. "At least she's down to one hobby now, though. Last year it was piano, dance, art class, and soccer. My wife was determined to find that one thing she was really good at, you know?"

*No, Greg, I don't know.* I feel like a tiny lightbulb goes off in my mind, but I can't quite put my finger on it. I stay still, pressing random buttons on the copier, trying to process their conversation without being too obvious.

Rita hums in agreement. "I know what you mean. My kids are in karate, gymnastics, and guitar lessons. It's so much! But how else will you know where they excel?"

"Exactly." Greg agrees, and the two of them walk out the door with a little wave at me. I wave back at them, but then I stare at the copier like I'm watching the sun rise for the first time.

Is that what parents do? Throw their kids in a ton of activities so they can find something they excel at?

When I was young, my parents couldn't afford to put me in classes. My mom was going to college, so our extra money went to her tuition. She did an amazing job at making sure we all excelled in school, which is why I eventually majored in structural engineering. There aren't many girls as good at math as me. But no one watches you solve an integral in calculus and says, "Wow! You're incredible!"

Those types of achievements?

They didn't happen for me.

By the time Mariam was old enough, though, there was a little extra money to use toward classes. She studied art and music, and, of course, she excelled at everything she tried. But at that point, I was so focused on school and making sure I had good grades that I didn't think it mattered anymore. Plus, once Jacob moved away, I lost my desire to try new things and get out of my comfort zone. And with everyone praising Mariam's natural talents, I figured I'd stick to what I knew. There was no need to add more fuel to my existing issues of being compared to her.

Maybe I was wrong. Maybe one of those hobbies would have been my "thing," the one chance I had for people to say, "Wow. Look at Emma. She's exceptional."

Did I miss my chance? Is it too late for me?

Or maybe…do I still have time to find my "thing"?

"Are you almost done?" A man's voice sounds over my shoulder.

Startled, I realize I haven't even started making my photocopies. "Sorry, Dan," I say, quickly feeding the originals through the machine and pressing the copy button. But inside, my mind is swirling through the possibilities.

What if I really, *really* tried to find what I was good at? What if there's something that's just been hiding under the surface this whole time, and I never got the opportunity to look for it?

Maybe there's a possibility that I'm actually *better* than average.

The copies finish, and I grab the warm papers from the machine, hugging them to my chest. This office is always frigid, and I take advantage of any opportunity to warm up. I head back to my desk and sit down, taking a moment to look around at the little stuffed animals, sticky notes, and pictures of Sharleen and my siblings.

*What am I doing here?*

Suddenly, I'm seeing my life through fresh eyes. Every day spent here in this office is a waste. Sure, I make enough money to buy adorable shoes and drive a cute, fancy car, but I've also got a decent savings account. Enough to support me for a few months.

I know what I need to do.

I'm being rash. I absolutely, positively know it.

But I don't care.

I stand up with renewed determination and head to Jeff's office. I poke my head in through the doorway. "Hey, Jeff. Do you have a minute?"

"Sure," he says with a smile, waving me in.

I step inside and speak before I can take a moment to reconsider. "I'm quitting."

His eyes bulge out of his head. "What?"

"I'm quitting," I repeat. "It has nothing to do with you or the company." That's kind of a lie, but I don't want to leave on a bad note. "This last week, I've been looking at my life through a different lens. It's like I'm watching myself wither away, slowly dying here in this office."

"Wow, that's quite a visual."

"Sorry, that might seem a little overdramatic." I take a deep breath, slowing myself down so I don't word vomit all over my poor boss. "I think I really need to take a chance on myself. Find what I'm meant to do."

Jeff watches me carefully, analyzing my expression. "Is this because we passed you on the promotion?"

"No! Well…" I don't want to lie, but I also don't want to make this more awkward than it already is. I brace myself. "In a way, yes. But it's a good thing. It made me realize I need to have more of a life outside of work. I've dedicated every waking hour to this job and I have nothing to show for it." I sigh. "I want passion and adventure. I want to find what makes me exceptional."

Jeff nods. He seems stunned, like my outpouring of passion has stilled him in his seat. He takes a moment to gather his words, and my heart drums in my chest while I wait for his response. "While I'm not thrilled with you throwing this on me at the last minute, I guess I understand where you're coming from."

I exhale, a weight off my shoulders. But, then again, what else was he going to do—fire me?

"Is there any way you'd be willing to stay for two more weeks until we find a replacement? At the very least, we need to transfer your clients to the remaining engineers."

I press my lips together. As much as I want to leave the office this second and never come back, I understand his problem. "I can accept that."

"Deal." Jeff holds out his hand and shakes mine.

I give him a tight smile and a wave, and head back to my desk. A nervous thrill passes through me. I'm on the cusp of something big, something new. I can feel it in my veins.

# *Chapter 6*

On the way home from work, I call Sharleen and tell her what happened. She's super sweet and supportive, but I worry she thinks I'm crazy. After that phone call, though, I decide I should call my parents. I know I'm twenty-eight, living on my own, and I can make my own decisions, but my parents are such an important part of my life and I want to share this news with them.

As soon as I walk through the door to my apartment, I dial my dad's number, because Mom usually leaves her phone plugged in and charging in her bedroom. Calling her is like making a call to the Twilight Zone.

"Hey, hon," he says. "What's going on?"

"Hey, Dad. Is Mom around?"

"Yep, we're all getting ready for dinner. Garen and Mariam, too. Here, I'll put you on speaker." He fiddles for a moment. "Everything okay?"

"Mm-hmm." Now that he's on the line, I feel like I'm going to throw up. I inhale and exhale, gripping the kitchen counter for strength. "I quit my job!"

Silence.

"Are...are you there?" I ask.

"Yep, we're here," Garen says.

"Is everything okay?" Mom asks.

"Yes. I didn't get fired, if that's what you're asking." I sigh. "I got passed for a promotion last week."

"Yes, I know. Your dad told me."

"You told?" I cry.

"You didn't say I couldn't!" Dad says. "I tell your mom everything."

I huff. "Fine. Well, it's easier if you know, I guess. I feel like I'm wasting my life there, trying to dedicate myself to a company, and for what?" I pause and take another deep breath. "I couldn't take it anymore. So I quit, and I'm going to have a fresh start."

"So, what are you going to do now?" Garen asks.

This is the part I'm most nervous about telling them. "I'm giving myself a few months to sort that out. And before you say anything—I have plenty of savings, and I've budgeted this out. I just won't buy shoes for a few months."

"I thought you were saving that money to take your engineering exam again." Mom says.

I sigh. "I'm not ready to try again. And I'm not about to flush a thousand dollars down the toilet, just to fail another time." I smirk. "I can send you my budget spreadsheet if you want."

"No, no, I trust you." *Sure you do, Mom.*

"Well, this sounds awesome," Garen says.

"I agree," Mariam chimes in.

"What, have you all been waiting for me to leave this job?" I ask.

"I mean..." Garen begins.

A knock sounds on my apartment door, scaring me half to death, and I scream. Who comes to people's doors these days?

"Emma? What's happening?" Dad says.

"Someone's at my door," I whisper.

My dad yells, "Stay on the line!"

"I'll call 911!" Garen chimes in.

"Emma, I know you're in there!" a voice calls through the door.

"Sharleen?" I tiptoe to the door, open it cautiously, and find my best friend at my door with ice cream, magazines, and her cosmetology bag.

"Emma? Is it her?" Dad asks, still on speaker.

"Yes, it's just Sharleen. Sorry for scaring you guys. Have a great dinner. We'll catch up later!"

My family choruses with goodbyes, and I hang up.

"What are you doing here?" I ask, my hand on my chest. My heart is still racing from the scare.

"Look, I know you're going through this soul-searching time, and what's better for that than ice cream?"

I exhale and laugh with relief, then let her in the door. "What are the magazines for?"

"Well, as I was in the grocery store line, this cover screamed your name." She holds out the glossy pages for me to see.

*40 Hobbies for Cool Women Looking to Spice Things Up!*

"Maybe you'll find some inspiration here."

Who knows? She could be right. I take the magazine and start thumbing through the pages, skipping the ads and perfume samples until I find the article.

"Phish Food or Chunky Monkey?" she asks, holding the two cartons in her hands.

"Phish Food." I open to the page with the article and sit down at my kitchen table, perusing the list.

"Any good ideas in there?" she asks, rifling through my drawers for a spoon.

I tilt my head from side to side, assessing. "Pottery could be cool."

"Ooh, cake decorating," she says, pointing at the page and taking a seat next to me.

"Eh, that's too much like Mariam's latest hobby."

"What's she up to now?"

"Cookie decorating."

Sharleen huffs a laugh. "I'm surprised you're not asking her for advice."

"No way. Then I'd have to compare myself to her the whole time. This is all about me, and I don't need to keep thinking about how much better than me she is at everything." I don't look up to see Sharleen's reaction. She knows the deep-seated issues I have, always feeling inferior to Mariam's natural talents.

I keep reading the list. "Makeup? That could be kind of fun."

Sharleen nods in agreement, then points at another item on the list. "You already tried dance classes."

"Don't remind me."

"You should come back!"

I twist my lips to the side of my mouth, thinking about dancing in Jacob's class again. "I don't think I could take another class from Jacob."

"Oh, really?" Sharleen says, raising her brows.

"Don't do that."

"What?" She blinks rapidly.

"Act like you don't know what I mean."

She opens her mouth in fake shock. "I would *think* that you'd be fine with taking a class from your dear childhood friend, who happens to be objectively drop-dead gorgeous."

I snort a laugh. "Yeah, that's an excellent description of him." I set the magazine down with a sigh. "He really is beautiful."

"Seriously." Sharleen puts another spoonful of ice cream in her mouth and watches me carefully. "You can't tell me there's not some spark between you two."

I sit back and cross my arms over my chest. "I don't think I should date right now."

"Oh?"

I nod. "I need to focus on myself. This is my moment. Dating is just going to confuse me. I don't want to change myself for anyone else. I want to find what makes me special."

"Wouldn't being with someone who already likes you for *you* make you feel special?"

"I'm *missing* something, Sharleen. And I don't need to add romantic feelings into the mix to confuse things more."

Sharleen purses her lips, not believing me. But that's fine. I believe me, and that's all that matters right now.

"Video games," I say, pointing back at the list. "Garen could help me with that one. Maybe it runs in the family."

Sharleen laughs out loud. "I would *love* to see that."

"Balloon animals."

"That is *not* on the list."

"No, it's not." I set the list down. "But I always thought that would be cool."

Sharleen snickers. "Let's make your own list, from best to worst, and you can try each hobby one at a time. If you find your thing, then you can stop. But if it doesn't work out, then you move to the next hobby on the list."

I nod in agreement. "That's a great idea."

"I'm glad you think it's a great idea. Because I'm full of them."

I laugh. "Oh, really?"

"Yep. And I have another great idea, too." She scurries back to the front door and picks up her cosmetology bag. "I think it's time for a haircut."

✦✦✦✦✦✦ ✦✦✦✦✦✦

"You're not going to chop it all off, right?" I ask, sitting in a chair in the middle of my kitchen.

"Stop being crazy. Trust my judgment." She snaps her shears a couple times and circles around me, like a lion prowling its prey. Inhaling deeply, I mentally prepare to get a cut other than straight across my shoulder blades.

"I've been waiting for this moment for *years*," Sharleen whispers like an evil genius.

"Years? You've only been in school for a few months."

"Yeah, but your boring hair has always bothered me."

I snicker. If it wasn't Sharleen, I'd be hurt.

She places her hands on my shoulders. "Okay, we'll do something simple to style, but still really chic."

She sections out my hair and combs the back down. I brace myself, and Sharleen takes a hold of a piece of my hair.

"Wait!" I screech.

Sharleen jumps and lets go of my hair. "Did that hurt? There's no way that hurt! It's only your hair!"

"No, no! It's just..." I take another deep breath, gathering myself together. "It's the symbolism. The old me is getting cut away, and the new me can shine."

Sharleen fans her face, blinking away mock tears and taking in a shuddering breath. "That was beautiful."

I smack her in the leg. "Don't make fun of me."

She cracks up. "Don't tease the hairdresser. I'm the one with the shears."

I gulp and nod, and she finally starts the haircut. I focus my attention on the magazine and notebook in front of me, working on my list.

"So, what should I try first?" I ask.

"What have you always wished you could do?" Sharleen asks. "What did you always dream of doing when you were a kid?"

"Ice-skating," I say instantly.

"Really?"

"Yep. I remember watching the Winter Olympics when I was little, and ever since then, I dreamed of being an ice-skater." I shake my head.

"Don't move your head! I almost gave you a bald spot."

Obediently, I sit still.

"Okay, so is there a class you can take for that?" she asks. "Or something you can try?"

"Let me look." I pull out my phone and do a quick search for ice rinks near me. "There's a place about ten minutes from here. Look! They have a class tomorrow!"

"Awesome. Sign us up."

I turn my head to look at her, and she hisses at me. I ignore her. "You want to come, too?"

"Of course! You need moral support."

My eyes glisten with tears. "You're the best."

"And don't you forget it. Now turn back around so I can finish your haircut."

Sharleen really worked a miracle.

She didn't color my hair, since I wasn't ready for a full makeover, but she gave me the most stylish haircut of my entire life. Which isn't really saying much, since I've had the same blunt cut across my shoulder blades since I was five. Even so, it's so stylish, I feel like I finally look good enough for the shoes I wear.

My shaggy, shoulder-length bob frames my face just right, and the soft curls she added make me feel glamorous. Maybe I should put makeup as one of the top things on my list of hobbies to try, because this hair deserves a show-stopping face.

I snap a quick picture of myself and consider posting it on my Photogram account. I rarely post anything there, because I don't have a lot of things to be proud of. But I spend an embarrassing amount of time scrolling through everyone else's accomplishments. Here's what's happening tonight:

Sarah Cooper got a promotion.

Ken Chavez hiked the entire John Muir trail.

Shawna Masterson's daughter is reading at only two years old (how?).

Devin Martinez posted an entire reel dedicated to her epic vacation to Fiji and New Zealand.

And me?

I quit my job. And I got a haircut.

Whoop-de-do.

I start drafting a caption. *Say hello to the new Emma! Can't believe I have my first new hairstyle after twenty-three years.*

But I can't press post. It feels so dumb.

If this really is the new Emma, doesn't that warrant a new account? Maybe I should start fresh. A place where I can document all of my adventures and attempts at finding what makes me special.

I poke around the app, searching for different usernames that might work for me. What describes me right now? *Average_emma* is already taken, as is *mediocre_emma*.

Wait a second.

Isn't the whole point that I want to be more than this? Better than average? Even more than that—extraordinary.

Exceptional.

With a tremble in my fingers, I type in the username *exceptional_emma*.

Available.

I squeal out loud, rush to make a new email account with the same username, and create my account. It's not that I think I'm going to become an influencer or anything. It's more the symbolism of starting fresh and accepting this new journey I'm on.

Setting up the profile doesn't take long, and I use the picture of me with my new haircut as my profile picture.

Now that that's done, I feel even more excited about starting this journey. Ice-skating, here I come.

# *Chapter 7*

"**Y**ou look cute," Sharleen comments as we walk inside the ice-skating rink on Friday afternoon.

"Thanks!" I smooth the purple, fuzzy sweater and scarf that I pulled out of my winter clothes. Here in southern California, we rarely have a need for cold weather clothes, unless we head to Mammoth or Big Bear in the mountains for a snow day. I have two scarves and three beanies that I save for these trips. Otherwise, I'm good with a light sweater and jacket for even the chilliest winter days.

"Hello. Welcome to Harbor Sands Ice Rink." The front desk attendant looks like she's about forty and not thrilled to be here. She reminds me of Sadness from Inside Out. I probably wouldn't be ecstatic to work in such a cold building, either. Although it might be nice in a few months, when we get our annual September heat wave.

"Hi! We're here for the beginner class at four thirty," I say.

She looks us up and down. "Do you have kids?"

"Uh, no. It's for us."

"The four thirty class is for kids, five to ten years old."

My heart sinks. Already I've made a mistake. "When is the adult beginner class?"

"Not until tomorrow." She checks the schedule. "We do have the beer and hockey league at six, if you want to join in with that group."

"I'm sorry, the *what* league?" Sharleen asks with a mischievous smile.

"Beer and hockey. They play hockey and drink beer out of a championship trophy."

Sharleen bursts out laughing. "Please, please, can we at *least* stay and watch that?"

I sigh, resigned. "Sure." I look around the ice rink, assessing my options. What a waste. My first childhood dream is already meeting an obstacle.

The receptionist clears her throat. "There's no rule that says you *can't* take the beginner class, if you don't mind being with a few kids."

My heart fills with hope, and I turn to face Sharleen. Her eyes widen and she shakes her head.

"Please, Sharleen," I plead. "I need to do this. Just today."

She shakes her head again.

"Okay, how about you just record it?" I ask. "You can be my paparazzi. I need to document it for my Photogram account, anyway."

She twists her lips, then smiles widely in a conspiratorial grin. "Now *that* is sure to get a lot of attention."

"Yes!" I pump my fist in the air. "Okay, one for the beginner class at four thirty."

The attendant gets me registered and fits me into the right size skates. I sit on a bench, tying the laces while Sharleen takes pictures and a quick video.

"Emma, tell me how you're feeling right now."

I look up as I finish my knots. "Super excited. And a little nervous."

"Are you ready for your very first ice-skating class? With children?"

I laugh nervously. "Well, I do wish I was a kid like them and didn't wait until I was going through a quarter-life crisis to take my first class. But either way, at least I'm getting to experience it for the first time."

Sharleen stops recording. "This is gold."

"We'll see." I stand up, testing out my skates. My ankles wobble a little, but the skates are tight and hold me in place.

A few kids start filtering into the waiting area, dressed in adorable snow clothes. Seeing them in front of me is like a bucket of ice water on my head.

"Oh, my goodness. What am I doing?" I whisper to Sharleen.

She puts a reassuring arm around my shoulder. "You're trying out your childhood dream. You're following your passions. You can do this!"

Right on cue, the instructor appears at the gate to the ice. "Everyone ready for beginner skating?"

The instructor is an older woman who looks like she's as comfortable on the ice as she is walking on the street. She has a kind, sweet face, blond hair pulled up in a high bun, and lean legs showcased in adorable black leggings with snowflakes. "You must be Emma," she says to me kindly. "They told me about you at the front desk. I'm Jessica."

I shuffle over to her as fast as my skates will allow me. "Is that okay?" I whisper. "For me to take the class?" I was so sure, so confident when I signed up at the front desk, but now I feel like I'm going to pass out.

"Yes," she says, smiling widely and squeezing my mittens with her gloves. "I'm always happy to help a beginner, no matter how old."

My heart slows its racing, and now it's more like a thumping rabbit than a thundering racehorse. I wave at Sharleen, who gives me a thumbs up with her free hand and keeps recording for evidence. Am I totally nuts for putting this on the Internet? Maybe. But at least it's giving me some accountability.

"We're actually going to start off the ice," Jessica says, stepping into the waiting area. I follow behind her as she takes attendance of the kids near me. "Charlie, Adele, Clara, and Phoebe. Perfect." She smiles at me. "And Emma."

"And me!" I say, putting my hands in the air and waving them around. That gets a giggle out of the kids. Oh man, I'm so weird.

"Let's practice our falls off the ice. Do you kids remember?"

As if on cue, all four of the little ones collapse to one side, then get on their hands and knees and stand up one leg at a time.

"Wow, impressive," I murmur.

"It's important to fall to the side whenever you can. And we'll practice getting up here, where it isn't slippery, before we practice on the ice."

I nod and brace myself to fall. "Oh, my!" I say as I pretend to fall, and the kids all giggle again. They should hire me as the entertainment.

"Perfect," Jessica says reassuringly. "Now get on all fours, step on one leg, and use your hands to help you stand on both feet."

I follow her instructions and stand up. "That wasn't so bad."

"Great. Do it one more time."

I do it once more, even better the second time, my confidence skyrocketing. I'm a natural.

"Wonderful. Now let's practice some marches." Jessica demonstrates marching on the ground, and the little ones follow suit. I imitate their movements, and although my ankles wobble a couple times, I'm able to stay standing.

Jessica watches me for another minute, then nods her head. "Wonderful. Let's get on the ice."

The little ones squeal and head to the gate, and I follow behind. I take my first step onto the ice and nearly fall backwards.

Jessica steadies me with a firm grip on my arm. "Have you ever ice-skated before?"

"Uh, once," I reply. "I was about eight and we went on a class field trip." The memory of my class all bundled up at the ice rink hits me hard. The excitement, more about the hot chocolate that was to come after the skating, fills my vision.

And Jacob.

Why didn't I remember skating with him until this moment?

*"I'm scared!" I whispered to him.*

*"Don't be," he said, smiling and showing off his missing teeth. He held out his mitten to me. "Hold my hand and don't let go. I won't let you fall."*

"You can do this, Emma," Jessica says, bringing me back to the present. She holds out her glove, and I hold tight as she leads me to the general area where the four little ones anxiously wait to begin skating.

"We'll start by practicing our falls again, so we're all able to get back up when we fall." She looks at me. "Because we're *all* going to fall, and that's okay."

I nod with determination, confident that I won't be the only disaster here on the ice. Maybe the only twenty-eight-year-old disaster, but I can deal with that.

We all do our pretend falls, and I try to stand back up. But I can't.

All fours, one foot down, hands on my knees, and…my foot slips out.

Again.

And again.

"Oh, Mylanta," I mutter.

"It's okay," Jessica says reassuringly. Now a little crowd of children has formed around me, crouched on all fours. "Use your butt and dig your foot into the ice."

Grunting, I push myself one last time, and finally make it to standing.

Except when I stand, my feet slip out from under me, and I land on my butt again. Frustrated, this time I lie all the way down on the ice. I need a moment.

"Try again," Jessica says reassuringly. The kids around me start to get impatient.

"Go ahead and practice your marches," Jessica says to the kids, showing them a little path to take. They follow each other in an adorable little duck line, marching on the ice.

"How long have they been taking lessons?" I ask from my starfish position. Apparently, this is where I live, whether in hip hop class or ice-skating.

"About two weeks," she says with a smile.

Despair sinks in my belly. "Is that supposed to make me feel better?"

"They're kids," she says gently. "They pick up on these things faster than we do as adults."

A wave of shame crashes over me. Of course. Of *course,* this isn't something I'd be able to pick up on as an adult. There are certain hobbies you need to start as a child while your body is still developing, and trying them as an adult is nearly impossible.

"But it doesn't mean you can't learn," she continues. "Now try to get up again."

And I do. After I'm up, she helps me through my marches and shows me another move called swizzles, where I wave my feet in and out. I keep falling, but I keep getting up. At one point, Jessica leads me over to a giant plastic seal on its belly. Its chest is on the ice, and its tail is up in the air around waist height.

"Here. You can hold on to the seal's tail and it helps you keep your balance as you try skating."

This is probably the most embarrassing moment of my life. I thought Jeff calling me "average" was bad, but this takes the cake. But pushing a seal is probably better than falling on my bottom for another fifteen minutes. I take the seal, who I've named Sam, and slowly glide around the ice as the kids literally skate circles around me.

The class continues through the hour, and I'm so sore and disappointed I want to cry.

"Thank you, everyone!" Jessica calls. "See you next week!"

I skate in her direction, pushing my new friend Sam the Seal, and nearly collide with her because I still haven't figured out the snowplow stop. She steadies me and gives me a tired smile.

"I really appreciate you helping me out," I say. "Thank you for being so kind."

She squeezes my arm. "I think you did an amazing job for a beginner. You probably wouldn't feel so out of place in an adult class. I'm really proud of you for trying."

Over her shoulder, I see what must be the beer hockey league putting on their gear and getting ready to go on the ice. There's about eight men and a woman, laughing and joking with each other.

Jessica helps me back to the gate, where Sharleen waits with a sympathetic smile on her face. "Hey," Sharleen says softly. "How's your butt?"

I snort. "I'll be so sore tomorrow. Again." I step out into the waiting area, eager to get these skates off my feet.

She pats my shoulder. "It'll be worth it for the views. I got some great shots of you falling."

Goodness gracious. I totally forgot that she was filming this whole thing. I slump down on the bench and put my head in my hands. "Please tell me you haven't posted yet."

"No, not yet. I'll let you approve it first. But don't you want to be honest about this whole thing? That's why you started the account, right?"

Is it? It's going to be *so* humiliating, putting videos of myself in a kids' skating class online for everyone to see.

But she's right.

"All right, we'll post it. But I still want to approve it first."

"No problem." Another man brushes past her to join the beer hockey league. Sharleen eyes them with a grin. "Now *that* looks awesome."

"Right?" I ask. We watch them pulling on their gear and lacing up their skates, all smiles and laughter. "I wish I was that happy knowing I was going to skate."

"Maybe you can be," Sharleen murmurs. A mischievous look glints in her eyes. "Hey!" she calls out to the group. "Can you take one more?"

"Sharleen, no!" I squeal.

"Sure!" a man with a bushy beard calls back. "You need gear, though. League rules."

"Not for me, for her." She stands and pulls me up with her, then shoves me toward them.

Bushy Beard Man looks me over. "You any good at skating?"

"Nope," I reply.

He narrows his eyes, then shrugs. "Check the lost and found for gear. Be on the ice in five minutes."

What in the world am I about to do?

# Chapter 8

Turns out Beer Hockey League is the coolest group of people I've met in a long time.

Do I still suck on the ice? Absolutely.

Do I fall? Absolutely.

But I fall because I'm trying my hardest to score a goal, so my feet slip out under me, and I land on my bottom. The protective gear cushions my body, though, so it doesn't hurt nearly as bad as all my falls in the kids' class.

And the best part? When I fall, all the league members hit their sticks on the ice and cheer.

"Get it, Emma!" Bushy Beard Man, whose name is Calvin, shouts.

Back in my standard starfish position, I smile at the ceiling. Yep, I fell, but I feel so happy.

Calvin helps me to my feet and guides me to the wall. "Time for a break?" he asks the group, who all cheer in agreement.

The gear is a little small on me. I'm pretty sure it belongs to a twelve-year-old boy, but at least it was a way for me to get on the ice with them. And thank goodness I did, because I would have left the rink sobbing otherwise.

We head back to the waiting area, where Sharleen films with a huge smile on her face.

"And now, for the beer part of the league." Calvin takes a championship trophy out of a display case, opens a can of beer, and pours its contents inside the trophy.

I gape at him. "Is that allowed?"

"Allowed? It's what we *do*." He picks up the trophy and hands it to me. "New girl first."

I peer cautiously at the trophy and the beer inside. This is definitely not sanitary. But I'm in too deep to back out now.

I lift the giant trophy to my mouth and take a huge gulp to the sound of cheers and applause. Beer dribbles down my face, and I swipe my mouth, then pump my fist in the air.

Sharleen sits on the bench laughing out loud and shaking her head, recording all the while. The members of the league each take turns drinking out of the trophy, smiling and laughing.

"So, what made you come here today?" the woman, Cynthia, asks. She holds an unopened can of beer in her hands and offers it to me. I take it, thankful for the sanitary can, and pop it open.

"Quarter life crisis," I reply.

She laughs. "Mine was a mid-life crisis."

I take a sip of beer. "Oh, yeah?"

She nods, her red curly hair bouncing around her freckled face. "My husband cheated on me after twenty-two years of marriage, and I was left alone for the first time in a long time. The kids were teenagers, and I needed something for myself. My daughter had been training here for years, and I saw these guys practicing a few times, so I decided to join in. It was just what I needed. There's no group of people like these guys here."

I look around the group, smiling and laughing, and can see how this could be an incredible community to be part of. It's not really my place, but I'm glad Cynthia found her home here.

"Besides, that's how I met my new husband," she says, pointing at Calvin.

I smile widely. "Ah, that's awesome." I can already tell that the two of them make a perfect match. "Everyone seems pretty amazing. And I'm really grateful you let me join today. I'm sorry if I ruined your usual game."

She shakes her head. "Sometimes it's more fun cheering for people than winning the game."

I take another slow sip of beer, not sure I completely agree with her. Winning *anything* sounds pretty nice right now. But I'm not about to contradict her out loud.

"So, who's your friend with the pictures?" she asks, pointing at Sharleen. "Are you famous or something?"

"No, no, not at all," I say with a laugh. "I'm trying out a bunch of hobbies to see if I can find something I'm actually good at. Sharleen is helping me make posts for my new Photogram account."

"Nice. What's your username? I'll add you." She pulls her phone out of her pocket.

"Exceptional Emma," I say, suddenly shy.

"What a name," she says with a wide smile.

"Yeah, it's a little tongue-in-cheek," I say, feeling the urge to explain myself. "I don't actually *think* I'm exceptional, but I'm hoping I'll find what makes me so along the way."

She nods. "I don't know. A girl who takes a kid's beginner skating class and then hops into beer league seems pretty exceptional to me." She pats my shoulder. "I'm following you now. Can't wait to see what else you end up doing." She heads back to Calvin and gives him a big, sloppy kiss on the lips. They seem like a match made in heaven.

I head back over to Sharleen and offer her my beer.

"No, thanks," she says. "I'd feel like a fraud. You deserve a whole can after drinking out of that disgusting trophy."

I laugh. "Worth it. Did you get it on video?"

"Oh, yes." She shows me the compilation of videos she got, starting with all my falls during the kids' class, more falls and cheers playing hockey, and me drinking out of the trophy.

"This will make an amazing reel," I say. "I'll have to figure out how to put that together tonight."

"I bet Jacob knows how to do it," she says with a wink.

"Why do you say that?" I ask, trying to sound innocent.

"He's posted all kinds of cool videos from dancing with Nova Sky. Haven't you followed him yet?"

"Nope." Followed? No. Stalked? Yep. I take a sip of my beer and shrug a shoulder. "I'll ask him if he can help."

Sharleen and I sit and watch the group for a few more minutes while I finish drinking my beer. The laughter and love are contagious, and I take a quick picture to capture the moment. I post it on my Photogram account, and then we agree that it's time to go home. Calvin and Cynthia wrap me in big hugs.

"Stay brave, Exceptional Emma," Cynthia says. "I can't wait to watch you shine."

"Thanks, Cynthia," I say with a smile. "And thank you for taking me in today," I say to Calvin.

He pinches my cheek, like a dad to a daughter. "No problem."

We wave goodbye and head out to our cars. I'd like to say that the wobble in my step is from being on solid ground again, without skates strapped to my feet, but it's more likely the beer.

Sharleen grabs my shoulders and steers me away from my car. "You're not driving, lightweight."

"What are we doing with my car?"

"We'll come get it tomorrow morning. Hop in." She opens the passenger side for me, and I drop into the seat, already feeling my legs stiffen from exhaustion. She closes the door and gets into the driver's seat, then drives toward my apartment.

"Lemme call Jacob," I say.

"Now?" she asks.

"I'm feeling brave." I pull out my phone and dial his number.

"That's the beer talking! Don't do anything stupid!"

"Shhh, it's ringing," I whisper.

"Hey, Emma," Jacob answers.

"Heyyyyyyy," I say, dragging out the word.

"Stop acting weird," Sharleen hisses at me.

I wave her away. "Do you know how to make reels for Photogram?"

"Uh, yeah. I do them all the time for dance."

"That's what Sharleen said. Awesome. So. I made an account, and I could use your help."

"Don't you already have a Photogram account?" he asks.

"That was my personal one. Wait. How do you know about that? We don't follow each other."

"I...uh..."

"Were you stalking me, too?" I giggle. "I stalked you."

"Oh, my goodness. *Stop talking!*" Sharleen says.

"You stop talking!" I say.

"Who, me?" Jacob asks.

"No, no, sorry. Not you. Okay, I'm going to send you some pictures and videos. Let me know if you can do it." I put him on speakerphone and text him everything from today.

"Okay, got it," Jacob says. He pauses a minute, probably looking through the pictures. "What...where...when was this?"

"Just now."

"Ah, I see. Feeling a little tipsy after that beer?"

"Yep." I pop the *p* a little extra.

"Well, I can definitely help you with that." He clears his throat. "Would you want to get dinner? We can talk about the project."

"That would be awesome." Turning to Sharleen, I whisper, "He wants to get dinner with me."

"I'm sure he just heard you say that," she whispers back.

"No. I'm *whispering*."

Sharleen shakes her head.

"Yes, I did hear that," Jacob says.

Shoot. I forgot he was on speakerphone.

"Okay, give me some time to get myself together and then we can get dinner." A thought pops into my brain, though. As much as I'm feeling romantic things about Jacob, I don't want him to assume I'm pursuing him. Just look at me, then look at him. He's a ten, I'm a six. I don't want to make him uncomfortable, so I decide to be upfront. "But just to be clear, it's not a date."

"Emma!" Sharleen squeals.

"What? It's better to be clear about these things."

"You can't just *assume* that's what he was looking for. Guys and girls can go out without it being romantic."

Oh, no. She's right. My mind went there because, well, *Jacob*.

"Forget I said that!" I exclaim. "Just kidding! It can totally be a date! Wait...no...uh, okay, just erase the last two minutes from your brain."

Jacob chuckles. "Done. Where should we meet for dinner?"

"Wherever," I reply.

"She doesn't have a car," Sharleen chimes in. "I have to drive her home. She's not drunk, just a little tipsy."

"I can hear that," Jacob replies. "Emma, I'll just pick you up at your place in an hour. Sound good?"

"Purr-fect. Like a cat."

He laughs again. "Text me your address. See you soon."

I hang up. "See? That wasn't so bad. I'm just a little tipsy."

"Still here." Jacob's voice comes through the speakerphone.

"Whoops! Byeee!"

Sharleen shakes her head at me. "You're a mess."

# Chapter 9

I take a quick shower and feel the alcohol exiting my pores and down the drain. The impact of my words to Jacob hit me like a ton of bricks. Oh, my goodness. Did I really make a point of saying that it's not a date?

I get dressed and do my hair, thoughts racing. Maybe he won't remember. Or maybe he won't bring it up.

But is it better if I just say something?

A knock sounds on my door. No more time to over-analyze the consequences of my tipsy conversation.

I unlock my door, poking my head out. Jacob stands there, looking as gorgeous as ever. Does he ever look the slightest bit imperfect?

All my analysis has led to this conclusion: handling the situation up-front is the best course of action. "Please, *please* forget everything that I said in that phone conversation."

Jacob smiles, infuriating me. "What if I don't want to?"

I groan, leaning my head against the doorjamb. "I am such a lightweight. One beer and I start spouting all kinds of ridiculous things."

"It's adorable," he says.

My eyes widen. He didn't mean that in the way I wish he did, right?

"But don't worry, in a platonic, adorable way," he clarifies. "Since this isn't a date."

Oh, right. That.

I roll my eyes. "I repeat, please forget that entire conversation."

He chuckles. "I get it. We're just friends. Let's go get dinner."

Relieved that he's not making a big deal out of this, but slightly disappointed that he's not saying, *'Are you out of your mind? I want you!'* I exhale and nod. "Give me a couple more minutes. I'll be right out." I close the door on him, not wanting him to see the inside of my apartment yet—it seems too intimate, right?—and finish getting myself together.

A couple minutes later, I reemerge and shut and lock the door behind me.

"Did you cut your hair?" Jacob asks.

"Oh, yeah." I feel a twinge of embarrassment. Why are all my life changes happening right when Jacob reenters my life? "Sharleen did it last night. I'm still not used to it yet."

"I like it. It suits you." He leads me to his truck, a tall, silver pickup. "Any preference for dinner?" he asks, leaning his hand on the door.

I shrug. "Not really. Anything you've been craving since you moved away?"

"In-N-Out," he says.

I smile widely, remembering all the chocolate shakes we shared in our younger years. "Yes! I'm always down for a double-double."

He grins back at me. "Let's go."

"You haven't gone since you moved back?" I ask. I'm surprised he waited this long.

"Oh, I have," he says. "I've been there three times in the last week. But I have a lot of time to make up for."

I laugh. He's not wrong; there's nothing like In-N-Out.

He opens the door for me, and I find myself wishing this really was a date. *No, Emma. Shut that down.* "You really don't need to do that," I say, climbing up into the truck.

"Yes, I do. You have no idea the training I received while on tour."

"Oh?" I hope I don't sound too curious. He's already mentioned Nova and his familiarity with her shoe closet. I'm sure dating her would have required some specific rules, too.

"Yeah, Nova was quite an educator on the importance of manners in gentlemen. She drilled those rules into all of us."

I smirk, hiding my jealousy. "You say it like it's not a big deal that the biggest pop star around gave you gentleman lessons."

He leans his arm on the open door. *Holy smokes.* I want to take a picture and remember this view forever. "She was really down to earth. Her husband is pretty awesome, too." On that note, Jacob closes the door.

It takes a moment for his words to sink in. *Wait, what?!*

The second he opens the door, I shriek. "Husband?! She's *married?*"

"Yep." He climbs in, and I wish I could say the smug grin makes him look annoying, but dang it, he's even hotter. "It's pretty incredible that she's kept it secret for this long. They've been married for over six months."

"That's wild," I whisper. The full effect of this news sinks in. Jacob *wasn't* dating Nova Sky, because she's MARRIED.

I'm still processing this news as Jacob begins the ten-minute drive to get burgers.

"So, when are you going to explain all of this hockey and ice-skating business?" he asks, interrupting my thoughts.

Here we go. When I decided to call him after beer hockey, I didn't realize how pathetic explaining my journey would seem, especially on the heels of the conversation we had when we went salsa dancing. We couldn't have ended up more opposite—he's a world-famous dancer, and I'm...just me. "This is so embarrassing."

He glances at me. "Why? It's just me."

"You're not *just* you," I say without thinking. I wave a hand up and down his body. *Great, Emma. Just make it worse.*

He furrows his brow. "What's that supposed to mean?"

How is it not obvious? I try to explain it without digging myself into a hole. "I haven't seen or talked to you since we were, what, nine? Ten?"

"Ten," he confirms.

"Right. So we've gone eighteen years without seeing each other. I'm not the same person I was when I was ten. And you're...all grown up." There. Hopefully that gets my point across without being too forward.

He pauses a moment. "Maybe you've grown up, but you're still Emma. Pretend I'm still Jakey."

As if I could. But the thought makes me laugh. "Fine." I can do this. It's just Jakey. The boy I shared my Armenian food with at lunch. The boy I defended from relentless teasing throughout our friendship. The boy who pulled me out of my shell, teaching me to dance in my living room, and eating dinner with our family whenever he could to avoid the dysfunction in his own home. I straighten in my seat. "Remember how last weekend I complained about being 'average'?"

"Yes."

"It all kind of came to a head yesterday when I quit my job."

His eyes widen as he looks over at me. "You quit?"

I nod. "Two of the other engineers were talking about their kids being in all these activities, and how they want to find what they're good at. And I realized that I never did that. My parents didn't have much money growing up, and by the time they had a little extra savings, I was too focused on school. So Mariam got to take all the classes." I pause a moment, trying not to get distracted by my personal issues with Mariam. "It was kind of a spur-of-the-moment thing yesterday. I realized I still have time and a life ahead of me, and I deserve to find the thing that makes me stand out. The thing that makes me special."

"You *are* special, Emma," he interrupts.

It's sweet of him to say that, but he doesn't know me. Not at this age or point in my life. I wave a hand at him. "You don't get it. But that's okay. I don't need you to understand the inner workings of my crazy mind. Besides, you're already incredible at dancing. I want to feel, for once in my life, like I can do something special."

"So explain how ice-skating and hockey fit into this."

Here we go. "Right. So last night, after I quit, Sharleen came over and gave me this haircut." I run my fingers through my hair. I've found myself doing it throughout the day, and I love the reminder that I'm starting fresh. "And she brought a magazine with a list of hobbies for 'cool women' to try out. We wrote all the ones I want to try, along with a few others that I think are feasible, and I'm going down the list, one by one, until I find the thing I'm really good at."

"And beer hockey was on there?"

"No, no," I laugh. "That was a happy coincidence. Not that I'm any good at it, but it was a blast."

Explaining this to him is surprisingly easy. And he's not judging me, which is an added weight lifted off my chest. I wasn't sure how he'd react to my insecurities and new life mission. But now that I'm sitting here, pouring out my heart to him, I realize he was right. He's just Jakey.

Jacob parks at In-N-Out, and I open my door to get out.

"Hey, I was supposed to get that," he protests.

I lean in toward him and whisper, "Don't worry, I won't tell Nova."

His eyes twinkle with mirth, and the moment lasts a little too long to be friendly. I clear my throat. "Let's eat. I'm starving."

We walk inside the restaurant and get in the long line. Jacob inhales deeply. "Mmm. Grilled onions and french fries."

I smile. "It's the simple things in life."

"You have no idea how much I missed this." He looks over at me, and I have to wonder if he means the food...or something else.

We get to the front of the line and place our separate orders. After we have our numbers, we find a booth and settle in across from each other.

"Let's see this list," Jacob says. He puts his hands on the table, curling his fingers in a "gimme" gesture, and a big smile is on his face.

Ugh. This will be humiliating. I grab the list from my purse and slowly slide it across the table, hoping he doesn't notice my shaky hand.

Jacob snatches it from me with a mischievous grin, then un-folds it and starts reading. "Is there any reason for the order of the items on this list?"

"Um, yes." I bite my lip, trying to convince my racing heart that this is fine. This is fine! He won't laugh or judge me. Just get the words out. "They're in order of things I'd like to be good at the most."

He pauses a moment, soaking it in, then looks back down at the list. He's quiet as he reads through. "So you really wanted to be good at ice-skating?"

Ice-skating. Safe. I shrug. "It was a childhood dream. Now I know that wasn't reality."

"And next up is...balloon animals?" He glances up at me. "Please tell me I can't read your handwriting correctly."

Aaaaand here we go. I try to explain as quickly as possible. "That's probably my most embarrassing item. I have this weird desire to be a clown. But, like, a cool clown who doesn't scare children and makes really intricate balloon animals."

He's not *laughing*, per se, but his lips are pressed so tightly together, I'm pretty sure he's holding it back. His attention goes back to the list. "So then it's calligraphy, pottery, painting, and your next highest goal is..." He looks up at me with wide eyes. "Video games?"

My face fills with heat. Is it that ridiculous? "My brother is a professional level gamer. I think it might be in my genes."

A sneaky grin lifts one side of his mouth. Holy smokes. He should not look at me that way. "No hip hop?"

I play off my attraction to him by rolling my eyes. "Already tried that."

He holds my gaze another moment, the smile still on his lips, then he looks back at the list. "So, wait. Where do the pictures and videos come in?"

"Ah." I grab my phone from my purse and go to the Photogram app, then hold it out for him to see. "I made a new account, called Exceptional Emma. I'm going to document all my attempts at rising above mediocrity."

"You should've included the dance class last week."

Why does he keep bringing that up? I roll my eyes again. "Thankfully, that wasn't recorded. It was a clear fail."

"And you think your ice-skating adventures weren't?"

If he didn't have a playful smile, I would feel offended.. Still, I gasp, pretending to be offended. "How dare you insult my skills on the ice!"

Jacob laughs out loud. "I will say, I was impressed with your championship trophy beer chugging skills."

I pretend to take a bow. "Thank you, thank you."

Our numbers get called, and Jacob offers to pick my food up with his. As he goes to the counter, I take a moment to process this exact moment. My former best friend is here. I'm having dinner with him. And sharing all my deepest feelings and fears.

Just another normal day.

Jacob sets the food down, interrupting my thoughts. "Still haven't grown out of those chocolate shakes, huh?"

I grab the shake. "Never." I take a long sip and feel the chocolaty goodness seep through to my bones. No, I know it doesn't really go into my bones, but I feel happiness in every part of my body.

"Man, I've missed you," Jacob says.

My eyes widen. Wow.

He rushes to explain. "It's just that, being away from home, I haven't had real friends. It's been a long time since I've settled somewhere long enough to enjoy being in one place, with people I know." He swallows. "And it's nice to have someone I can trust."

Friends. Yes. That's what we were before, and that's what we are now.

And that's how it should stay. I can't imagine how much of a distraction it would be if I keep wondering if he likes me or not. I need to focus on myself right now.

I smile at him. He's not meeting my eyes, so I reach my hand across the table and take his to ease his discomfort, squeezing it tight.

"I'm glad you're home, too," I say.

He looks up at me, his expression visibly relaxed, and we both dig into our burgers. Just like we did when we were ten.

# Chapter 10

While we eat our dinners, I pull up the Photogram app. To my surprise, the picture I posted of the league laughing together has gotten thirty likes, more than the number of followers I have. I hand Jacob my phone, and he shows me how to make a reel from the videos Sharleen took earlier today.

"You'll want a catchy song to go with it too, unless the audio is good enough on its own," he says, tapping around and editing the different clips.

"Do you mind doing it for me this time? I really want to make sure it looks good."

"Not at all," he says, looking up with a smile. "My days are pretty light. I can be your social media manager."

I laugh. "That's a little much. Don't get ahead of yourself there."

He smirks and hands me back my phone. "Do you want to post it now?"

I rewatch the compiled video, so embarrassed by my lack of skill. But this is what I promised, right? My five followers are begging for an update.

"Sure. I should probably write some kind of caption, huh?"

"Yeah. Just speak from the heart. People love that."

I take in a deep breath, then start typing.

*Turns out ice-skating is not my calling, but I'm excellent at drinking beer out of a championship trophy and finding new friends. Many thanks to the Harbor Sands Beer Hockey League for helping me find some gear in the lost and found, teaching me to play, and cheering me on. Now for my next hobby!*

I hold my phone out to Jacob, who smiles as he reads the caption. "Perfect," he says.

I tap the "post" button and set my phone down. "Now all five of my followers will get to see me slipping on the ice."

Jacob shrugs. "If nothing else, you're keeping track of this for yourself. It's like a journal." He laughs. "Remember the journal that you had when we were kids? The one where you'd draw a picture each day and write about what you did? It was so cute how you kept doing that as we got older."

I laugh tightly. "Uh-huh, yep, I remember."

His eyes narrow. "Why are you being so weird?"

"Weird? I'm not being weird. You're weird."

He smiles. "You're being really weird. What is it? Do you still write in a journal?"

I contemplate my words. "Well, sure, yeah. Lots of people write in journals."

"But it's not just that you write in a journal... You write in the *same* kind of journal, don't you? The one with the big space for a picture and the guided lines to learn how to write your letters properly."

I bury my face in my hands. How did he figure it out? "Ugh, yes. Yes, I do. And no one else knows that."

He peels my hands off of my face, his warmth and gentle touch flooding the rest of my body. "I love it. That's awesome. It's innocent and sweet, and I'm glad you still do it." He doesn't let go of my hands, and I swear this would be the best date I've ever been on, if it was a date.

But it's not. Right? I pull my hands away slowly. "Thanks," I say, giving my hair a quick fluff. "We should probably get going."

He looks a little disappointed at the change in conversation. We stand up together and start carrying our trays to the trash can, but Jacob goes back to the conversation at hand. "Since ice-skating clearly was not your calling—"

"Clearly," I confirm.

"When are you going to try some video games? I'd love to be there for that."

A slight warmth creeps up to my cheeks, but I hide it by taking my trash to the bin. "Are you a gamer?"

He shrugs. "I dabble. What game does your brother play?"

"Heroes of the Kingdom," I reply. "He and his friend Aaron are ranked super high, and they compete."

Jacob's eyes widen. "That's so cool. Do they make money?"

"Some," I say. "They get lots of free stuff from sponsors, though. My mom doesn't love it, but at least it's not a super violent game. I figured that's what I'd try out."

"I've played before," he says. "Can I join in on this one? I can record you, too. Social media manager, right?"

"Right," I say with a laugh. "Sure. Let me text Garen and see when he's available."

We walk out of In-N-Out and back to his truck, the moon shining above us in the darkness, and I text Garen on the way home. We talk about a few of the other items on the list for the next ten minutes, and I'm disappointed when he pulls into my parking lot. I don't get to spend any more time with him. My heart sinks a little.

When he parks the car, he opens the door to get out of the truck.

"You don't have to do that," I say quickly.

"Walk you to your door?" he asks.

I nod.

"Emma." He fixes me with a serious look. "It's very dark. I'd like to make sure you get home safely."

I exhale. "Okay."

The walk to my door is quiet, except for the voice in my head that keeps screaming, *This is not a date! Don't get your hopes up!*

We arrive at my door, and I fish my keys out of my purse. "Well, you saw me safely here, so now you can go."

He raises a brow at me. "That's all I get?"

My heart stops. "W-what do you mean?" What does he want, a *kiss*?

He pauses a moment, taking in my panicked expression, then opens his arms wide. "I figured friends can hug goodbye."

"Right. Of course." I step close to him and wrap my arms around his waist, his arms encircling my shoulders. This hug does *not* feel like the hugs when we were ten. For one, I'm pretty sure I was a little taller than him back then. Now, he's a good five inches taller than me. But he's not angles and bones anymore. Oh, no, he's full of tight, firm muscles that are twisting my stomach into knots.

But it's a friendly hug, nothing romantic. He holds tight to me. It's like he *needs* this hug, like my physical contact is keeping him together. I squeeze him back, resting my head on his chest. Despite my physical attraction to him, there's something so much deeper between us. Something I've never experienced with anyone I've dated before.

He pulls back and looks at me, a twinkle in his piercing green eyes. "I'm so glad we did this." He squeezes me one more time and whispers in my ear, "You're already exceptional, Emma."

Shivers run down my spine. When he says it, I can almost believe it.

Almost.

And then he kisses my cheek. His soft lips just barely graze my cheekbone, and I think I could melt on the spot. But he pulls away before I can say or do anything, a sly grin on his lips. He knows exactly what he's doing to me.

"Bye, Emma," he says with a wink. "Don't forget to go inside."

Oh, my.

"Bye, Jakey!" I squeak, shoving the key into the lock with a shaky hand and waving a quick goodbye. As soon as the door closes, I lean my back against the door and take a few deep breaths.

Holy. Smokes.

It takes a few minutes to calm myself down, but I manage. After getting a glass of water and fanning myself off, I get ready for bed and pull out my journal. I'm in the middle of sketching out a picture of myself drinking from the championship trophy, Sharleen filming on the side, and Cynthia and the guys cheering me on, when my brother's name flashes across my phone screen. I pick it up and check the text.

*Hey, sis. I can't believe you want to play. I'm going on a trip to the river this week with Aaron's family, but we can definitely play after that. Jacob can come too. Are you guys dating?*

I furiously type out my reply. *No, no. He's just helping me get my social media account going.*

*What social media account?*

I push the palm of my hand into my forehead.

I guess I couldn't hide it from my family forever. I take a screenshot of my account and send it over to him.

My phone rings almost immediately with a call from Garen.

"Hey," I answer.

"Hey, Exceptional Emma," he says slowly. "So, how did that beer taste? Like the sweat of a thousand men before you?"

"Ugh, disgusting. And yes, it did. But it was worth it."

He laughs out loud. "I don't know what brought this on, but I support it."

"Really?"

"Really." He pauses a moment, and I get a little uncomfortable. It isn't like my little brother to get all emotional on me, and I wonder what he's hesitating to say.

"I don't think you're average," he finally says. "You're more than that. But I think you deserve to take this time to find yourself."

"Well, thank you," I say, surprised that my little brother can pull out such an emotional statement. Tears gather in my eyes, brought on by pride in the man he's becoming. "I'm glad I have your support."

"Okay, that's enough of that," he says quickly, and I laugh. He's still nineteen, after all.

"I'll check with Jacob to see when he's free and let you know," I say. "And I'll try to do some research on Heroes of the Kingdom so I'm ready."

"That is an excellent plan. I look forward to teaching you my ways."

"We'll see about that. Bye baby brother."

"Yuck. Bye, old lady."

Laughing, we both hang up. I finish my journal entry and tuck it inside my desk. Realization dawns on me that posting on Photogram isn't so different from writing in my journal; it's just writing a caption about a picture. How hard could it be? Maybe I'll be pretty good at social media, after all. I climb under the covers, then decide to text Jacob with the plan for gaming. *Garen is gone until next weekend. So maybe next Saturday we can plan on gaming?*

As soon as I send the message, I realize how disappointed I am that it's so far away. I don't know if it's because I think I'll actually be good at video games or if I wish I could see Jacob sooner.

Almost immediately, a response comes back. *That sounds perfect. What will you do until then?*

I reply. *I'll try out the other hobbies on the list to fill my time.*

I set the phone down and pull out my list, seeing what's next. As if he's reading my mind, the next message reads, *Okay. Bummer that it's such a long wait. What was next again?*

I scan the items and smile at the next one down.

*Balloon animals.*

The three dots appear, disappear, and reappear. *That's right. I guess that could be cool.* He includes a couple of clown emojis, and I giggle.

I don't really know what to say to that, but his next message comes in before I have a chance to respond.

*What's your favorite animal? Is it still a panda?*

I smile at the memory. I used to draw pandas constantly when we were in school. Every time I did a project, I would draw my panda logo and write "Panda Publishing" across the top. *I guess so. I haven't really thought about my favorite animal in years.*

I wait a moment, then realize I should ask him the same question. *How about you? Still a tiger?*

While I'm waiting for him to respond, I find a tiger emoji and send it to him, hoping it'll make him smile.

*Nah, I grew out of tigers when I was about fifteen. They're cool, but I watched a documentary about octopuses and I'm kind of obsessed now. I want to get scuba certified one of these days.*

I search for an octopus emoji and he laughs back at it.

*I got another question for you. Favorite time of day?* He writes.

I wiggle under my covers, getting that giddy feeling I haven't had in years. I don't know if he's just trying to get to know me after all this time, or if he feels even a small twinge of the attraction I feel toward him, but this attention makes me feel more special than I can remember in a long time.

*I love early mornings—that first sip of coffee, the fresh possibilities, and the feeling that no one else is awake. You?*

The three dots scroll over and over, and waiting feels like torture. Just when I'm about to switch to a different app, he responds. *I'm a night owl. I get a crazy rush of energy after ten pm.*

I snort out loud. That's the exact opposite of how I feel. But I guess I did have a really fun time going out dancing with him last week. Maybe when I'm with the right person, I can enjoy nights, too.

*But I also love a quiet night in,* he writes. Maybe he realized how different his response was from mine.

*And I guess I had fun going out late with you last week.* I send a winking face after that, then wish I could take it back because it sounds so flirty.

*So did I,* he writes back.

A moment passes where I don't know what to say, but Jacob fills it. *What's your favorite food?*

*Oh, that's so hard. But probably my mom's dolma. It's the best. Lemme guess, yours is In-N-Out?*

He laughs at that. *Guilty,* he says. Then a moment later, *I haven't had good Armenian dolma since I left. I think I'll have to remedy that.*

I smirk. *Are you inviting yourself over for a family dinner?*

*I used to eat at your house all the time. Why would it be different now?*

Uh, because you're a gorgeous, grown man who will get my mom way too excited about the potential of grandchildren.

Don't worry, I won't write that.

He keeps asking more favorites—color, season, sibling (as if that's a question, when Mariam drives me crazy and I adore Garen), and before I know it, it's midnight and my eyes are drooping.

*I don't want you to think I'm ghosting you, but I'm about to fall asleep,* I write.

*No worries,* he says. *You had a busy day. When are you doing balloon animals? I wouldn't mind seeing that.*

I smile. *No plan yet. But it's a date.*

And I fall asleep immediately after I press send.

Chapter 11

*It's a date?!*

Oh, my goodness. Sleepy Emma is just as dangerous as tipsy Emma. I really need to be more careful with my words around Jacob, whether spoken or typed. Besides, I should stick to my goal of no romantic entanglements. Jacob will just distract me from my end goal!

Tell that to my heart.

Because it's Sunday afternoon, and I'm heading over to his apartment to make some balloon animals. Well, technically, it's Sara's apartment, since he's staying with her and Cami. I picked up a balloon animal making kit from the local party store on Saturday, and Jacob said he was free on Sunday, so here I am at his door.

I ring the bell and hear the pitter-patter of little feet. "I got it, I got it!" a little voice squeals.

"Cami, no!" Sara's voice says.

But Cami flings the door open wide. I'm greeted by long, bouncy brown curls on the most adorable little girl with big, brown eyes and cheeks that deserve to be squished. "Hi! I'm Cami."

"Hello, Cami. It's nice to meet you." I'm not really sure what to do with four-year-olds. That's more my sister's area. But I put my hand out to shake hers, and she seems to enjoy the grown-up treatment.

"Cami. How many times have I told you not to open the door to strangers?" Sara appears around the corner, drying her hands on a dishrag.

"But it's not a stranger! It's Emma! And we knew she was coming!"

"She's not wrong." Jacob appears, and I swear, my body has a physical reaction to just seeing him. Does he lift weights or just dance? That's not a question I'm about to ask out loud, but whatever he does, he should keep doing it forever.

"It doesn't matter if she's not wrong," Sara says, shaking a finger at Jacob. "She needs to listen."

"But she's my little *princesa*. She can do no wrong." He picks Cami up and swings her around, and she squeals.

Oh.

My.

Ovaries.

Sara shakes her head at them. "I can't discipline her anymore with him around," she says to me.

I laugh and take a couple of steps in, observing my surroundings. Scents of chilis and garlic waft through the air. The decor in the apartment is lively, but clearly the home of an active kid. Toys litter the floor, but the majority of the mess is paper, crayons, and markers.

"Cami, do you like to make crafts?" I ask.

"I do!" She runs over to a sheet of paper and shows it to me. "Look, I drew Tío and Mamá."

I don't know anything about art skills in children, but it looks pretty good to me. She nailed Jacob's physique and curly hair. "I love it," I say. "Are you going to make balloon animals with us?"

"I want to try!"

"What about you, Sara?" I ask.

Sara waves her hands. "That's okay. I'm working on dinner for tonight, anyway."

"What are you making? It smells incredible."

"Enchiladas. You should stay and have some."

I look over at Jacob, who watches our interaction with a smile on his face. I grin. "That sounds great."

"Let's get this going, shall we?" Jacob asks. He takes his phone out of his pocket and props it up on the kitchen table. He presses the record button, and I open the box.

"It says there are instructional videos we can watch," I say. I brought a laptop with me, so I pull out the instruction manual and type the URL into my browser. A slew of videos show on my screen. "What should we try first?"

Jacob leans over my shoulder, and I can feel the weight of his chest behind me. I have to remind myself to breathe.

"The bear is listed first. Maybe we'll try that one? It shouldn't be too hard." He bumps my shoulder with his chest. "It's the closest to a panda."

I swallow and nod, alarmed at my body's reaction to being so close to him again. Jacob moves away from me, and I click the play button.

The video begins with loud trumpet sounds heralding the parade of balloon animals. I can barely hear the man introducing himself over the music, but I'm getting in the mood to learn some party tricks, so I guess it works. The man in the video is wearing a bowling shirt and a fedora, and he starts by blowing up his balloon with the pump and tying it off. Then he shows how to make a slew of twists of various lengths, and after a few minutes, it magically turns into a bear.

"That's kind of crazy," I say.

"It looks fun! Let's do it." Jacob grabs a brown balloon and starts blowing it up. He pinches the top and hands me the pump.

I grab a white balloon. "I'm gonna make a polar bear."

"Closest thing to a panda, huh?"

"Yep." I start blowing up my white balloon and notice that Jacob is struggling to tie his balloon. "Having a problem?"

"This is way harder to tie than I expected." He struggles for another minute.

"Careful! You're being kind of rough!"

"These can't pop." The second the words are out of his mouth, a loud POP fills the room, and Cami and I scream.

"You said they can't pop!" Cami exclaims.

"Yeah!" I'm still holding my white balloon pinched shut, a little concerned now that we're already off to such a rough start.

He shrugs. "Just gotta try again." He picks up another brown balloon and starts filling it with air.

I focus on my white balloon instead of the way his biceps and forearms flex. The one benefit I have is that my fingers are smaller than his, so even though tying mine is a struggle, I get it done.

"There!" I say proudly.

"I want one!" Cami says. I set mine down, blow up a purple one for her, and tie it off. My finger is already red from the lack of circulation in tying these knots, but the smile on her little face makes it worth it.

"Okay, so now I have to make a few twists at two fingers' length," I murmur, trying to estimate the right size.

Jacob has finally figured out how to tie his balloon and reaches over to me, placing two of his fingers over mine, measuring out the distance to the twist. "This should be good. Your fingers are a little small."

I suck in a breath, my heart racing from this tiny touch of our hands. What is going on? Making balloon animals is supposed to be dorky, not sexy. I have major problems.

"Mmmmkay," I say, and start twisting. I'm a little paranoid that my balloon is going to pop, but the twist ends up working fine.

Jacob and I twist our balloons silently, and after making my first four twists, the whole thing untwists into its original shape.

"Why does it keep doing that?" I ask, frustrated.

"Because you're supposed to hold it like this," Jacob says, showing me how he's using one finger to hold each of his twists.

"That's not what the guy did!" I complain.

"Yes, he did," Jacob says patiently.

I shake my head and restart the video.

Whoops. Sure enough, Jacob is right.

"Oh. I guess he does."

"See?" Jacob says, but it's all good-natured and smiles, and I can't be upset with him. I sigh and start twisting again.

Cami already lost interest in making actual balloon animals and is happy with her "worm." She put some eyeball stickers on it and drew a mouth. But now she's looking through the instruction booklet at all the options.

"Look at that puppy!" she squeals. "Mamá, come look! It looks just like the one Abuela wanted."

Ever-patient Sara peeks her head over the counter and smiles. "You're right, it does."

Jacob looks over at Cami and Sara. "What puppy?"

"Oh." Sara looks at Cami sadly, then back at me and Jacob. "Mom was looking at getting a little poodle. She had one picked out at the shelter that she wanted, but then...you know."

Jacob nods. The silence hangs thick in the air.

"Then what?" I ask.

Jacob turns his head to me, then fiddles with his balloon. "Then she got sick."

Oh.

*Oh.*

I look around the apartment that clearly wasn't decorated by Sara and Cami. There are touches everywhere of Jacob and Sara's childhood, and the blankets their mom would crochet when we were kids are all over the furniture.

This wasn't just Sara's apartment. It was Sara's...and their mom's.

I feel so embarrassed that I didn't realize this until *right now*, but I also don't want to make this about myself. The pieces of the puzzle are clicking together, including the fact that Jacob suddenly quit his dream job and moved back home—the question all his Photogram followers have been asking for weeks.

I drop my voice to a whisper. "Is that why you came back home?"

Jacob keeps playing with the balloon, twisting and pinching in different places. He nods, then smiles sadly at me. "Sara and Cami needed me."

I don't push him, because I can tell he's already fighting his inclination to shut down with these little pieces of information. Instead, I gently place one hand on his arm, giving it a light squeeze. He looks over at me with a grateful smile.

"I *really* wanted a puppy," Cami says, breaking the silence. I pull my arm away and try to twist my bear.

"And maybe we'll get you one," Jacob says.

"Is that so?" Sara asks, her eyebrow arched.

"You know I can't say no to my *princesa*," he replies.

Sara rolls her eyes but smiles. And just like that, the tension is gone.

Jacob finishes the face of his bear and hands it to Cami, who runs around the apartment with it, making growling noises. He starts making a dog next, and within minutes, it looks amazing. But I'm determined to finish this polar bear, no matter what it takes.

About half an hour later, I'm making a twist to create the front legs when I feel Jacob wrapping a balloon around my head. The nearness of his body behind mine sends my heart racing.

"Wh-what are you doing?" I ask.

"Measuring you for a hat."

"A...hat?"

"Mm-hmm. It's gonna go great with those shoes you're always wearing."

I snort a laugh, and he moves away, satisfied with his measurement. I don't pay much attention to him, now that I'm so focused on my bear. I can't get distracted this close to the end.

Finally, I make the last twist to create the back legs. "I did it!" I squeal, holding it up proudly.

Jacob looks up from his hat, and I watch as his eyes widen and his lips twitch. "That's a...bear?"

"Yeah!" I turn it around, admiring it from every angle. "It's good, right?"

"Why are its ears lopsided?" Cami asks.

"Cami!" Jacob says in a hushed tone.

Cami narrows her eyes. "And the back legs are so much shorter than the front legs. Ohhhh, is that his butt? It's his butt, right? He just has front legs and a butt?"

I look at my bear a little more closely and swallow hard. "No, those are his legs."

Cami blinks a few times. "Uh-huh."

"It's really great," Jacob says slowly, and I look up at him. His face is turning red, and I know he's trying to hold his laughter in.

"Let it out, Jakey," I say. "You can laugh."

He doubles over, his hands on his knees, his laughter echoing off the walls. "Oh, Emma. It's deformed!"

I want to be offended, but the more I look at it, the more I agree. A giggle erupts from my mouth, then an actual laugh, and then I'm laughing so hard, tears are streaming down my face.

"What's so funny?" Sara asks, coming out of the kitchen. I hold up my polar bear, still unable to say any words.

"Oh, that's...lovely," Sara says.

"You don't have to pull your Mom-act on her," Jacob says breathlessly. "She's not Cami."

Cami gasps behind us. "You don't think my drawings are beautiful?"

"No!" we all three chorus.

"I love your drawings," Sara says. She eyes my creation, a twinkle in her eye. "And...yes, this polar bear looks a little...misshapen."

We all laugh for a few more minutes, but then the moment winds down, and now the disappointment sets in. "I guess this wasn't my thing, either."

"Thank goodness," Jacob mutters.

"Hey!" I say, shoving his arm.

"Don't mess up my beautiful hat!" he says.

"You know, I read an article about something called the 100-hour-rule, that if you spend just one hundred hours on a skill, with really dedicated practice, you can become an expert."

"Yeah, but do you really want to spend one hundred hours making balloon animals?" Jacob asks.

"I thought I might," I say. I look at my misshapen bear, and while I kind of love him, I don't have a desire to try again. "But not anymore. That's okay. That's why I have my list. I can just move on to the next thing."

"But will you really be amazing at something on the first try?" Sara presses.

I shrug. "I have to hope I will."

# Chapter 12

After balloon animal Sunday, I posted a compilation reel of our attempts, plus a picture of me modeling Jacob's hat. I look like a complete joke, but we had so much fun, I don't even care. But then it was time to go back to work. Everyone acted awkward and weird. I only went through the motions, spending any free moment researching my next hobbies. Monday and Tuesday evenings were for calligraphy. I watched some basic calligraphy YouTube videos by someone named Amy Carter, but my attempts looked like a second-grader learning cursive. I know it would take more time to become an expert, but I didn't have the patience for it.

Thursday evening was a beginner's pottery class. I won't go into the details, but let's just say my mug looks deformed, just like my balloon animals. I even tried hand embroidery, and now I have bandages all over my fingers from the needle. I actually got blood on my fabric, which isn't even funny, it's just gross.

My posts are getting attention, though, which is both cool and embarrassing. Jacob helped me create a few reels of my calligraphy, including a pretty obvious mistake where I misspelled the word "calligraphy," and that got a decent amount of views and likes. I also posted a few pictures of the other students in pottery class, which got more attention than my misshapen mug. I was right about the similarities with journaling, though; writing captions has been coming easily, and people seem to enjoy what I have to say.

Now it's Saturday, and I'm sitting with Garen at the kitchen table of my parents' house, learning the basics of his video game. My parents know the general idea of what I'm up to, and while they're not completely supportive, they respect my decisions as an adult. Especially since I'm not asking them to bankroll me while I'm jobless.

The front doorbell rings, and Sparky rushes over to the door, barking loudly on his mission to save us all from the dangerous intruder.

"Everyone!" I announce loudly. My parents, who are watching tv, look over in alarm. "I am begging you. Please do not be weird in front of Jacob."

"You mean Jakey," my mom says with a sly grin.

"Yes, Mom. Jakey. Just...please don't be weird."

"I don't understand why you're so worried," my dad says. "He was your friend, and now you're hanging out again. Don't be so paranoid."

I sigh, hoping that he's right and I *am* just being paranoid.

But one individual is missing from this pow-wow, and as soon as I hear the front door open, I realize where she is.

"Holy smokes," I hear Mariam's voice at the front entryway.

"Uh, hey Mariam," Jacob says. I run to the front door, a little breathless when I reach the two of them as they're reconnecting. Sparky stands by Jacob, barking loudly.

"Don't look at him," I command Jacob.

Jacob raises his hands. "I remember your *very* specific instructions."

Sparky keeps barking. "Sparky, hush!" I scold. He finally quiets down but is still on high alert.

I sigh. "I'm sure you remember each other. Jacob, Mariam. Mariam, Jacob." I give Mariam a sweet, fake smile. "Now, bye, Mariam."

Garen shows up at the front door and shakes Jacob's hand, introducing himself for the first time.

"You did NOT say how hot he was now!" Mariam hisses at me.

"Why would I have said that?" I whisper back, knowing full well that Jacob is looking over and hears the entire conversation.

"Uh, hello!" She gestures at her outfit, another flour-stained ensemble. "I would have dressed up a little for him."

I roll my eyes. "He's not here for you."

"Not yet." She waggles her eyebrows at me.

I decide it's best to just ignore her. "Come on, Jacob." I pull him by the arm and toward the living room so he can quickly say hi to my parents.

*Please don't embarrass me.*

"Hi, Jakey!" my mom calls. "Look at you! You're so grown up. You're such a man now!"

I think I'm dying.

"Hello, everyone! I like how you've redecorated, Mrs. Nazarian!" he calls and waves, but I don't let go of his arm, and Garen leads the way to his room.

"Whoa," Jacob says as we enter his cave. "How many monitors do you have on your computer?"

"Four." Garen beams with pride. "I built the setup myself."

"That's amazing." Jacob looks around the room, taking in all the medals and computer equipment. "You must be really good at Heroes of the Kingdom."

Garen shrugs as if he hasn't won every local tournament for the last six months. "I'm all right."

"Well, let's see how our Emma does, huh?" Jacob squeezes my arm, and now I'm feeling nervous. Maybe I shouldn't have had him come after all. I have no clue how this will go, and having Jacob watch *and* document it all seems a little overwhelming.

But there's no time to lose. Garen guides me to his super fancy gamer chair and sets me up with a practice round. We're on teams of five, starting on opposing sides of the virtual map. I have to shoot bubbles at woodland creatures for points to get stronger, but avoid getting shot by bubbles from the opposing team, otherwise I'll float away into time-out. The goal is for the entire team to make it to the other side of the map, and then we'd win.

Garen teaches me the keys to press and the way to click my mouse to move around the board and target my bubbles at the right person. I play around for a few minutes, and I kind of feel like I'm getting the hang of it.

"You're doing great!" he says. "Wanna try an actual match?"

"Uh...not really," I say. The idea of playing with other people is a little nauseating.

"You got this. We won't put you in a ranked game, so your teammates shouldn't be too upset if you lose. It's a good experience."

I take a deep breath and wait as he cues up the game. When the match begins, I feel a rush of adrenaline and try to channel it into my fingers on the mouse and keyboard. The first few minutes pass peacefully, but then I get put in time-out a few times for getting shot with too many bubbles. Each time compounds my frustration and boils my blood. I've been playing for ten minutes, in time-out three times, and I keep getting pelted with bubbles.

"Oh my goodness, *what is happening*?" I squeal.

"Jeez, Emma, it's just a game," Garen says.

"Just a game? *Just a game?* This is a fight for survival!" I keep pushing buttons on the keyboard and clicking my mouse, but nothing is working. Another three seconds, and my character is in a thirty-second time-out.

"You've got to be kidding me," I say, burying my head in my hands.

"Does she normally get this worked up?" Jacob whispers to Garen.

"Never," Garen replies.

"I can hear you," I growl in what (hopefully) sounds like a menacing voice.

"Easy there, tiger," Jacob says, rubbing my shoulder with his free hand. I'm too upset to enjoy the massage that would normally send me into a spiral.

"You're actually doing really well," Garen says.

"You're kidding, right?" I exclaim. "I've been in time-out four times in this match alone."

"That's not bad for your first attempt," Jacob says. "The first time I played, I think I was in time-out for more than half of the game."

I shake my head. "This is infuriating." I hear a snort from Garen's direction and look over at my brother. "What's so amusing?"

"You rarely get worked up like this," he says. "This must be really bothering you."

"Well, yeah!" I turn back to my computer, where I'm finally out of time-out and can start playing again. "My team is counting on me." I click around with my mouse, moving my avatar throughout the map, shooting bubbles at the woodland creatures to earn gold.

I notice the chat box in the corner of the screen, and I try to decipher all the acronyms my team is typing at me. "What are they saying?"

Garen and Jacob exchange a glance.

"Uh." Garen smirks. "You don't want to know."

I gasp. "Are they being mean to me?"

Jacob bursts out laughing. "Yes. And pretty crude, too."

I slam the mouse down. Not only do *I* know how badly I'm playing, my teammates are talking trash about me! "I can't believe this."

"Whoa, there," Jacob says. "You don't want to break your mouse."

I narrow my eyes at Garen. "I know full well that Garen has slammed a mouse or two in his time playing."

"And you've always yelled at me for it," Garen retorts.

"Well, now I get it!" The adrenaline is pulsing through my veins, making me feel and act in ways I normally wouldn't. All this conversation distracts me from the game, and a player on the other team traps me in a bubble. "Ugh! Now I'm in time-out again. I shouldn't be talking to you guys."

"You're so tilted," Garen comments.

"Tilted?" I ask.

"Yeah, like you're getting so upset by the game, and it's making you play worse."

He's not wrong, but I don't know how else to feel or act. I sit back in my brother's gaming chair, close my eyes, and take a moment to gather myself. When I open my eyes, I see the word "DEFEAT."

"That was a disaster," I mutter.

"Did you expect to win your first game?" Garen asks.

I shrug. "I thought maybe I'd be good at it."

"You *are* good at it," Garen says. "But you won't be professional level on your first try."

I rub my forehead with the heels of my hands, willing myself to take deep breaths and calm my racing heart.

"So, Emma," Jacob asks, "how do you feel about playing video games?"

I turn my head and glare at him, finally aware that this is all being recorded to post tonight for my hundred followers. "Pass."

He laughs and ends the recording, then squeezes me in a hug. "You did really well."

I lean my head on his chest, reveling in the embrace of a friend. "Thanks." The beat of his heart calms my nerves, giving me a steady rhythm to focus on. Another memory floods my vision.

*I throw my Guess Who? game board on the ground and squeal. "It's not fair!"*

*Jacob pats my shoulder. "It's okay, Emma. It's just a game."*

*I shake my head, my seven-year-old body unable to handle the frustration. My hands clench into fists. "I was so close to winning that time. If only I'd asked their hair color instead of eye color."*

*"I know." He gives me a hug, squeezing me tight. The beat of his heart calms my body, and I relax into him. "I'm still proud of you."*

Garen clears his throat. "Uh...do you guys need a minute?"

My head pops up, realizing how intimate this looks, and my cheeks redden. "Yeah, no."

Jacob releases me and sits back, fiddling with my phone. He's probably putting the different clips together to make another reel for me.

"Honestly, Em, you did really well," Garen says. "I could totally train you and—"

"Heck. No." I shake my head vehemently. "There is no way I'm doing that again. My body cannot handle the emotional turmoil."

Garen laughs and rubs my neck. "It does take a special breed to handle the pressure of video games."

I narrow my eyes at him. "I wouldn't say you're the perfect example."

"No, I'm not. I get tilted, too. But I'm typically able to manage myself and my emotions."

I nod in agreement. He's right. Overall, he's a sweet, happy-go-lucky kid. He gets frustrated, but he doesn't let it take over his life.

But me? If I were to keep playing, I think it would consume me. No, thank you. I don't think that's worth it.

"All done," Jacob says, offering my phone to me. I take it in my hands and watch the reel he put together.

"Oh, my word," I murmur. I look wild. My eyes are crazed, my hair flying, and, of course, I act like a three-year-old throwing a tantrum.

"Want to post it, or no?" Jacob asks, his lips tilted in a crooked grin.

"You know I'm going to." I click *post*. "All one hundred of my followers will love it."

He huffs a laugh. "It's real. People like that."

"I guess." I scroll through my posts from the last few days, the pictures and reels from ice-skating, balloon animals, calligraphy, and pottery. The comments are generally kind. People have been supportive of my attempts, even though I look like a fool. Hopefully this reel won't be any different.

Sounds of a violin filter in through the door, and Jacob looks out into the hallway. "Is someone listening to music?"

I sigh. "No. That's Mariam practicing."

"Really?" He tilts his head, listening more carefully. "Wow. She's really good."

"Yep." I shut my mouth so I don't say something I'll regret. Like how it feels as if she's playing to get his attention, and that aggravates me more than I'd like to admit.

"She's playing Adoration by Borowski," Garen chimes in. "I play the piano part with her."

"I want to hear," Jacob says. He looks over at me for confirmation, and I smile tightly. I don't really need to hear it again. They've been playing together for years. But if Jacob wants to hear it, I'll suffer through it one more time.

"Cool." Garen closes out the game from his computer, and we follow him into the music room where Mariam is finishing the piece.

"Hey, sis," Garen says, and she stops playing. "Can I play with you?"

"Sure!" She shuffles out of the way, and Garen takes a seat at the piano, rifling through the sheet music until he comes to the piece they've been perfecting together since they were kids. Mariam has it memorized, though, so she stands, patiently waiting for him.

Jacob and I sit on the little sofa my mom placed in the music room, along with the painting of a little girl playing the violin and a little boy playing the piano. Just another indicator that I don't belong here.

They begin playing together, the familiar, beautiful notes frustrating me further. Jacob watches them, completely awed by their performance.

"So, they play instruments," he whispers to me.

I nod.

"What about you?"

I shake my head. "No music for me, remember? I didn't take any classes."

"But it's not even on your list. You didn't want to ask your brother and sister to teach you how to play?"

I turn to face him, a blank expression on my face.

Jacob just smiles. Thankfully, he also knows not to press when I'm feeling like this. So he sits back and listens to the music, leaving me to wonder what it must feel like to be this good at something. It's probably the extra adrenaline from playing the game, but I'm more aggravated than usual by their display of talent.

Finally, they finish playing, and I clap politely while Jacob cheers.

"That was incredible!" he says. "Fantastic."

"Thanks," Mariam says shyly, wiping away a tear.

Seriously? She's *that* emotional over playing a piece? I thought it was bad enough that she cried while *listening* to music, but this just takes it to another level. Jacob doesn't seem phased by it, though, which irritates me to no end.

"That was beautiful," my mom says from behind us. I don't know when my parents joined the party, but it figures. They're never far from their incredibly talented children.

"How did video games go?" Dad asks me.

I shake my head. "I don't want to talk about it."

"Well, I was thinking," my mom says, "since you'll have more time on your hands, do you think you could design the deck that we're going to add from our bedroom?"

They've been talking about adding this deck for *years*, and I've always said I had too much work to design it for them.

"Yeah, that might work," I say. I don't really want to commit to anything, because the point of quitting my job is to focus on myself and my journey. But I'm sure I can find some pockets of time to design it for them.

"So if it's not video games, what's next?" my dad asks.

"Um…" I hesitate, knowing exactly what it is.

"Surfing," Jacob supplies with a huge smile.

I nudge him with my shoulder. "Why do you look so happy about that?"

"Because I can teach you."

# Chapter 13

It turns out Jacob had a camping trip planned for the beach in Carlsbad, about thirty miles south of Harbor Sands.

Well, not just Jacob. Sara and Cami are coming, along with Ricardo and a few other guys. But apparently Sara is thrilled for me to come too, since she's dying for a girl to hang out with. These guys, and even Sara, all know how to surf and are willing to teach me.

That's why one week later, at four in the afternoon the next Friday, I'm waiting outside my apartment for Jacob to pick me up. I'm a ball of freaking nerves. Two nights with Jacob. At least we won't be in tents. There is some company that sets up a trailer for you at the site, and all you have to do is clean it up when you leave, and they come pick it up and take it back. I'm not sure I could handle *actually* camping at the beach without an indoor shower and a proper bed.

Am I going to have my own *room*? That was something I should have asked ahead of time.

I asked Sharleen to come along, but she's busy on Saturday mornings with her cosmetology classes and can't miss. So it's just me.

And Jacob.

And Sara, Cami, and a bunch of guys I don't know.

No problem.

I'm about to dash back inside and text Jacob that I'm…I don't know, some version of sick, when his truck pulls into the parking lot. Dang it. Missed my moment of escape.

But this is what being "exceptional" is all about, right? Going outside of my comfort zone, embracing the hard and scary parts of life, and finding out what I'm meant to do here on this earth.

Jacob parks the truck at the curb in front of me and hops out, grabbing my bags.

"You don't have to do that," I protest.

"I insist," he says with a wide smile that makes me a little weak in the knees. He hefts up my bags like they're nothing and throws them in the cab. I open the back door to climb in, but I'm greeted by Sara and Cami.

"Hop in the front," Sara says cheerily.

Cami sighs. "She's so pretty."

I blush furiously, even though it's just a four-year-old's compliment, but hide it by closing the door quickly and opening the front passenger side.

"You're right, Cami," Jacob says, sliding into the driver's seat. "She is pretty."

Aaaand there comes the blush again. But that doesn't mean anything. He's been around stunning, drop-dead gorgeous women for the last ten years. I'm just…me.

"Everyone ready?" Jacob asks.

"Ready!" Cami and Sara chirp.

"Anyone need to use the bathroom?" he asks.

I look over in alarm. "Uh, no, I'm good."

He laughs. "I'm asking for Cami. I've learned already that long car rides are not a good idea for a four-year-old's bladder."

"Ah."

"I'm good!" Cami says.

"Excellent." Jacob shifts the truck to drive and pulls out of the parking lot.

I settle back in my seat and try to relax. Jacob puts on some Jack Johnson—"mood music," he calls it—and we enjoy the ambiance.

The drive down to Carlsbad is beautiful. The five freeway going south is on a ledge overlooking the ocean, and on a day like today, the sun is shining like diamonds on the waves. I gaze out my window, keeping myself from staring at Jacob's perfect face or worrying about how awkward this weekend will be.

"Today was your last day at work, right?" Jacob asks, breaking the silence.

I nod. "I left at lunch, though."

"How was it?"

I shrug. "It's been weird, since everyone knows that I'm leaving, but they don't understand why. And it's especially awkward because everyone can tell I was upset about not getting the promotion. But it's still not keeping me from pursuing my goals." I run my fingers through my hair, not sure if I should share the next part. "My coworker asked me out as I was leaving...the one who got the promotion."

"Wait, what?" Sara squeals in the backseat.

Jacob looks over at me, his sunglasses blocking his eyes, but he seems alarmed, too.

"Uh, yeah. It was really awkward. But I told him I'm focusing on myself and I'm not getting romantically entangled."

Sara sits back in her seat. "Good one. That sounds pretty believable."

Jacob glances over at me again, but I say nothing.

"Wait... You're not serious, right?" Sara asks.

What do I say to that? That's exactly what I told Sharleen when we first sat down to make the list. I wanted to focus on feeling good about myself, not whether I was good enough for someone else. But after spending all of this time with Jacob, I know my heart is already tangled romantically.

I still don't know what to say to Sara, though. "Uh..."

"Emma?" Cami's voice peeps from the backseat, oblivious to the conversation around her.

I turn around in my seat to face her, relieved at the change. "Yes, Cami?"

"What's your favorite movie?"

Oh. I don't think she'll share my love of the Hunger Games trilogy. "Well, when I was a little girl, my favorite movie was—"

"The Fox and the Hound," Jacob cuts me off.

I look over at him, surprised he remembers.

He continues, keeping his eyes on the road. "Your backpack and pencil case had the fox and the dog on them. And whenever you had a bad day, that's the movie you wanted us to watch." Finally, he chances a glance over at me. "Right?"

I swallow hard, my heart racing a little bit. He really remembers everything about me. About *us*. "Right," I say softly.

"I don't like that movie very much," Cami chimes in, unaware of what's brewing between us. Sara shushes her, but she doesn't pay attention. "It's too sad at the end."

I turn back to Cami with a small smile. "Sometimes we need the sad parts to teach us how to be happy. And sad things help us remember what's most important."

She studies me for a moment, thinking about it. Then she shakes her head. "Nope. I'd rather just be happy."

I chuckle and turn forward in my seat again, but I catch a glimpse of Jacob. He looks over at me again, his expression sad.

"What did I say?" I ask softly.

He simply shakes his head and focuses on the drive.

But a minute later, something unthinkable happens.

He reaches his hand over to my seat and grabs my hand decisively. There's no hesitation. He *wants* to hold my hand. He takes it firmly in his and holds on tight. I look over at him, surprised. But he doesn't look back. He keeps focusing on the road, acting like nothing monumental has happened.

But something monumental is happening to me.

We arrive at the campsite nearly two hours later. The drive normally only takes forty-five minutes, but the traffic going down to San Diego on Friday afternoons, especially in the summer, can be brutal. Our campsite is a dirt rectangle up on a ledge overlooking the ocean. There's a chain-link fence separating us and the bushes below, but we can hear the crashing waves and smell the salty air, and it's pretty incredible. I'm bound to get super dirty, but I can manage that.

The trailer is already on the site, and it's pretty tiny. Sara and Cami step inside first and assess the sleeping situation—a master bedroom with a queen-sized bed and a set of bunks. Well, shoot. Three beds and four people?

"Cami and I can sleep together in one bed," Sara offers. "If you don't mind giving us the bedroom, then there's enough for you to each have an actual bed."

I glance over at Jacob, who nods. "Sounds like a good plan. Which bunk do you want, Emma?"

"Bottom," I say quickly.

"Afraid you'll fall out again?" he asks with a smirk.

"It was one time!" I insist. But he's right. I fell out of a bunk bed at a sleepover when I was eight, and the fear of falling has followed me around for twenty years.

He snorts. "Sure, sure. Whatever your reasons, I'll take the top bunk."

The tiny bathroom is right next to the bunk beds, but thankfully there's another camp bathroom across from our site. There's no way I'm going to poop next door to Jacob's bed.

We spend the next half hour unpacking everything from the bed of the truck for camping—coolers of food, tables, chairs, an easy-up tent, and games for Cami. When everything is finally ready, Sara's friends pull into their spot.

"Uncle Ricardo!" Cami cries, running over to their SUV, as Sara follows behind, trying to keep her from getting run over.

"Uncle?" I ask Jacob. "Are you related to him?"

He shakes his head. "Sara and Ricardo have a...complicated rela-tionship."

I tilt my head, waiting for an explanation.

He sighs. "They dated in high school. He broke up with her, but they stayed friends. Then she had Cami, and her dad is clearly not around. So Ricardo picked up a lot of the slack while I was gone."

I hear a twinge of bitterness in his voice. "Does that make you...jealous?"

He opens his mouth to protest, then shuts it. "Maybe. A little."

I nod. "It makes sense. You're her actual uncle. But it's not your fault that you weren't around. You had a job to do."

He looks back over at Cami and Ricardo, him twirling her around. "Some things aren't worth it."

A pang fills my heart. Which would I have chosen in his situation, an extraordinary career as a backup dancer for Nova Sky, or being ordinary back home with my family?

At this moment, I can't say for sure.

I feel the desperate need to comfort him, to reassure him he's not a bad uncle, and that he's genuinely a good person. Tentatively, I raise my hand and start to rub his back. I feel and hear him sigh, and he wraps his arm around my waist and pulls me into a side hug. "Thanks, Emma. I'm glad you don't think I'm a terrible person."

I look up at him, trying to slow my heart from racing at being this close to him. "You're not a terrible person. And for what it's worth, I'm glad you're back home."

The side of his mouth lifts in a grin. "Me too."

Ricardo spots us then and calls us over. Jacob lets go of me, and I follow him over to the other campsite with Ricardo and his three friends.

"Emma! So glad you could make it!" Ricardo says. I met him briefly at the salsa party, and I'm thankful for the friendly face. He's on the shorter side and wears thick-framed glasses. Next to Sara, I can see that they'd make an adorable couple.

"Thanks for including me," I say. "It's good to see you again."

"I hope you're ready to dance again tonight. We just have to get our site set up."

I glance up at Jacob, who smiles encouragingly at me. "I think I might." I look around his site, realizing they didn't rent a trailer and will be staying in tents. I gesture at their setup. "You're brave! No trailer?"

"It's not so bad," Ricardo says. "There's nothing like waking up to the sounds of the waves and the smell of the ocean air."

I guess that could be nice. Maybe one day I'll try it. But one thing at a time. Right now, my focus is on finding the one thing that makes me exceptional, and I hope it's surfing.

I shake hands with Ricardo's friends Ted and Seth, but Frank pulls me in for a hug and a big kiss on the cheek. I'm only slightly startled, because Armenians love to give cheek kisses in greeting, as well. But I don't miss the flash of anger in Jacob's eyes when I pull away. Jealousy, maybe? I file that away for analysis later.

Jacob helps the guys get their tents set up, and Sara, Cami, and I head back to our trailer. Cami busies herself digging a hole in the dirt with her sand toys, and Sara and I sit in the chairs facing the ocean. I breathe in the ocean air, the calm entering every inch of my body. This is heaven.

"You haven't been camping before?" Sara asks.

I shake my head. "Unless you count sleeping for an hour in my backyard, then deciding I'd rather sleep in my own bed, nope."

She smiles. "Being in the trailer isn't so bad. It's better than tents. That's what we always did with my dad."

I remember Jacob talking about camping when we were little, but I didn't think much about what that entailed. "Your dad liked to go camping?"

Sara nods. "We used to go all the time before he left with Jacob." She glances over at him, setting up the tent with the guys. "After they left, Mama and I never went again. But Ricardo thought it might be fun to try now."

"Ricardo, huh?" I ask.

Her cheeks redden at the mention of his name, but she passes it off. "Yeah, he's been a big help to me and Cami. And he's right. A lot of my best memories from being a kid were camping here."

"I can understand that," I say. We fall into a moment of silence, watching the waves.

I clear my throat. "Can I ask you a question?"

"Yeah, of course." Sara turns to look at me.

"Where's your dad now?"

"LA." Her eyes take on a steely gaze. "My dad has always had a single goal: to make Jacob a star. So after they left, I saw him maybe once or twice. When I got pregnant with Cami, he just sent a gift card. He's never even met her." She looks over at her beautiful daughter playing in the sand and smiles. "He doesn't know what he's missing."

"That's awful," I say. "I can't believe he hasn't even met his own granddaughter."

"No kidding." She turns back to me. "He's selfish and manipulative. My mom only put up with him for our sake. She begged him not to take Jacob away. But Jacob loved dance so much, he thought it would be fun. And I think my mom knew Jacob would resent her forever if she didn't let him go."

"And now?"

She sighs. "Dad ended up becoming Jacob's manager. When Jacob decided to come home, they got into a huge argument. Dad doesn't agree with his decision, and he keeps pressuring Jacob to come back on the road. That's why he's in LA, trying to set up auditions for him."

I watch Jacob working with the guys and setting up the tent. "What's he going to do?" I ask, feeling a slight twinge of anxiety at the thought of him leaving again.

She follows my gaze over to Jacob. She doesn't answer for a moment. The sound of the crashing waves is the only thing we hear, and then she looks back at me. "I think you should ask him."

# Chapter 14

At seven the next morning, I follow the group of guys down the scary looking wooden stairs to the beach. I didn't realize we'd be climbing down three flights of stairs while holding surfboards. Thankfully mine is foam, borrowed from Sara. I'm also wearing her wetsuit over my favorite retro one-piece, since the water will be too cold for just a bathing suit. Sara said she'd stay back, and she's enjoying a quiet morning in the trailer while Cami sleeps.

We ate some spaghetti last night and stayed up late, talking and listening to the ocean. We were a little too tired to dance, but we still have tonight. I haven't felt so relaxed in ages.

Sleeping in the trailer was…interesting. I actually really enjoyed the loud sound of the ocean waves. It was like a white noise machine, but better, because it was real. But sleeping under Jacob was so strange. I still don't understand the relationship between us. We were best friends before crushes were even a thing, and now he's back and gorgeous and perfect and helpful, and knowing that he was lying just a few feet above me was so unsettling.

Needless to say, I didn't sleep well last night. So now I'm trying my best to put one foot in front of the other, battling between drowsiness and the nervous rush of adrenaline.

The steps lead to a few crazy rocks. The guys have no problem jumping over, leaving me staring at them and trying to figure out where to step without dropping the surfboard. Before I can make a plan of attack, Jacob's hands firmly grab my waist and pick me up and over the rocks.

He sets me down on the sand but doesn't let go right away.

"Thank you," I say breathlessly.

He smiles, then removes his hands and takes a step back, grabbing his surfboard from the sand. "We should do a quick lesson here before going out in the water. Did you want to set up the phone first, though?"

That's right. I'm recording this whole ordeal for my Photogram account. After all, that's the point of it. I nod in agreement, and he pulls his tiny tripod out of his pocket for my camera. "You should be fine leaving your camera here," he says. "It's early enough, and the surfers usually look out for each other."

After the camera is all set up, he shows me how to paddle and pop up on the sand. It reminds me of my ice-skating lesson, how we practiced falls and marches off the ice, first. Hopefully, this lesson translates better. We practice for about ten minutes, and then he deems me ready.

My heart races with excitement. Maybe this is it. Maybe I'll be a world class surfer. How cool would that be? Every girl would be so jealous.

We walk to the waves, and I take a peek at Ricardo and his friends. They're just hanging out on their boards in the water, but I did see a couple of them surfing toward the shore before.

"I should've asked this sooner, but how comfortable are you swimming in the ocean?" Jacob asks.

"Um, I'm okay," I say slowly. "I go to the beach with Sharleen in the summer, but I'm not the type to go swimming out really far or anything."

He nods. "We'll stick to the shallow water so you won't get too disoriented."

We reach the water, and the icy cold shocks my feet. I didn't realize how cold the water would be in July. I jump back in alarm. "Holy smokes! I'm supposed to put my whole body in that water?"

Jacob laughs. "That's why you're wearing the wetsuit."

Gulping, I channel my bravest energy and step into the ocean. I follow Jacob past the first few little breaks, then we climb on our boards and paddle a little further until we reach Ricardo and his friends.

"You ready, Exceptional Emma?" Ricardo asks.

I roll my eyes. "If I'd known people would use that name regularly, I would've chosen something different."

He smiles. "It suits you."

Jacob sits on his board and turns himself around to face the beach, and I do my best to copy him.

"Now what?" I ask.

"We wait," he replies, keeping an eye behind us.

I nod, my heart continuing to race in my chest. I turn and look behind us, too, seeing...nothing. No waves, just calm water.

"How long does this normally take?" I ask.

He shrugs. "It depends on the day. But this is part of the experience. Living in the moment and enjoying what's around you."

I'm not sure I can do that right now. I'm full of tense energy, waiting for my chance to catch a wave and see if this is my calling.

"But when we find one," Jacob continues, "I'll stay back here to watch you and give you pointers."

I nod, taking deep breaths through my nose to calm myself down. Time stretches on, the water bobbing us up and down. Instead of focusing on myself, I listen to Ricardo and his friends laughing and making jabs at each other.

"Ten bucks says you face plant on the first wave," Frank says to Ricardo.

"Fifteen says you burn the carne asada tonight," Ricardo replies.

"Twenty says you make out with Sara tonight," Frank retorts.

"Hey! That's my sister!" Jacob exclaims.

The guys all crack up at him.

Jacob glances behind him. "Okay, Emma. Here's one!"

Yes! Perfect! I look behind me and see a wave coming toward us. I flop onto my stomach, start paddling, and...

I miss it.

I groan in disappointment as the wave passes under me.

"It's okay, Emma. We'll get one," Jacob calls reassuringly. The guys all cheer for me, which is nice but almost makes things worse. I don't really want an audience watching me fail, other than, you know, my followers on Photogram. I turn the board around and paddle back to our spot.

The next few waves are the same. I try to catch them and fail, then paddle back to the guys. Jacob keeps saying that I'll get one, but I'm not so sure. Frustration starts to take over. If I can't even catch a wave, how will I actually surf?

"Okay, here we go!" Jacob says, pointing out one I can catch.

I'm going to do it. I swear, this is it.

I paddle, and finally, I feel the wave pushing me forward. I caught it! What now?

"Yeah, girl!" Jacob calls. "Pop up!"

I grab the rails and lift my chest, then pop up to standing. *I'm doing it!* But as soon as I get a solid half second on my feet, I lose my balance and fall backwards. Salt water shoots up my nose, and, because I'm super talented like that, I do a full backwards somersault under the water. Just when I think I'm coming up, I hit my head on my surfboard. Alarmed, I pop back under the water, and another wave crashes over me, sending me spinning under the water again.

The wave passes and I finally stand up out of the water, snot pouring from my nose, my hair a crazy mess all over my face. Taking in a deep, shaky breath, thankful that I'm no longer tumbling under the waves, I look around the ocean.

And start to cry.

I give myself a minute of standing in the waves before I grab the board and stomp back to my phone, shutting off the recording. I'm sure I look completely crazy, with my hair all over my face and sand covering the left half of my body, but I don't care. Because I failed again. And not just failed, but *epically*.

The wetsuit is suffocating me, so I unzip the top half and pull my arms out, folding it down to my waist. I sit in the sand, rest my arms on my knees, and lean my head down on my folded forearms, hiding myself from the world. My nose burns, my side hurts, and my ego is bruised most of all. The tears running down my cheeks blend in with the salt water from the ocean, and I can't tell the difference, so I don't bother wiping my face at all.

A minute later, I hear someone sit next to me. "Are you okay?" Jacob asks.

I keep my head down. I can't stand to look at him right now. All I can do is quietly say, "No."

He doesn't respond, just lifts a hand to my back and rubs it, like I did for him yesterday. And the gesture makes me cry even harder, but he keeps rubbing my back, letting me get all my frustration out of my system. Finally, I run out of tears and look over at him. He's pulled the top half of his wetsuit down, too, and *holy abs and arms.*

I shake my head and refocus on the situation at hand. "Why are you doing this?"

He tilts his head, urging me to explain more.

"Why are you trying to help me? Aren't you sick of seeing me fail?"

He watches me carefully. "You're not failing, Emma," he says gently. "You're learning."

I scoff and turn to look back at the ocean.

"Do you think I was always a good dancer?" he asks.

I turn back to him, raising a brow. "Uh, yes. You always told me you were the best student in your class."

"Okay, when we were kids here in Harbor Sands, sure. That was small time. But when I went to LA, and New York, and even on tour with Nova, do you really think I was always the best dancer?"

"Yes." I don't hesitate. Come on, he's basically perfection personified.

"I wasn't." He rubs my back a little harder, getting into his story. "I spent so many nights alone in the studio, perfecting my steps. Being a male dancer is a novelty here, but there are hundreds, maybe thousands, of guys all over this country, dying for the same jobs I got. And I had to work like crazy to get the spots I wanted."

"But you got them!" I exclaim. "You don't get it! I've got *nothing*. I have no credibility, no accolades, nothing that separates me from everyone else. I'm just average." Tears fill my eyes again, and I look out at the ocean to avoid his gaze. "All I want is to be better than average. Is that so much to ask? I don't even need to be exceptional. I just want to be more than this."

"Emma." Jacob's voice is soft and tender, and I turn to look at him again. "You are so much more than average. In every way that matters, you are absolutely exceptional."

I search his eyes, desperate to see the truth in them.

He's not lying.

And in that moment, with our eyes locked on each other, the morning breeze whipping my hair and his arm on my back, he kisses me.

# Chapter 15

Our lips move together, and finally I feel myself relax. I'm in the moment, just like Jacob told me to be when we were waiting to catch waves. But this...this is different. I could kiss him forever.

Jacob puts one of his hands around the back of my head, gently drawing me closer to him. I lean into his kiss, finally getting to show him exactly what I think of how incredible he is with my lips.

But we're cut short by a whistle. I pull back and look for the source of the sound: Ricardo and his buddies, clapping and waving at us from the ocean.

My cheeks turn fire hot. I can't believe I was kissing Jacob in public! I bury my head in Jacob's shoulder. "Oh, my goodness. What are we doing?"

He pulls me tighter, and I could get used to this feeling forever.

Jacob. Kissed. Me.

What is happening?

I burst into laughter, lifting my head to look at him. "I can't believe you kissed me!"

His lips pull in a sly grin. "Well, if I need to convince you again..." He leans in and kisses me softly again, and I lose all coherent thought.

He pulls away, and I slowly open my eyes, taking in the glorious sight that is Jacob Perez.

"I have no business kissing someone as hot as you," I say.

He raises a brow. "You absolutely do. Because you are incredible." He lifts one hand and brushes my cheek with his thumb. "And you're really hot, too."

Say *what*? Jacob thinks *I'm* hot? This day needs to be memorialized for the rest of eternity. Jacob Perez thinks Emma Nazarian is hot. I feel my cheeks flame with heat, and I bury my face in his shoulder again. He holds me tight, and we sit in a comfortable silence for a few minutes, watching the waves and the guys surfing a few of them.

My mind tries to process this information. Why did Jacob decide to kiss me? Why now? I replay the conversation in my mind and inwardly cringe, remembering how whiny I was about being average. Did he just want me to stop talking?

I have to know. "Why *did* you kiss me?"

"I thought it was pretty obvious," he says with a laugh.

"No, seriously." I sit up and look him straight in the eye. I need to know the truth. "Was that a pity kiss?"

He snorts. "A *pity* kiss? What's that?"

I cringe a little. "You know, you feel sorry for the other person, and to make them stop feeling sorry for themselves, you kiss them to shut them up."

He huffs a laugh. "I mean, kind of."

I smack his shoulder. "Hey!"

"Well, I did feel sorry for you and wanted you to stop feeling sorry for yourself. But I also truly believe that you're more than you think you are. And I don't want you to head down a dangerous line of thinking."

I tilt my head. I'm not sure I like where this is leading. "What do you mean?"

He studies me for a moment. "You're incredible, Emma."

I roll my eyes, tired of everyone teasing me for my new username. "You mean exceptional."

"No, I don't mean it in the sarcastic way at all. You're kind, intelligent, determined... There's so much of you I admire. You have such a fiery spirit. And to see you being so hard on yourself... I just want to make sure you understand exactly how special you are. Just being you."

It's almost too much. I turn my head away from him, unsure I can face him after all those compliments.

"Are you embarrassed?" he asks.

"A little," I admit. I look back up at him. "I've never been good at taking compliments."

"Maybe that's because you haven't received enough in your lifetime."

"Maybe." I wrap my arms around my knees and watch the waves, thinking back on my childhood and the accolades I didn't receive. "I got complimented on my grades, sure, but Mariam and Garen got all the admiration. But it doesn't mean I don't wonder what it would feel like to get those compliments myself." I look back at Jacob. "*You* know, though."

And he does. I don't fault him for it. There's a little jealousy, but I'm not angry with him. I just wish I could experience knowing that people admired me.

So I ask. "What's it like? To *really* be good at something?"

He pauses to think, looking out at the ocean. "There are moments when I'm on top of the world. After a show, when I've done my best, I feel like I'm electric. I'm on fire. Nothing can touch me, and I know I'm one of the best there is." He pauses. "There's nothing like it."

It almost hurts more, having him confirm all my dreams and wishes about being exceptional. I sigh. "I knew it."

"But there's another side to it, Emma," he continues. "There's always someone gunning for your spot. If you get injured, you have to be replaced. You live in fear of losing your position, because everyone is watching and waiting for you to fail."

I nod, but it still doesn't seem that terrible. Jacob never got injured or replaced. I'd rather be afraid of losing something precious than never having it at all.

"And there's more." He takes a deep breath, as if willing himself to get this part out. "Being on top means you're removed from reality. You lose all of your grounding." He pauses again. "I've been gone for eighteen years. Do you know how many times I've been back home?"

I shake my head. "No."

"Once."

I furrow my brow. "What? But what about your mom and Sara?"

"They came and visited me a few times. My dad kept me on a tight schedule. Training, auditions, rehearsals all came first. There wasn't time for visiting family. But it was expensive for Mom and Sara to visit, so we rarely saw each other. I sent money home once Sara had Cami, and I convinced myself that I was doing everything I could for them." He swallows hard. "I didn't even know my mom was sick until a month before she died. Sara called and told me."

My heart completely breaks for him. How would I feel if I hadn't seen my mother in years, and Mariam or Garen called to tell me she only had a month to live? Completely shattered. My eyes fill with tears, and I reach a hand over and rub Jacob's shoulder. "I'm so sorry."

He nods. "My mom didn't want to upset me while I was on tour with Nova. But Sara knew that I would have regrets for the rest of my life if I wasn't there for her last few days." He sucks in a breath and lets it out slowly. "So I quit my job and came back. I was able to be with her for the last three weeks, and then I helped Sara with the funeral arrangements."

He doesn't say anything for a few beats. I can't think of anything to say, so the sound of the waves fills the silence. It's not uncomfortable; it's pensive and emotional.

"I think I'll regret not being home more often for the rest of my life," he says softly, just loud enough to be heard over the waves. "I didn't *know* her. She was part of my childhood, but after I left, there was a void in my life where a mother should be. I don't blame her for that—I blame my father and myself. And I know that for the rest of my life, I'll wish I had come back more often. Because now I'll never get another chance."

I trace my fingers down the back of his arm, feeling goosebumps rise on his skin. Jacob grabs my hand and holds it tight, like I'm the only thing keeping him from running off. Just like he grabbed my hand in the car.

"I haven't shared this much of myself with anyone," he says.

"What about your dad?" I ask.

He scoffs. "My dad looks at me like I'm covered in dollar signs. He doesn't care what I think or how I feel. It doesn't matter to him. All that matters is practicing, auditioning, and rehearsing."

My heart breaks for little Jacob. The bright spot in my childhood days, whisked off to LA with his greedy dad. "And what's your relationship with him like now?"

"It's the same." He uses his free hand to dig into the sand, grabbing fists of sand and letting it fall through his fingers. "After I quit Nova's show, he thinks it's his life's goal to get me another gig. He's trying to set me up with an audition to dance for the boy band Rivera, even though I keep telling him no. It's probably my fault for telling him that money is tight right now."

That's news to me. "Is it?"

He nods. "Teaching at the studio is great, but the pay isn't enough. Sara contributes by working at the restaurant, but we're still coming up short." He looks at me again, intensity in his expression. "But I'm not leaving again. I'll do whatever it takes to stay here. Because nothing matters more than being home with them." He pauses, running the back of his hand down my cheek. "With you."

I suck in a breath. As much as I feel a deep connection with Jacob, that was pretty bold to say. I'm not sure how to respond.

"You don't have to say anything," he says quickly. "But you're important to me, Emma. And every day that I'm here, I'm more thankful that you're in my life again."

I exhale, relieved that he knew exactly what to say to make me relax. This is why I love being around Jacob, and why I have such deep feelings for him. I smile widely, lean in to Jacob, and just before kissing him again, say, "I'm so thankful for you, too."

After a kissing session that makes the seagulls blush, we try catching a few more waves again, and I do much better. I'm able to stand for a few seconds and don't cry at all. But at the end of the morning, I'm not sure I want to keep surfing.

"It's fun," I say to Jacob and the guys. "But I don't think it's anything special, you know?"

"No, I don't know," Jacob teases with a grin. "What do you mean?"

"I don't feel any fire," I reply. "And I'm scared that I'm about to fall every second."

"But that's part of the thrill. Maybe you just need to keep trying. Not everyone is perfect at things the first time they try."

"Yeah, but the point of my journey is finding *the* hobby that I'm naturally good at, right? And I think I'm still pretty average at this, for a first-timer."

"I don't know," Ricardo chimes in. "I've tried to teach a few girls who couldn't stand up at all. You've got it in you."

I shrug. "Maybe. But I don't want to commit. Early mornings, all the prep and driving...I think I'll move on to something else."

"But you'll try it again, right?" Jacob presses. "Just for fun?"

I turn to him. "I don't know. I don't think it's worth my time."

Jacob furrows his brow at me, and I know this is one point we won't agree on. I have a mission, and that mission doesn't include doing things "just for fun."

I still need to find what makes me exceptional.

<h1 style="text-align:center">Chapter 16</h1>

The rest of the day camping is bliss. We have breakfast with Sara and Cami, then go back down to the beach and build sand castles. Jacob tosses a football around with the guys, and I don't mind watching. Neither does Sara. She's not very good at hiding the way she watches Ricardo.

I still can't believe Jacob is actually interested in *me*. Maybe I took on the username Exceptional Emma, but I don't feel exceptional at all. When Jacob looks at me, though, I feel like I could be.

I didn't realize he was still having financial issues, though. And as much as it pains me to say, I do wonder if going back on the road is the best option for him right now. He's so talented, and staying in Harbor Sands isn't utilizing all of his options. But I'm not sure I can say that to him. Not yet.

That evening, the guys grill up some carne asada and Sara works on making side dishes in the trailer. I offer to help and get assigned to chop tomatoes. Thankfully, I make an excellent sous chef—my mom trained me well.

"So...what's the deal with Ricardo?" I dare to ask her.

Her eyes flick to me, then back to her cutting board. "So...what's the deal with my brother?" she replies.

I pop my head up and see her teasing smile. "I think we both know what's going on," she says.

I nod in agreement and grin. Apparently, I'm not the only one with a crush at this camp.

We eat our dinner together, the guys' conversation loud and teasing, and it feels so comfortable and right. After we're done eating, Ricardo turns on some salsa music and everyone starts to dance. Ricardo grabs Cami and twirls her around. Frank pulls Sara by the hand (and I don't miss Ricardo's watching glare), and Jacob tugs me close to him as we move to the rhythm.

I laugh and dance, stepping on Jacob's toes, but I don't care, and neither does he. He holds me a little closer than is probably required for the dance, and my heart flutters a little more with each beat of the music.

I look up at him, his hair messy from the day, but the light in his eyes is unmistakable. I'm smiling so hard, my cheeks hurt. "This is the best day."

He smiles down at me, then presses his smiling lips to mine. My heart is so full, I feel like it might burst.

"Tío is kissing Emma!" Cami squeals. "Oooh!"

"Cami, shh!" Sara scolds.

We break apart in laughter, and I try to tell Sara that it's fine. We probably shouldn't have been kissing in front of her, anyway. It's not like we've decided if this is anything serious.

I mean, I want it to be.

Jacob was my best friend for the pivotal years of my childhood, and his heart has remained unchanged. It seems like fate brought us back together, right where we belong.

Right here, right now, is exactly where we belong.

The next morning, I get up with the sunrise. No one else is awake; the guys decided to sleep in, but I'm determined to soak in every moment I can. I sit in one of the chairs with my journal, watching the waves through the chain-link fence. Ever since I started my Photogram account, I haven't been writing in my journal as much, and I feel the need to ground myself a bit. I'm about to start writing when I hear the trailer door open behind me.

I turn to see Jacob walking down the steps. "Hey, there," he says.

I smile widely. "Good morning."

"Wanna go down to the beach? This view could be much better."

"Really?"

He nods. "Really. I'll even carry the chairs down for us."

I grab my journal and follow him down the thousand steps to the beach.

He sets up the chairs right by the shoreline, then notices what I'm holding. "Is that your journal?"

I nod, a tiny bit embarrassed but also glad that I can share this part of myself with him. "I was going to write about this weekend."

He pulls me by the waist and gives me a sweet, quick kiss. "I love that. I'll play a game on my phone so you can write."

I beam. Weird as it sounds, I love the idea that we can sit together without talking, but comfortable and secure in each other's company.

I work on a drawing of our kiss at the beach the morning before and write a little bit about us. In ten years, I'll probably cringe at all the things I'm writing about our first kiss and the way he makes me feel, but I'm giddy like a teenager right now. I glance over at him, his handsome face marked with stubble, his curly hair unkempt, and my heart fills with joy.

He must feel my attention on him, because he looks over just then. "What's up?"

I shrug. "Nothing. Just happy to be here with you."

That puts a huge smile on his face. He turns off his phone and holds his hand out to me, and I put my hand in his. We lean back in our chairs and watch the waves, content to just be.

***

"You ready to go?" Jacob asks a few hours later, after we're all packed up and about to leave.

"No," I grumble.

He smiles teasingly at me. "Me neither." He kisses my forehead, then opens the passenger door of the truck for me to climb in.

I'm not ready to leave this paradise. It's dirty and messy, but it's heavenly. This weekend has been the refresh and reset that I've needed. I tried surfing one more time, and it was fun, but I could feel that it wasn't my "thing." Maybe I'm crazy, but I'm waiting for some kind of spiritual connection to whatever I try that I'm good at. And without that connection, I know I need to move on to something else.

I settle in the passenger seat of the car. Cami and Sara are already waiting for us in the backseat. Jacob says goodbye to the guys, and then we're on our way. Once we're on the freeway, I look over at the ocean through Jacob's window. It doesn't hurt that Jacob is in my line of sight, too. I feel like it will make a cool picture, so I snap one.

"What was that?" Jacob asks.

I shrug, suddenly embarrassed that I was taking a picture of him. But man, does he look gorgeous with the sun and the ocean behind him. "It seemed like a cool picture."

"Can I see?" Sara asks.

I hand my phone over to her. Her eyes widen as she looks at the picture. "Wow. This is a really cool shot." She hands the phone back to me.

I look at it again. It is pretty good. "Do you mind if I post it?" I ask Jacob.

He glances at the phone, then smirks. "You're sure you want to post a picture of me on your Photogram account?"

"You're a big part of my life now," I reply.

His lips turn back into a wide grin. "Sure. Go ahead and post it."

I nod, then open my Photogram account. After I posted a little video of me surfing yesterday, I spent the rest of the time offline and haven't checked for the response.

"Holy smokes," I murmur.

"What?" Jacob asks. "Are people being mean about your surfing video?"

"No, no, it's not that." Well, some might be, but I haven't had a chance to check the comments yet. "I have two hundred more followers."

"In one day?" Sara asks.

I just nod and show her my phone. "It's up to seven hundred now." I click on the video from yesterday and see that it went semi-viral. "The surfing video got fifteen thousand views." I click the comments to read what people are saying.

*Get it, girl!*

*Love this!*

*Yikes, epic fail.*

*You should never surf again.*

*She is so inspirational!* That one has a bunch of tags, probably to other friends.

The comments send waves of conflicting emotions through me. Elation that people are watching my videos and connecting with my journey, and then terror that fifteen thousand people watched me fall into the ocean. And a bit of humiliation that someone felt compelled to say that I shouldn't ever surf again.

"You okay?" Jacob's voice pulls me out of my daze.

"Uh, yeah. I'm okay." I close out of the video and focus on posting the picture of Jacob. I write the caption: *Not a bad view* and hit post. Then I lock the phone and throw it in my purse.

"You're sure?" he asks. "You got a little pale there for a moment."

I shrug. "Just your typical range of people being varying degrees of nice and mean." Even though I got more friendly comments than mean, I can't shake the mean ones from my head.

*You should never surf again.*

That shouldn't hurt, right? I basically said the same thing myself. But...what if I *wanted* to surf again? Shouldn't I be allowed to do whatever I want, as long as I'm enjoying it?

Jacob reaches his hand over to my side, his palm facing up. An invitation. I turn my head to him, and he's glancing over at me, then he wiggles his fingers in a "gimme" gesture. With a smile, I put my hand in his. I settle back into my seat and relax, feeling the comfort that at least I've got him on my side.

"So what's next?" Sara asks. "Is photography on your list? Because that picture was pretty good."

I press my lips together, trying to remember. What was next? "I think it was running."

Jacob snorts. "Running? You could barely run a lap in PE."

"Hey!" I let go of his hand to smack him on the shoulder, but he just laughs. "Maybe I was just growing into my legs."

"There's no way. You'd get a stitch in your side one minute into our laps."

I huff and sit back in my seat, but Jacob grabs my hand and kisses it, then puts it over the shifter in the center.

"Fine. Maybe I should skip running." I sigh. "All the runners rave about getting a high when running, though. I thought maybe I'd get to experience that."

"I really think you should try photography," Sara says. "I know one mom at Cami's school runs a photography program, and she does workshops on the weekends. Maybe you should try one of those."

I look over at Jacob, and he shrugs. "Considering how well your pictures are doing on Photogram, maybe you already have a knack for it. Might as well try it out."

I pull my phone back out of my purse and type in the name Sara gives me. On her website, she has a workshop next Saturday morning for photography with your phone. Within a few minutes, I'm signed up.

"All set." I say. I settle back in my seat and enjoy the view.

And by the view, I don't just mean the ocean.

# Chapter 17

"All right, class, let's begin!" The photography instructor stands in front of the ten of us in the workshop. Her waist-length, black hair sways as she moves from side to side, getting everyone's attention.

I glance around the room, taking in the group that I'll be spending the next three hours with. Two of them look like Photogram "models," trying to get free stuff by posting perfect pictures online. But they're sitting on opposite sides of the room and glaring at each other, so they must know one another, and not in a good way. There's a group of three older ladies who are chatting and laughing together, and a couple of middle-aged men sitting on their own, as well.

My phone buzzes with a text from Jacob. *Have a great time! Can't wait to hear all about it tonight!*

I smile widely. He promised Cami that he'd take her to the park this morning, and I told him I didn't need anyone for moral support today. But we're getting dinner tonight, and I can't wait to see him. This week has been amazing. He sent me gorgeous white flowers on Tuesday morning, and we've spent every day and night talking and texting.

I write him back. *So nervous but excited! See you tonight!*

"My name is Mona," the instructor says, drawing my attention back to the class, "and I figured we'd start by introducing ourselves and why we're here today. This is a safe space, and everyone is welcome."

One of the "models" named Tiphani (she spelled it for us) goes first, and her introduction confirms my suspicions of her intentions here. Then the group of older women introduce themselves and explain that they want to take better pictures of their grandchildren, which is so sweet. One man lives in an RV and wants to take better pictures of the incredible landscapes. Another one says his wife is undergoing cancer treatment, and he wants to document her journey. That gets a few sympathetic murmurs from the others in the class. The other "model," Nicolette, says the same as the first, and shoots daggers at the first girl.

And then it's my turn.

"Um, hi, I'm Emma." I wave awkwardly. "I'm on a...personal journey, trying to find out what I'm good at. Nothing has clicked so far, and a friend of mine recommended photography."

"I thought I recognized you," Tiphani says. "You're Exceptional Emma."

"*Exceptional* Emma?" Nicolette snorts.

"Uh, yes. That's me." I wave my hands by my shoulders, like a *surprise!* gesture. "But the username is kind of a joke. I'm trying to find what makes me exceptional."

"Her account is hilarious," Tiphani says. "You should have seen her try beer hockey."

"Oh, that's you?" The man whose wife is in cancer treatment chimes in. "I saw that video."

I give a tight-lipped grin. "Yep."

"And your surfing fails," Tiphani continues. "Hilarious."

"Yep. Hilarious." I look up at Mona, begging her with my eyes to move on.

"Okay!" she says, clapping her hands. Bless her. "Let's get started with some basics of photography. Then we'll learn how we can use certain settings on our phones to achieve the shots we desire."

We spend the next thirty minutes covering the rule of thirds, lighting, exposure, and lots of other things I've never heard of. We analyze two pictures taken just steps away from each other and how different the overall effect is. It seems like a lot of analysis, more than I was expecting.

"And now, we experiment!" Mona says at the end of the slideshow. "We're going to take a walk outside, and I want you all to apply the principles we learned to take your own pictures. When we come back, we'll look at the different photos and share what we like about them all."

We walk out of the room and into the bright sunlight. We're not in the most exciting part of the city. It's just sidewalks, streetlights, and a few strategically placed shrubs to make us feel like there's some sense of greenery in our little suburb.

The Photogram models set up little stands for their phones and start taking selfies. I'm not sure they learned anything.

The older ladies take pictures of each other in groups, which warms my heart. They tell each other to pose in certain ways, adjusting to the background behind them, and then take different pictures.

The men venture off on their own, taking pictures of the scenery and the cars driving by.

And me?

I'm watching everyone, trying to figure out where I belong. If that's not a metaphor for my life, I don't know what is.

"Anything good yet?" Mona's voice sounds over my shoulder.

I turn to look at her, phone in hand. "Not yet. I can't figure out what to take pictures of."

She shrugs. "What do you notice here?"

I look around at everyone, the way they mill around, almost like pigeons in a park. "The people."

"Then capture that." She smiles, then walks away to help one of the "models." I overhear her encouraging Tiphani to take something other than a selfie.

I guess I can try capturing the people. I start snapping pictures of the people taking pictures, which seems kind of meta. Even though I'm trying to apply the things we learned in class, each picture isn't turning out right.

Looking around for something to change my perspective, I find a bench at the bus stop. Perfect. I climb all the way to the top of the back of the bench, holding my phone above my head. It's probably dangerous, but it's worth it for the shot. From this angle, everyone looks a little bit like birds. I snap a few pictures of the people taking pictures of each other.

After that, I hop down and take pictures of the individual groups. I capture the models with no one around them, trying to get the perspective that there's a bunch of empty space. Then I fill my screen with the older women, laughing and holding each other. I try to capture the men along with the backgrounds they're capturing, to get the full effect of their experience.

All too soon, Mona calls time and gathers us back into her studio. We file back in, and she asks us to AirDrop our five favorite pictures to her. After a few moments, she hooks up her computer to the projector and shows the pictures on the screen.

She puts up the first set of pictures, some landscapes done by one of the men. We all ooh and ahh, because they really do look nice. After a few minutes of pointing out some things he did well, Mona asks for any suggestions.

I feel like he could have tilted the angle of the camera just a bit to capture the vastness of the sky, but I feel dumb saying it, because who am I to know anything about photography? So I stay quiet.

"Anyone?" Mona asks. Still, no one responds. "Well, I'm thinking if you barely shifted the angle of your camera to show the sky and how expansive it is, that would really give a great perspective shift."

Hold up. Seriously? She said exactly what I was thinking?

Huh.

She moves through the rest of his pictures quickly, then continues with the other set of landscape pictures that the other men did. Again, she has a couple of comments that I thought of but am too afraid to say out loud.

Then she pulls up the pictures of the older ladies. They giggle and cheer in their little corner, and I love them already.

"These are lovely," Mona comments. "There's so much life in these. Any suggestions for these pictures?"

I look around, and everyone is too afraid to say anything again. Tentatively, I raise my hand.

"Yes, Emma?"

"Um...I was thinking the camera could crop out some of the background and focus in on the ladies, to really get the full feeling of life and love in the picture."

Mona nods approvingly at me. "I was going to say the same thing." She uses her computer to crop the picture and shows the result. "I think this is what Emma means, right?"

I nod enthusiastically. And the ladies all murmur approvingly.

"That's lovely," one of them says. She reaches over the empty seats and squeezes my shoulder and whispers, "Good job."

I grin. Plus one for me!

Mona goes through the rest of their pictures quickly, commenting on how well they captured the light and surroundings. The ladies all smile and laugh together, and I hope that when I'm older, I'll have a friend group like them, too. I've got Sharleen, and maybe even Sara, so hopefully I'm on my way.

Next up are the Photogram "models." Mona pulls up Tiphani's pictures, and bless her heart, she finds some amazing things to say. "The perspective is great. Look how long your legs look," she says. Tiphani flips her hair over her shoulder as if to say, *tell me something I don't know.*

"But maybe you could work on the lighting. See the shadows here? You could eliminate those if you had come from a different angle."

Tiphani scoffs and pulls out her phone.

"Rude," I mutter.

Nicolette titters a laugh. But then it's her turn.

Mona puts the pictures up on the screen, and she's at a loss for words. I kind of love it.

"So this is...interesting," Mona says slowly.

It's literally a shot of her pinky toe.

That's it.

And it's not well done, either. It looks like a two-year-old got a hold of her phone and started running around with the camera app open, and just happened to get a picture of her foot cut off on the side.

"Is this the picture you meant to send?" Mona asks.

Nicolette rolls her eyes. "Of course it is. I'm not an idiot."

"Mm-hmm." Mona's eyes dart around the room.

I feel the urge to help her out. "Maybe if you had used the rule of thirds," I offer, "it would seem a little more...intentional."

"Yes. Intentional. Exactly." Mona nods, then mouths *keep going*.

Oh, jeez. What else can I say? "And, uh, your lighting is good. No shadows or anything. That's actually pretty impressive."

Nicolette scoffs and slumps back in her chair. "This is a waste of time."

"Not necessarily," Mona consoles her. "I bet your pictures tomorrow will be incredible. Just you wait."

Nicolette rolls her eyes but doesn't say anything else.

"One more set of pictures left," Mona murmurs, then pulls up my bird's-eye view picture of everyone taking pictures.

The room is silent.

Oh, no. Please tell me this isn't worse than the pinky toe.

My eyes dart around the room, desperately seeking any sign of whether or not they all hate it.

The silence is killing me. I have to say something. "I thought it might be cool to take pictures of you all," I blurt. "And I got up on the bench because you kind of looked like pigeons. Not in a bad way! Oh, my goodness, that came out wrong. But it was a cool sight watching you all taking pictures of each other and...oh, if it's terrible, someone just say something."

"This is amazing," one of the older ladies breathes.

"Stunning," one of the men agrees.

Mona keeps looking at the projector, but she still hasn't said anything. The anticipation is driving me nuts. Finally, she speaks. "I love it."

Heat rushes to my cheeks, and now I'm speechless.

"The way you captured the angle and the space of people... It's beautiful," Mona continues. She clicks to the next picture. It's my shot of the older ladies huddled together. "And this is beautiful, as well."

The lady who grabbed my shoulder earlier squeezes it again. "Please send that to me," she whispers. I look back at her and smile, and notice that she has tears welling up in her eyes.

Mona switches to my pictures of the models with the empty space around them. No one says anything, but it's not an uncomfortable silence.

And then she pulls up the pictures of the men and their landscapes.

"You got a better shot of the mountains and the sun than I did," the man in front of me comments.

*What. Is. Happening??*

"You have a talent for this, Emma," Mona comments. "Have you done this before?"

I shake my head, unable to express myself.

"Let's talk after the workshop," she says.

It's all I can do to keep from bursting out laughing, crying, and cheering, all at the same time.

I did it.

I found my thing.

# Chapter 18

## One Month Later

AUGUST

Hand in hand, Jacob and I walk the cobblestone path to the front door of my parents' house. It's family cooking day, and Jacob's finally coming to hang out—as my boyfriend. I'm not going to lie; I'm nervous. The last time Jacob was here, Mariam stared at him like her favorite magazine model come to life. And then he watched her in amazement as she played the violin. So, yes. I'm a little insecure. But Jacob has never given me a reason to feel this way. Whenever we're together, I feel like the center of his universe.

And for once, I'm starting to believe that I might be worthy of those feelings.

We open the door and walk right in, and on command, Sparky rushes over, barking like he's going to kill us both.

"Don't look at him," I remind Jacob.

"Oh, I remember." He follows my lead in taking off our shoes, pretending we don't see him.

Garen comes out to greet us. "Jacob, my man!" He holds his hand out, and they perform an elaborate handshake.

My eyes widen. "Where the heck did that come from?"

"Bros never tell," Garen says, beaming at Jacob.

"Hmph." I glance around the living room. "Is everyone else rolling dolma already?"

"Yep," he says. "Come join the party."

We follow Garen to the kitchen, where my parents and Mariam sit around the table. Sparky follows us, his barks slowly spacing out until he lays down next to Mom's feet.

"Hey, you two," she says, looking up at us. "Emma! Where are your socks?"

I sigh. Not this again. "Mom. It's August."

"You need to protect your ovaries!"

She did *not* just say that in front of Jacob.

Garen chokes a little, and Mariam giggles behind her hand.

"Mom!" I hiss, my face flaming with embarrassment.

Jacob looks over at me, his brow furrowed. I didn't have a chance to explain the weird Armenian traditions my mom loves to hold on to. Maybe he'll forget about that comment.

"Go wash your hands and take a seat," Mom commands.

We obediently follow her instructions. At the kitchen sink, Jacob whispers to me, "What was that about your ovaries?"

I swallow. "It's an Armenian old wives' tale. They think keeping your feet warm protects your ovaries."

"Ah." Jacob smiles. At least he's not too weirded out.

We finish washing and sit at the table. Jacob takes the spot next to Dad, I sit next to Mariam, and Garen and Mom are across from us.

"So, how do I roll a dolma?" Jacob asks, rubbing his hands together.

I grab a grape leaf from the plate in the middle of the table and set it on my own. "Make sure the veins are facing up, so the outside is smooth."

He follows my lead, grabbing a leaf of his own and checking that the vein side is facing up.

"Then grab some of the filling." I reach into the giant bowl filled with a mixture of ground beef, onion, rice, parsley, and spices. "This part is key. You have to get the right amount."

Carefully, he tries to imitate the amount I grabbed and mold it at the top of the leaf into a little three-inch log.

It's not bad for his first attempt. I nod in approval. "Now you roll." I show him how to fold down the top, then the sides, then roll the rest of the way down to make the little stuffed grape leaf.

"You have to roll it tight," Dad chimes in, holding his up. "Like mine."

"Yours are too tight," Mom protests. "They explode when I cook them."

He waves a hand at her. "Don't listen to her, Jacob. Mine are always the best."

She clicks her tongue but smiles as she grabs a handful of the filling and makes her own.

I shake my head at my parents' banter, then glance over at Jacob. He looks thoughtful, but happy. I wonder what he's thinking.

Jacob makes his best attempt at rolling a dolma, but the edges are a little misshapen. "How's this?"

"Not bad," I say. "Here." I unroll it and show him how to tuck the edges in a little tighter.

He sighs dramatically. "I guess rolling dolma isn't my 'thing,' huh?"

What a stinker. I roll my eyes at him. "That was your first one!"

"And that's what I told you the whole time you were trying hobbies," he retorts.

I shrug and return to my dolma. "Whatever. At least I found something I'm good at."

"Speaking of which," Dad says. "How's photography going?"

"Great!" I sit up, so excited to talk about my accomplishments. I finally have something exciting to share around the family dinner table. "My Photogram account has really taken off. I have about five thousand followers now."

"Daaaang," Garen chimes in.

I beam at him. Of everyone in my family, he's been the most supportive. "Mona has taken me as an assistant for the last few sessions, and one of them referred me to her friend. So I'm going to have my own photography job next week."

"That's great," Dad says. "So you'll start getting paid soon?"

"Yes, Dad." I sigh. Their enthusiasm for my accomplishments is always tempered with a side of realism. I don't fault them for it; that's how they've built a successful life for me and my siblings. But sometimes I wish they'd be a little more...generous in their compliments and excitement for me. "And I still have enough in savings to make it another few months without a job."

"Not with those shoes, you don't," he says.

"I bought these *before* I quit!" I protest. "I was wearing these when..." I let my voice trail off and look down at my plate.

"When what?" Garen asks the question they're all wondering.

"When I got passed for the promotion." It's been a couple of months, so you'd think it wouldn't sting. But it still does. I straighten and paste on a smile. "But no big deal. I'm on to better things now."

Awkward silence fills the kitchen.

"Do you miss engineering at all?" Mariam asks.

I continue rolling my dolma, not meeting Mariam's eyes. "A little, I guess. I don't miss the office so much, but I liked designing." I swallow. "Not that I was any good at it."

"You were, Emma-jan," Mom says. "Have you had a chance to start designing the deck for us?"

Guilt washes over me. I promised her I'd do it, but I'm not exactly itching to work on a project for her. I love her and want to help, but when photography consumes all my spare thoughts, it's hard to concentrate on drawings and calculations again.

I shake my head, hoping I can give a passable explanation. "I've been so busy with photography. There's so much to learn about cameras and lighting and editing, not to mention marketing and all of that. It's taking up all of my free time."

Mom just nods, and Garen starts talking about his upcoming classes at the community college for the fall, taking the attention away from me and my inability to measure up to my family's standards. I thought they'd be proud of me for photography, but there's always a reason I'm disappointing them.

We finish the last of the dolma, and Mom takes the giant pot to the stove. She pours a can of tomato sauce and water over the top and sets the burner to low, and Dad comes up to Jacob, squeezing him on the shoulder.

"Jacob, come have a drink in my office."

What.

Is.

Happening.

Mariam and Garen's eyes are bugging out of their heads. I'm sure I look the same. Jacob turns to me and startles at my expression.

"Uh, sure," he says. He starts to stand, but he doesn't understand the gravity of what's happening here.

I tug on his arm and pull him back down to me.

"This. Is. Huge," I whisper in his ear. "We aren't even allowed in there unless invited."

He swallows hard. "Message received." He gives me a quick kiss on the cheek, then follows Dad up to his lair.

"What do you think that's about?" Mariam asks.

"Probably a 'touch her and you die' conversation," Garen says.

Mom snorts a laugh in the kitchen.

"Excuse me, I'm right here!" I wave my hands around, slumping back in my seat. "So awkward."

Mariam heads to the kitchen to help Mom, and Garen turns on the TV. I figure I have a spare moment to myself, so I grab my phone out of my purse and sit on the couch with Garen to check my Photogram notifications.

I have fifteen new followers from the last time I checked about an hour ago.

Fifteen!

I squeal out loud and realize I was tagged in a post by *photographers_daily*, an account that shares some of their favorite photos, which must be where all the new followers came from. They shared a picture of Sharleen at the park, and her now purple-tipped hair popped perfectly against the bright yellow bench. She was staring off into the distance, and the colors all contrasted vibrantly against each other to make a stunning shot. At least I thought so. But apparently, so did the admins of *photographers_daily*.

"What's going on?" Garen asks.

I show him my phone. "This picture got shared, and I'm getting new followers!"

He pushes my shoulder. "No way! That's such a cool shot. Great job, sis!"

"Thanks." I'm beaming, and these are the moments when I re-member how happy I am that I went on this journey and finally, *finally* found what I'm good at.

"What is it?" Mom asks, chopping up cucumbers for a salad.

"A picture I took." I scoot over to the kitchen, proudly showing my mom the picture on the screen. "It got shared by this huge account, so I'm getting a bunch of new followers."

She pauses her chopping and peers at my screen. There's very little expression on her face. She simply nods and goes back to her work. "Very nice."

The balloon in my chest deflates.

"Let me see," Mariam says, noting the exchange.

I show her the picture.

"That's lovely, Emma! I don't know much about photography, but I love the color."

"Thanks." I walk back to the kitchen table and sit next to Garen on the couch. I spend the next few minutes busying myself with notifications and messages, then scrolling to see what everyone else is taking pictures of lately. It's a hard line, the balance between feeling inspired by others' work and, well, jealousy.

Dad and Jacob emerge a little while later, smiling and laughing. I hop off the couch and rush to Jacob, squeezing his hand. "So?"

"I hate whiskey," he whispers, a faint smell of alcohol on his breath. "But don't tell your dad."

"He has *booze* up there?" I whisper-squeal.

He nods.

I grin. "Is everything okay?"

"Oh, yeah. He said he just wanted to get to know me better." Something about the way he won't meet my eyes tells me there was more to that conversation. Well, either that, or he's a little tipsy. So I decide to drop it for now.

"Who's ready for dolma?" Mom asks.

"Me!" everyone chimes in.

I look up at Jacob, and he wraps an arm around my waist and squeezes me tight. As he kisses the top of my head, I feel a sense of contentment.

Yes. Things are just fine.

# Chapter 19

## Three Months Later

NOVEMBER

"**B**eautiful! Keep laughing and looking at each other naturally." I continue snapping pictures of the family with two kids on their white bed, while they giggle and tickle each other.

"Now look at the person with the stinkiest feet!"

There's a pause, as usual, before everyone looks at the dad and bursts out laughing.

"No, Emma!" the dad calls. "Bad girl!"

No, he's not talking to me. Their bulldog, also named Emma, has taken a liking to my camera bag and equipment, and keeps sniffing around while I try to work.

Emma the dog reluctantly waddles away from my bag and miraculously hefts her overweight body onto the bed with the family. The little girl and boy squeal, the parents laugh, and I snap a few more perfect shots. My followers will *love* this.

I take a few more pictures, and, finally satisfied, call it a day. I promise to get their gallery of images ready in the next week and head out into the cool November air.

It's not until I sit in my car that I realize how exhausted I am. My new sneakers save my back, because there's no way I could wear heels and take pictures. Trust me, I tried. But beyond being on my feet all day, interacting with people and taking pictures is emotionally exhausting.

I pull my phone out of my bag and check Photogram—a few new followers, bringing my grand total to 17,000. Yep, after just a few months of focusing on photography, I've gained a significant following.

I've made new friends, too. Scarlett, a fellow new photographer, is awesome. I replied to one of her stories a month ago, and we created a great friendship. She just messaged me a shot of the Eiffel Tower lit up at night, along with well-wishes for my shoot today. *I don't know how you deal with people. I can't stand anyone,* her message says.

I smile. *I'm "people." We seem to get along just fine.*

*You don't count,* she replies. *You're cool.*

I snort, then get distracted with a few more messages and comments. I try to respond to everyone, being authentic and genuine, but sometimes it's a bit…exhausting. I'm so thankful for all the encouragement and support, but social media is turning into a job of its own.

My phone buzzes with a text from Jacob. *You still coming?*

I write him back. *Yep! Leaving my job now.*

He sends back an emoji with heart eyes, and I smile through my nerves. He's right to ask if I'll still show up for his studio party. We've hardly seen each other lately. It's not that I don't want to be with him. But with most of my free time now spent taking pictures or learning about taking pictures, we haven't been able to hang out much.

Add to my schedule the fact that Jacob is taking on extra classes at the studio to fill the financial need for Sara and Cami. It's a sore spot of conversation for us. While I hate the way his dad has treated him over the last eighteen years, I kind of agree with his suggestion for Jacob to go back on the road with the band Rivera and make some money to send home to Sara and Cami.

But from the way his dad talks to him, "suggestion" might be too kind of a word. Jacob has shown me the texts. His dad says things like, *Don't forget who made you famous,* and *You owe me.*

Just your typical, functional, father-son relationship.

As expected, Jacob isn't budging. But it hurts me to see him wasting his talents here in Harbor Sands. He could get all the praise he deserves for his incredible skill, and instead, he's here. I admire his devotion to Sara and Cami, but...

Sometimes I wonder if he's making the right choice.

I tried to bring it up a few weeks ago, and it turned into a tense discussion. Things have felt a little strained between us since then, so a fun night out is exactly what we need. Besides, we've been dating for four months now, and Jacob wants to introduce me to everyone at the studio.

For all these reasons, I grab my red Louboutins from the backseat and slip them onto my feet, then drive over to the dance studio. It's an open party for all the students and teachers, and Sharleen said she'd be there, too. As little as I've been going out with Jacob, I see Sharleen even less. So despite my itch to get home and start editing these photos, I push myself to the studio to see them.

I haven't been back to the studio since the night I took Jacob's hip hop class with Sharleen, AKA, the day I got passed for the promotion. It's weird coming here, only a few months later, and feeling like a completely different person. I'm not lost anymore; I know what makes me special. The drive takes about half an hour because my client was further away, and by the time I get to the studio, it's already dark.

I should probably let my followers know why I won't be responding much tonight. It might sound silly, but I have obligations now that I have a significant following. Messages need to be answered, tags should be responded to in a timely manner. I open the "stories" section of Photogram, the posts that only last for twenty-four hours, and start recording myself talking to the camera. "Hey, everyone! I'm heading to a party tonight so I won't be around much, if anyone messages me or tags me in anything. But I have some incredible pictures that I can't wait to share from my job today. Hope you're all having a great Saturday evening!" I hit post, then step out of my car and into the studio.

Kids and adults are milling around the studio, eating pizza and talking excitedly. It's packed in here, even more than I expected. Music is playing loudly in the background, and one room has a group of girls recording dance videos on their phones.

I look around desperately for Jacob or Sharleen when I'm suddenly tackled around the legs. I look down to see a mass of brown curls attached to a tiny body—Cami.

"Emma!!" she squeals.

"Hey, Cami!" I bend down and give her a big hug. "Having fun?"

She nods. "Mama says I can start taking classes soon, too. But she wants me to do ballet, not hip hop."

I snort a laugh. "I'm sure your Tío will gladly teach you some hip hop moves. I think ballet would be a great choice."

She bounces on her toes and looks around the room. "There's Ms. Laurie, the ballet teacher! Bye, Emma!" She scurries off, and I watch her run up to a gorgeous blonde who's talking to Jacob.

My Jacob.

A twinge of jealousy rushes through me, tightening in my chest. Who is this girl? Why have I never heard about her?

And why is she laughing and touching Jacob's arm now?

Heck no. I follow Cami over to the pair and run my hand down Jacob's back. "Hey, you."

He turns to look at me, and his whole face lights up. The knot in my chest loosens, and I feel like an idiot for being jealous. "Emma!" He puts his hands on my waist and pulls me up against his body, giving me a kiss on the lips.

Now I *really* feel like an idiot for being jealous.

He doesn't go too crazy on the PDA, pulling away after a moment, but I get the idea. He's trying to make it clear to this Laurie girl that we're together. With one arm around my waist, he holds me tight against him.

"Laurie, this is my girlfriend, Emma," he says.

"Hi, nice to meet you!" I put my hand out and shake hers, and I can see the enthusiasm deflating from her face.

"Nice to meet you, too," she says.

"Laurie is the studio owner's daughter. She was a backup dancer for Rivera."

Laurie beams. "And, like Jacob, it was time to come off the road and make a home. So I'm teaching ballet here as I get my bearings."

I put my hand on Jacob's chest. "Isn't that who your dad is trying to get you to dance for?"

Jacob's arm tenses around my waist. "Mm-hmm," he says tightly.

Clearly not the right time or place for this conversation.

"It was nice to meet you, Laurie," I say.

She gets the hint and gives me a fake smile. "I'm going to go check on the pizza." We wave goodbye to her as she leaves.

"I'm so glad you came," he says, gently running his fingers down my cheek. "I've missed you."

"I've missed you, too," I say. My heart warms being this close to him. "How is everything going?"

"Good so far," he says. "I've been chatting with some parents, and it's been going well. Everyone's happy to have a relaxing evening together."

I nod. "Have you seen Sharleen?"

"No, not yet. But a few of the adult students have been milling around, so I'm sure she'll be here soon."

"Jacob!" A woman in her thirties waves at him and walks over. "How are you doing?"

"Great, thanks. Kate, this is my girlfriend, Emma."

I smile. I love when he calls me that.

Jacob continues. "Kate's daughter is on the hip hop team."

"It's nice to meet you, Kate," I say.

"*Exceptional* Emma?" she asks with a wink.

"Uh, yes," I say, feeling a blush creep up on my cheeks. At least it's pretty dark in here.

"Oh, my goodness, I can't tell you how much I laughed watching your fails. I can't decide if beer hockey or video games were my favorite."

My heart sinks. Is that all people remember about me? Not the fact that I'm great at photography? "Thanks, I guess?"

Kate's eyes widen as she realizes her mistake and waves her hands. "Not that your photography isn't incredible. You're doing great. But I miss all your trials."

I smile tightly, then look up at Jacob. "I'm going to go outside and try calling Sharleen."

He presses his lips together, then he glances between me and Kate. I can tell he's trying to decide if he should follow me or continue mingling with Kate.

"I'll be back in a minute," I say, trying to convey that it's okay for him to stay here.

He nods. "Sounds good."

I give him a quick peck on the cheek and head outside.

The evening air is a little chilly, and I always forget to pack a sweater this time of year. With a shiver, I pull my phone out of my purse to text Sharleen, but I notice some Photogram notifications first. I decide to check them quickly before texting her. I need a little boost after Kate's comments, some kind of reassurance that my followers aren't there just because I made a fool of myself a few months ago.

There are a few likes on my story, a few messages saying *Have fun!* and a few new comments on my latest photography post, which give me that little bit of validation I needed.

Then there's a message from Scarlett. *I know you're busy, but I have to send this to you now. Check this out! We should both enter!!*

She sent me a post from The Shutter Society, an organization that runs photography competitions. The post is about their latest competition, called Focus First: a challenge for new photographers to find the most unique perspectives in their images. They're especially looking for photographers who have been in business for one year or less.

The winner gets showcased in front of their 1.5 million followers *and* wins a brand new camera.

My heart flutters with the excitement of possibility. This could be a way for me to prove myself and get a little more recognition than just likes and shares. I respond to Scarlett.

*Heck, yes! I bet we've got a shot!*

She writes back, and I spend the next few minutes messaging her about potential photos and ideas.

"Hey, Em," Jacob's voice sounds behind me.

I turn around quickly, slipping my phone into my back pocket. "Hey."

"You've been gone a while. I thought you'd be right back."

"I got a little...distracted, I guess."

"What did Sharleen say?" he asks.

Oh, shoot. After all that time, I forgot to text her. "I haven't heard from her yet," I say. Which is true. Just...not the whole truth.

He smirks at me. "Anything interesting on Photogram?"

I sigh. Of course, he knows what I was really doing. "Scarlett just sent me a competition that I think I'm going to enter."

"That's cool. When is it?"

"The entries aren't due until January, so I have a couple of months. I think I really have a chance. But it'll take more learning and practice to get the type of shot that will win."

I see the muscle in his jaw twitch.

"What?" I ask.

Indecision flickers in his eyes, and I see the moment he decides to go ahead with what he wants to say. He steps closer to me, taking my hands in his. "I'm so proud of you, Emma. You're so talented, and your passion and dedication are incredible. But it feels like you're becoming really...single-minded."

"Single-minded?" I say with a laugh, pulling my hands from his. "What, have you been talking to my dad?"

One look at his face, and I know he has.

"When?" I ask, my voice small.

"It was just a few months ago. When we were rolling dolma, remember? He asked me to go into his office."

The time he drank whiskey with my dad. I knew something was missing, but I never thought to ask for more details.

"And what did he say?" I ask.

Jacob runs a hand through his hair, taking a few steps away and then back. "He said that you can get really focused on certain things. Like you did about school, and engineering, and then finding your 'thing.' He asked me to look out for you. I said I would." He looks me in the eye, his jaw clenched. "And I worry I failed him."

"Failed him? Why does it matter what my dad thinks, as long as I'm happy?"

He steps toward me again, taking my hands in his. "*Are* you happy?" he asks softly.

I laugh. "Of course I am! I'm finally getting recognized for being good at something. Why do you even ask?"

"You're always so distracted. You don't seem to pay attention to what's happening around you. Whenever we're together, you're constantly on your phone, messaging other people."

"Because there's so much going on online!"

"But that's not reality!" He puts his hands on my waist and pulls me close to him, passion seeping through his fingers. "I'm here, right now, in front of you. How much of your attention is on me?"

I look him in the eyes. "All of it. I swear."

And then my phone buzzes in my pocket, and, out of habit, I look down.

"And how much attention is on me now?" he asks.

My heart sinks. "Don't do that to me," I whisper.

"If you could just take a step away from social media," he pleads, "take a break and focus on what's more important—"

Heat rushes to my cheeks. "You don't get it. I have obligations now." I shake my head. "I thought you'd understand."

"Me?"

I nod. "You have a ton of followers on your own account. People asking questions and wondering what you're doing."

"And I don't respond to them. Maybe you think you have an obligation to answer and respond, but you *don't*. Your life is your own."

"But where is that getting you?"

His eyes widen. "What is that supposed to mean?"

My heart is racing, frustration with the way he sees me and the way he doesn't understand his own situation. I take a step back from him. "You're an incredible performer. And you're wasting your talent and passion, staying here instead of going on tour. You'd be more helpful to Sara and Cami if you left and sent money home to them."

His jaw clenches. "You know exactly why I'm here. After everything I've been through and experienced, I wish you would listen to me instead of getting sucked into the flash of fame." He pauses, then speaks in a softer tone. "And what about us?"

"We'd be fine!" I say.

"Would we?" He raises a brow. "We hardly spend time together. And when we do, you can't even spend two minutes without checking your phone. *That's* with us living in the same town." He runs his hand down my arm, locking with my hand. "Why can't you be happy with what's right in front of you?"

My heart drops into my stomach. I can't believe I'm having this conversation with him. After all the attempts we went through together to find my calling, he still doesn't support my journey.

"I can't do this," I whisper.

His hands tighten around my waist. "Do what?"

I take a step back from him and gesture between us. "Me and you. I can't be with you if you won't accept me the way I am."

"What are you talking about?" he says, his voice rising. "All I've done is accept you for who you are, *before* you found your calling."

"And now? You're just trying to hold me back." I shake my head. "I can't be with someone who won't have my back one hundred percent."

"Emma." He takes a step toward me, pulling me into his arms. "I support you. And supporting you means seeing when you're turning into something you're not. Because I love you."

I gasp and look up into his eyes. That's the first time he's said that to me. Does he really mean it?

Do I love him back?

"I love you, Emma," he repeats, and he kisses my forehead. "You are everything I've wanted, just the way you are." He kisses one cheek, and I close my eyes. "And loving someone means being there for them, even if you have to say something they don't want to hear."

Tears prick my eyes. Because as much as I want to believe him, I can't help feeling like he doesn't understand me anymore.

"And I can choose to not hear it," I say. "Do you really love *me*, or the person I was before?" I pull his arms from around me, and he doesn't resist. I think he knows now that I mean it.

"I wish they were the same person," he says, not breaking eye contact.

I suck in a breath, and my heart sinks. "We're done."

We stand there, staring at each other for another moment, and he exhales a deep breath. "If that's the way you feel," he finally says. And then he turns and walks back into the studio.

My hands are shaking, my breaths uneven, and my eyes are burning with tears. I'm angry and disappointed in him. Of all people, he was supposed to understand! He wasn't supposed to hold me back; he was supposed to love me and be proud of me through it all.

Breaking from my daze, I finally realize that people are watching me, and I turn and head back to my car. Pulling my phone out of my pocket, I see another message from Scarlett. I could tell her about the breakup, but this is something I need Sharleen for. I turn on my car and call her number.

Her phone goes straight to voicemail. Strange. I leave her a message. "Hey, Sharleen. I thought you said you were coming to the dance studio, but I didn't see you. I really need you right now. I just broke up with Jacob and...I need my best friend. Call me back." I hang up and hope she'll get back to me.

I'm pulling into my apartment parking lot when my phone rings. It's Sharleen.

"Hey," I say, so desperate to talk to her. "Can you come over?"

"Not right now," she says, her voice short.

"Why not?"

She pauses. "Pancake died."

I gasp. "Not Pancake!"

She sniffs. "She's been sick all week. I took her to the vet yesterday, and she gave us the choice to keep up her doggy dialysis or put her down. She's been in so much pain." She starts to cry, loudly, and my heart breaks for her.

"Sharleen, I'm so, so sorry. I can't even imagine how I'll feel when Sparky passes." I take in a deep breath. "Why didn't you tell me?"

She's silent for a moment. "You haven't asked me about my life in weeks. You only call when you need something. Even now, you only called because you wanted me to come over and help you feel better."

I suck in a breath. "That's not true."

"It is," she insists, and in my heart, I can't say she's completely wrong.

"Can you come over? Or I can come there! We can do whatever you want and be sad together."

I wait patiently for her answer. "No."

"No?"

"No. I think...I need some time alone."

My stomach turns, and I feel like I'm going to be sick. "Okay. Please call me when you need anything, or when you want to hang out."

"Okay."

And she hangs up.

A wave of emptiness fills my heart. I sit in the parking lot and rest my head on the steering wheel, feeling the loss of my boyfriend and my best friend, all in one hour. I don't know what to do now.

My phone buzzes.

A Photogram alert—a new comment on my latest post.

*Wow. This is stunning. You have such a gift!*

And just like that, I feel a little bit better.

# Chapter 20

## Two Months Later

JANUARY

*B*eep, *beep, beep.*

I reach toward my nightstand and find the "stop" button on my alarm. 6:30—time to get moving. I may not have an office to go to anymore, but I've learned through experience that sleeping in late means more work on social media later.

My eyes blink blearily as I adjust to my phone screen. First things first: Photogram. There are ten messages from friends and fifteen new message requests. I scan through them quickly but don't open the messages, so the notifications stay on and I'll remember to respond later.

Then I go to the notifications. It's all a blur now; I don't notice the exact numbers of likes and comments and tags when I first wake up. I scroll down the seemingly endless list of likes, trying to pick out the few comments that might actually apply to me.

I have another thirty followers, which is kind of a slow morning.

After all, what's thirty people when your total is eighty thousand?

A comment catches my eye. *This is incredible. You have a true talent for capturing the human experience.*

I feel a flutter in my chest, that stirring that makes it all feel worth it. This is what I was hoping for. This is what I've been dreaming of for years.

I send a heart to that user and write back a comment. *Thank you so much. You made my morning!*

I scroll a bit more through the app, checking what my friends are posting. Scarlett is taking pictures of the Leaning Tower of Pisa. She asked me to join her, but I had too many events lined up for this week. Jenessa, an older woman who lives on the East Coast, did another family session in the park. Jonah is focused, as usual, on the ducks at Big Bear Lake. Thankfully, they got a good amount of snow recently, unlike the drought we've experienced the last few years here in Southern California. He loves bringing some bread and feeding them, then taking pictures of the kids squealing in delight.

I'll admit, they're sweet, happy pictures. I laugh out loud, but no one hears. Because, as usual, I'm alone.

But even in my solitude, my apartment has some incredible upgrades. These sheets, for example, are a gift from Barney Textiles. I never could have afforded them on my own. All I have to do is tell my followers how soft they are and that I feel like I'm sleeping on a cloud. And the robe I wrap myself in as soon as I get out of bed? From Rosanne Lingerie. It makes me feel like a movie star. At least, that's what I tell my followers.

I flip open my stories and pick the perfect filter to disguise the bags under my eyes and the blemishes on my cheeks. No amount of skin cream from Derma New has gotten rid of those, especially with how hard it is to sleep. I'm awake for a few hours every night around 2:00 a.m., thoughts racing about what to post next and how to book more clients. It's exhausting, but sometimes my best ideas come in the middle of the night, and I have to appreciate the fact that I can be creative at any hour. But my caffeine addiction and the bags under my eyes are telling a story that I don't want to share.

"Good morning, my lovely followers! I hope you're having a gorgeous day. It's a little chilly here, but I know January in Southern California is nothing compared to what you all are dealing with in the Midwest! I hope you stay safe in that storm. I would hate for any of my friends to be hurt! Today, I'm going to take some pictures at the local ice rink." I pause for a moment, not sure if I want to share my last experience there. It's been seven months since beer hockey, and I feel like so much has changed since then. "I've been there a few times in the past, but it's been a little while. I hope to have those pictures uploaded tomorrow! Later today, I'll choose which picture I want to enter in Focus First, the latest competition by the Shutter Society. The winning entry is half determined by likes, and half by the judges' decision, so I'll let you all know how and when to vote! Thanks so much for being here!" I blow a kiss at the camera, then shut it off.

Sharing myself online hasn't been as difficult as I expected. I just pretend I'm talking to myself about my day, and it goes well. It turns out that the years I spent writing in my journal were the perfect practice. But I haven't touched it in the last month or so. It's fine, though, because everything I used to write in my journal is saved in my Photogram account. Instead of writing it down, I just share it with eighty thousand people.

No big deal, right?

After making myself a cup of coffee, I sit down at the computer and start editing the pictures from yesterday. The pictures I shoot are considered "lifestyle photography," meaning I take everyday situations and make them artistic. I didn't realize that's what I was doing already, taking pictures of the beer hockey league, dancing, the guys surfing...and even Jacob.

Jacob.

I feel a pang in my chest at the thought of him, but I push it aside. I don't have time for that right now. I have work to do.

On the way to the rink, I stop at the local coffee shop. It's a ritual I've adopted since I started getting paid jobs, and it helps compensate for my insomnia.

I wait for my drink at the counter and flip through my digital portfolio on my phone, trying and failing (again) to find the right picture for the Focus First competition. While I'm proud of my work, and it's clearly good enough to earn followers, I still can't find the right one that completely encapsulates my skill.

"Emma?"

I look up in confusion, trying to find who said my name.

It's Samuel.

AKA promotion stealing, back-stabbing Samuel.

Okay, fine, he didn't intentionally steal the promotion. But seeing him still stings. And don't forget it's awkward, since he asked me out on my last day of work.

"Hey, Samuel," I say, locking my phone. "What are you doing here?"

"I'm on my way back to the office after a site visit and figured I'd grab a drink." He looks me up and down, dressed in my all-black pants and shirt, the uniform I decided would be best as a photographer. "You look different."

"You only saw me in business wear, I guess."

"You're missing your shoes."

I laugh and look down at my Skechers. "True. I do miss wearing my Louboutins."

He laughs, and we awkwardly look around the coffee shop in silence.

"So, how have you been?" he asks.

"I'm good," I reply. It's weird explaining the whole "Exceptional Emma" thing to people who I know in real life, so it's easier to avoid the subject altogether. "How's the office?"

"Going really well, actually. We still haven't found someone to replace you, though."

"Oh?" I can't help a little smirk that emerges. As petty as it seems, I feel good that I wasn't easily replaceable. Maybe my work wasn't so average after all.

"I was actually thinking about sending you an email. I know you're on this...spiritual journey...but if you could even come back part time as a consultant, that would be awesome."

Why does that idea get me excited? Is there a part of me that actually *misses* engineering? Or the office?

No, Emma. Don't be crazy. You're happy now. Things are good. You're on your way toward being exceptional.

"Thanks, but I've got a lot on my plate," I say. The barista calls my name, and I wave to acknowledge that I heard her. "I hope you guys find someone soon."

Samuel holds up a hand to say goodbye. "Let me know if anything changes. Bye, Exceptional Emma." And the glimmer in his eye tells me he knows *exactly* what I'm up to these days.

I cringe as I get my drink, but I paste on a huge smile when I turn around and head out of the store. I can't let him see how much he affected me.

Once I get to the ice rink, a weird sense of déjà vu from nearly seven months ago passes through me. I walk in the front doors, again blasted with frigid air, and the receptionist isn't paying attention to anything.

I clear my throat. "Hi, I'm here to photograph Rose."

She looks up, her bored expression reminding me of the last time I was here and took the kids' class. But I see the moment she registers who I am, and her eyes light up. "Emma! How have you been?"

My eyes widen in surprise. I didn't think she'd remember my name. "Oh. I'm doing well, thank you."

"That night you came in was so much fun. I know you didn't love the kids' class, but we were all so impressed that you still tried. And then when you did the beer hockey league..." She shakes her head. "That was awesome. I started following you on Photogram after that. Looks like you're doing well for yourself now."

"Thanks."

"Are you ever going to try anything new again?"

I shake my head. "No, I'm good. I took down all those posts of my failed attempts."

"Oh, really? Why?"

I shrug, looking around the rink. For some reason, I can't meet her eye. And I definitely don't want to tell her I deleted them the night that Jacob and I broke up, when that mom at the studio only remembered me for my fails and not my photography. "I don't know. They don't fit into what I'm doing now."

"I thought that's what got you all those followers. When they saw how you were willing to try and fail."

I feel a flush rise on my cheeks and shake my head. "Those followers didn't stick around. Now it's all about the photography." I take in a deep breath, pasting on a smile and looking at her again. "And that's what the journey was for, right? Finding what made me exceptional."

She blinks at me a few times, and I see her expression change into something a little less friendly. Is she...disappointed? She clears her throat and goes back to her computer, typing a few things. "Rose is here. She's warming up. Cynthia is here, too. You can go meet them."

"Thanks." Cynthia? As in...beer hockey Cynthia? I almost hope it *isn't* her. Because being at the ice-skating rink is already bringing back some weird feelings and memories.

I wander over to the benches, and even though her back is to me, I can tell that it *is* beer hockey Cynthia. The woman who hugged me and told me she was proud of me, and encouraged me to keep trying.

She'll be proud of me now, right?

"Hi, Cynthia," I say, and she turns around, a wide smile on her face.

"Exceptional Emma!" She stands and wraps me in a big hug. "I'm glad you're here." She points at the ice, where a woman spins on one leg at a scary rate. "That's my daughter."

"Wow," I murmur. Rose stops on a dime, her hands raised in the air, her chest heaving with exertion. "I didn't realize your daughter was so good at this."

"Thank you." Cynthia beams. "She's been on tour with Disney On Ice for the last year, so I haven't gotten to see her much. Now that she's home, I promised I'd get her a photography session."

"Well, I'm glad she called." I pull my camera out of my bag, the gorgeous new Canon EOS R5 I bought after my first few commissions. Before that, I was just borrowing one of Mona's cameras.

"Looks like you're doing well for yourself," Cynthia comments. "I've been following your journey."

I smile at her. "It's going well. I found something I'm really good at now." I fasten the lens on the camera body, then hold it up to my eye to check the settings.

"I bet your friend is so proud of you."

"Hmm?" I put the camera down and look over at her.

"Your friend. The one who was here recording you. She must be really proud of you."

Two pangs in one day. But I don't really want to explain the situation with Sharleen to sweet Cynthia. "Yep." I press my lips together and fiddle with more settings on my camera.

Rose skates over, thankfully breaking the conversation. "Hi! You must be Exceptional Emma!"

"That's me!" It feels weird acknowledging when people call me that now, but I've come to embrace it.

I shake her gloved hand, and I see the resemblance in her bright blue eyes and flushed cheeks. Her hair is more of a chestnut color, as opposed to Cynthia's bright red, but the family similarities are clear.

"You're incredible," I say, gesturing at the ice. "I wasn't expecting this."

"Thank you." She smiles. "I've got plenty of posed and planned pictures, but my mom wanted to catch some regular shots, too. She says I'll look back and remember what the everyday aspects were like."

"I love that," I say. "And she's right. That's what I like to capture. Life's realities and the little moments."

"So, I guess I'll..." Rose looks back at the ice. "Practice?"

"Yep! Just pretend I'm not here."

She smiles and waves, then heads back out.

"Man. She's so good. I couldn't even skate without using that plastic seal."

Cynthia laughs out loud. "I remember watching you. I thought, 'That has to be one determined cookie.'"

"That I was," I agree. I capture some shots of Rose, intentionally keeping the glass in view of the camera. It feels almost like a spy shot, but I love that part. "I had to go through quite a few hobbies until I got to photography."

"That's right. I remember seeing your balloon animals. That was an interesting one."

I snort. "It was fun, but I was terrible at it." A pang appears in my chest again, reminding me of the bear I made for Jacob.

Jacob.

"But surfing. That was emotional." Cynthia continues, unaware of the pain in my chest.

"Yep." I don't want to talk about what happened on that trip, and especially not what happened after the camera stopped recording. I still dream about kissing Jacob on that beach. "I'm gonna go take some pictures over there." I gesture at the tables, where I plan to stand and get some more shots of Rose.

"Oh, sure." I think she knows I don't want to talk any more, because she lets me leave and doesn't follow me.

I spend the next hour snapping shots of Rose practicing, resting and taking a water break, talking and laughing with her mom, and finally taking off her skates and resting.

I scroll through the previews on my camera, feeling that tingle when I feel like I get the perfect pictures. That's what this is all about. "I think we got some really great shots," I say. "I should have them ready in about a week."

"I can't wait! Thanks so much!" Rose squeezes me in a hug, all of her muscles pulling tight on my frame. But I have to admit, it feels nice to be hugged.

"You're welcome." I turn to Cynthia. "It was great to see you again."

"You too, Exceptional Emma." But when she says it this time, it's missing some of the warmth. She almost seems...sad? Before I can wonder too much about it, she squeezes me tightly. "Remember what made you exceptional in the first place."

I pull back and smile at her, even though I'm not sure what she means. "I'll send you the pictures soon."

With a wave, I head out of the rink and back to my car. I pull out my phone and check my notifications. I have an email from a client, one who was particularly difficult to please during the session, and as I read, a pit forms in my stomach.

*Hi Emma,*

*Thanks for sending over the gallery. But I have to say, I'm really disappointed in these pictures. The shadows are really intense, and we're all squinting because of the bright sun.*

Well, yeah. That's because you showed up a full hour before I told you to, while I was setting up and finding my light, and insisted on starting then. If we had started when I said to, one hour before sunset, the lighting would have been perfect.

*I'm also very disappointed in the editing. Can you send over the raw originals? I have a photographer friend who said she would fix them up for me. I'm really bummed, because I was so excited to secure a shoot with Exceptional Emma and I feel let down.*

I set the phone down and close my eyes. Every client until this point has been super kind and supportive, but this was bound to happen at some point, right? Even if it's not my fault, this is the business of dealing with people. I have to say, at times like these, I miss working in engineering. At least buildings didn't fight back about your artistic vision.

I shoot a text to Mona asking for her advice, and then I post in the Lifestyle Photographers Chat group on Facebook. There are a ton of experienced photographers there who can help me out, too. Then it's time to check my Photogram notifications. It's crazy how much can happen in just one hour away from the app, which is why I check it regularly when I'm not working. I filter to just the comments and scroll through. There are a few sweet comments on my latest pictures, questions about where I live and how much I charge (and I direct them to my website), but then one comment catches my eye.

It's on one of the few pictures I left from my "Exceptional Emma" journey. The one of Jacob driving up the 5 freeway on our way home from camping.

*What happened to this guy?*

That's a great question. I've intentionally stayed away from anything that has to do with Jacob because of the pang that hits my chest every time I hear his name. I don't know what sadistic torture I'm craving, but I click the comment and see a thread of replies has formed underneath it.

*I don't think they're dating anymore. She hasn't posted about him in a while.*

*It's Jacob Perez. He was a backup dancer for Nova Sky.*

*Sooooo hot! She's an idiot for letting him go.*

*Have you seen his latest YouTube video?*

YouTube video?

Do I want to know what they're talking about?

I don't think, just tap. I switch to the YouTube app and type in "Jacob Perez." And there he is, in all his glory. His channel is called Jam with Jacob, and he has four thousand subscribers. I click the top video, and he smiles at the camera with two girls behind him at the dance studio. I recognize one of them as Laurie.

Are they dating now?

The background music is Nova Sky's latest hit.

"Hey everyone! Welcome back to Jam with Jacob, where we get our bodies moving while having fun!"

And as I watch him teach a dance routine, smiling and joking the whole while, I start to cry.

# Chapter 21

On Saturday morning, I take a sip of my hot coffee, letting the warmth seep into my bones. My fuzzy panda slippers and robe help a little, and I settle in at my kitchen table for a morning of edits.

I think weekend mornings are my favorite. This is when I get to look through everything I've shot this week and decide which ones are worth running through my editing software. I have a couple in-home family sessions, one family working in their vegetable garden, and Rose at the ice rink.

I spend a couple hours editing the family sessions first, getting into my groove, and I'm pretty happy with the pictures. I always see something I can improve, though, but doesn't everyone? Even so, I finally feel that pride in having something I'm actually good at.

Finally, I pull up Rose's session. Scanning through the pictures, I feel half pride, half disappointment. The pictures aren't quite as good as I thought they were. This was my first attempt at sports photography, and I didn't consider all the factors as I should have. Many of my pictures are blurry, and the lighting is off. I can fix some of the lighting issues, but not all. The best pictures are the ones of her standing still, grabbing a drink of water, or coming over to the side and talking to her mom. I'm glad I grabbed a few of those shots.

And then I see one of the last pictures I took: Cynthia is in focus, looking through the glass into the rink, and the delight in her eyes is contagious. You can see an outline of Rose in the background, but the focus is on Cynthia and her admiration of her exceptional daughter.

This is it. My entry for the contest. How much better could I get at showing perspective?

Ignoring all the other pictures, I load this one into my editing software and start working. A few touch ups here and there, and twenty minutes later, I think I've got it.

I stare at my computer screen, my heart racing with excitement. I've been waiting for the right picture. This picture isn't just beautiful, but it has a story and a heart behind it too. I download it to my computer, email it to myself, then open my Photogram app and send it to Scarlett, Jonah, and Jenessa. *What do you think? My entry in the competition?*

It doesn't take long for their responses to come in.

*OMG YES!!!*

*Gorgeous. Maybe up the warmth a little, but otherwise perfection.*

*Beautiful, Emma.*

The smile on my face grows larger and larger with each message. I follow Jonah's advice and up the warmth a teensy bit. As usual, he's right. I'm really thankful I found these friends who completely support my journey and make it feel worthwhile.

I can't say the same for everyone else in my life.

Shaking those thoughts from my head, I open the entry form for the competition on my web browser. They ask for very little information—Photogram account, name of the photographer, upload the picture, and the title of the picture.

I breeze through the first parts, then hesitate at the title. What was it that Cynthia was feeling in that moment? Delight, yes. Admiration. But something a little bigger than that.

Adoration.

She *adores* her daughter.

I type in the word *Adoration* as the title of the photo and hit submit. Violin notes fill my memory. Just like Mariam and Garen's piece.

A pang fills my chest, remembering the last time I heard them play it at my parents' house, Jacob by my side, wishing that someone adored me the way everyone adored my siblings.

But I'm on my way. I really think I have a shot at this competition. And if I make it, then maybe I'll be adored, too.

Two weeks later, I'm sitting at my kitchen table, editing as usual. The Focus First competition closed a week ago. I posted every day asking for votes, and I can only hope that my followers came through. But it's not *just* up to the number of votes. The judges also have to agree that it's the best photo out of them all.

I'm trying to tell myself that it'll be okay either way. I mean, of course I'll be thrilled if I win. But if I don't, it's not the end of the world. Sure, I've been working hard at this for a few months now. But other entrants have been studying photography for years and are just now taking it to a professional level. Who am I to think that

I would win over them? To be honest, when I scrolled through the other entries, I felt a little sick to my stomach. But it can be really hard to judge your own work, especially when it's a photograph and you've seen the original scene before it came into your frame.

The competition organizers haven't said when they'll announce the winner, but I've been checking the website every chance I get. Yes, I've already checked it this morning. So now, I'm trying to distract myself with some editing. Which has really turned into scrolling through Photogram, looking at other people's work, and trying to see what I can learn. It's research, right? And if I happen to respond to someone's comment along the way, there's some networking.

Boom. Productive.

I keep scrolling through, and am about to type a comment with some heart-eye emojis on Scarlett's latest post, when a notification pops at the top of my screen.

*Shutter Society has tagged you in a post.*

Holy smokes.

What does this mean?

My fingers are shaking, my heart is racing, and I feel like I'm about to throw up. I click the notification and arrive at the post. I read it once, but it doesn't compute at first. So I read it again, more slowly.

"Congratulations to our first place winner, Exceptional Emma, for her photo titled *Adoration*. We loved the depth of emotion and perspective that she captured, and so did all our voters!"

I won.

I WON.

I WON!!!!

I squeal out loud, dropping my phone on the table. Unable to stay still, I jump out of my chair and start dancing around my kitchen. I look like a fool. I absolutely know it. Of course I do.

But do I care?

Not at all, because I WON!

Dancing is a lot more strenuous than I remembered, though, and exercise has not been a priority in the last few months. Maybe I should have been *doing* Jacob's dance exercise videos instead of just watching them. I hold on to my kitchen counter, panting like a dog, but I can't shake the smile from my face.

"I *won*," I whisper to myself, shaking my head. I can't believe it.

I squeal again, then cover my mouth with my hands, but I can't contain the grin that's spread across my face and hurting my cheeks. I did it. I finally did it. I finally found something that makes me stand out, something that I'm really good at.

Something that makes me exceptional.

The realization brings on a whole new wave of emotion. My chest tightens and tears fill my eyes, but they're not tears of sadness. It's bittersweet, the accomplishment of a goal I've held for so long, mixed with wishing I'd been doing this longer so I could have experienced this moment before.

I grab my phone and open Photogram. As weird as it may seem, this very real moment would make a great post.

"Hey everyone!" My reflection is bursting with emotion, eyes shining with tears but a giant smile on my face from ear to ear. "I just got a notification that I won the Shutter Society's Focus First competition and I wanted to thank you, from the bottom of my heart, for voting and supporting me on my journey. I can't believe

what it's taken to get here, and I love you all so much. Thank you!"
I squeal one more time and blow a kiss at the camera, then post it.

I take a few minutes to do more "business" on the app—commenting on Shutter Society's post to thank them for awarding me first place and replying to a few comments from people who already congratulated me. I think about sending a message to my photographer friends, but I'm not sure if it will come off as bragging. I know they were hoping to win, too. It's a little awkward, being friends with people who are your competition in some ways, and I don't want them to feel like I'm shoving it in their faces. So I leave it alone for now, figuring they'll reach out to me. But I want to share the news with someone I know... Who?

Closing the app, I go back to my home screen and think about whom to call. Garen would be excited for me, I know that. He's been my biggest supporter this whole time. We haven't talked much lately, but he's there for me. So I call him. The phone rings five times, and then his voicemail comes on. I remember he said he was busy with something this morning but would be back in the evening for family dinner. I can't remember what it was, though. His voice rings through my ear: *Hey, sorry you missed me. I'm probably gaming. Leave me a message! GG!*

"Hey, Garen! I have some exciting news I wanted to share with you... I guess I can just tell you tonight at dinner. I feel like you said you were busy this morning, but I can't remember what it was. Anyway, call me back if you can! Or I'll see you later!"

I hang up, a little bummed. But I'm sure there's someone else to call, right?

I open my text messages, hoping I'll get an indication of a friend I've been talking to lately. But as I scroll...and scroll...and scroll, the only messages I find are conversations with clients and annoying marketing texts I forget to unsubscribe to. *No, I don't need another shade of quick-dry nail polish.* I go back and back, until I hit two months ago, and see my last conversation with Jacob.

*You still coming to the studio tonight?*

And that was the beginning of the end.

I take in a shaky breath, wondering if he'd be interested in knowing that I won. No, that's stupid. Of course he wouldn't. The whole reason we broke up was because of my "single-mindedness" with being exceptional. Winning would be the last thing he'd want to hear about.

Above that conversation is my last message with Sharleen. A few days after she put Pancake down, she messaged me and asked if we could get our nails done. It was a clear sign of peace that she was trying to make a truce.

But I got distracted and forgot to reply.

And I still haven't replied.

I bite my lip, pushing down the waves of emotion. I guess there isn't really anyone to share the news with, other than my Photogram friends. But that's okay.

At least I can tell Garen tonight.

"Hey, everyone, sorry I'm late," I say, sitting down at the dining table. "I got caught up editing and lost track of time."

"Sit, Emma-jan," my mom says, even though I'm already sitting. She starts serving manti, Armenian meat-filled dumplings, on my plate, layering garlic and tomato sauces over the top.

I look over at Garen, who's shoveling food in his mouth and won't meet my eyes. "Amazing manti, Ma," he says with a mouth full of food.

Mom smiles at him and pats his cheek. "Anoush," she says, which basically means *enjoy, sweetheart.*

"Garen, you never called me back," I say.

He looks over at me, and his eyes are missing their usual twinkle. "I was busy."

"Yes, he was!" Mariam says. She squeezes his arm. "He did so well today."

Garen meets her with a smile. So apparently he's only mad at me, not everyone.

I furrow my brow, racking my brain for what they're talking about. "So well at what?"

He looks back at me, the irritated expression back on his face. "My regional tournament. It was the biggest competition for Heroes of the Kingdom. I told you about it last week, and you promised you'd be there."

My heart sinks completely into my stomach, and I feel the blood rush out of my face. "Garen, I'm so sorry. I completely forgot."

He nods. "I figured."

"Truly." I reach across the table for his hand, but he keeps his in his lap. Slowly and awkwardly, I pull my hand back. "I really am sorry. I wanted to be there."

"Not enough," he mutters, then goes back to eating.

I swallow down my guilt, then start eating, too. Manti is usually one of my favorite meals, but right now, I can't taste anything. Because the one person I wanted to share my excitement with looks like he wants nothing to do with me right now.

The conversation swirls around me, and I feel like I could be anywhere else, and no one would notice. Emma the Spare, surrounded by her extraordinary siblings and doting parents. Sparky prances over to me and starts begging for food.

"Hey, dude," I say. He promptly sits at my feet, thinking that sitting without a command is the magic key to getting a treat. He's not completely wrong. I look for a scrap on my plate to feed him. Normally, I scold my mom for doing this exact thing, because it just teaches him that begging is okay. But right now, I feel like I need a friend. And even though Sparky is psychotic, I'll take it. I take a piece of meat out of one dumpling and give him a little piece. He gobbles it up and patiently waits for more.

"That's enough, Sparky," I whisper to him. So he lays down, thinking the next trick, even without a command, will get him a treat.

"I'm not giving you any more food," I say.

And then he rolls over onto his back. I sigh and start to rub his belly. He relaxes for a moment, closing his eyes and letting me massage him.

But, because he's Sparky, the moment ends in an instant. His eyes pop open and he eyes my hand. I try to pull my hand back quickly, knowing what he's thinking, but his teeth nip my fingers and I scream.

"Sparky!" I jump up out of my seat, shaking my hand. "Why did you bite me, you crazy dog?"

"Oh, Emma, be kind," my mom says, rubbing Sparky between the ears. "You should have known not to pull your hand away like that from him."

"I should have known?!" I put my fingers in my mouth, giving them momentary relief from the pain. There isn't too much blood, but given the events of the day, just that little prick of pain has sent me over the edge. "He's literally insane! Why am *I* the one getting in trouble?"

"He doesn't know better. When we rescued him—"

"He had been attacked by a cat, I know. But he *still* shouldn't be allowed to do that! Especially not to me!" Hot, angry tears fill my eyes. "Especially not to your *daughter*!"

My mom stares at me for a moment, and I realize how quiet everyone has gotten. No one speaks, chews, or drinks.

"You care more about Sparky than you do about me," I say, willing my voice to stop shaking and commanding the tears to stay in my eyes.

"That's not true," my mom says gently, reaching for my arm.

I pull it away quickly. "Even if it's not Sparky, it's Mariam or Garen. Your two perfect, incredible children."

"Emma, no," my dad jumps in.

"You don't care about me either!" I say. "None of you ask about my photography! That's the *one* thing I'm *finally* good at, and do any of you care? No!" I face Garen. "You know why I called you today? Because I won the Focus First competition. I flipping *won*. I finally did something exceptional. But does it matter? No." The tears I was holding back are streaming down my cheeks now. "None of you care. Because I don't matter to any of you."

I turn and leave, and no one says a word. No one follows me or tells me to come back. I don't know what I expected. Maybe for someone to tell me I'm wrong, and that they love me and love my photography. That I'm important, too.

I guess I'm not.

As soon as I slam the front door shut behind me, a wracking sob runs through my body. I crouch down on the ground, my high heels supporting my seat, and I try to catch my breath, but I can't.

I don't hear the door open, but I see Garen's shoes next to me.

"I knew you won," he says.

I suck in a breath and look up at him from my spot on the ground. "You did?"

He nods. "I saw it on Photogram."

"Then...why didn't you say anything?"

He watches me for a moment, then crouches down next to me. "You might think we don't care about you, but the truth is that you don't care about anyone or anything other than yourself." He holds my gaze for another moment. "You're not yourself anymore."

Anger boils through me. "You're right. I'm not sad, pathetic, mediocre Emma. I'm *Exceptional* Emma now."

His features harden at the use of my nickname. "Exceptional, how? Exceptional in the things you do? Or in the type of person you are? Because the old Emma was exceptional in every way that mattered. And this new Emma..." He waves his hand at me. "I don't know her anymore. And I don't want to."

My heart tightens at his words. I want to tell him he's wrong. That this was the piece of me that had been missing all along. But before I can protest, he stands and goes back into the house, slamming the door behind him.

I'm too tired to cry again. But it's clear that I'm not wanted here. So I stand, make my way to my car, and slump in the driver's seat. I just need a minute to feel like myself. I pull out my phone and open the Photogram app, smiling at the new comments on my post. There are thousands of new likes, and over a hundred comments congratulating me on my win. I take in a shaky breath and start replying to the comments, thanking them for all their support.

But one comment stands out.

*This is crap. I can't believe this picture beat out Scarlett's entry.*

My heart drops. Not only because I wondered the same thing myself...but because his comment has 154 likes.

154 other people agree my picture is crap.

I try not to let it get to me. I've dealt with trolls and nasty comments before. Even back when I was attempting all my hobbies, I had some weird comments. But for some reason, this one is striking even harder. And it's probably because I'm in a vulnerable place.

Since the comment is on my account, I can delete it. I wait a moment, trying to decide what the best move is. The words sting, since so many people agreed with this person, but at least it won't give anyone else new ideas. With renewed determination, I block the user and delete the comment. There. Now they can't bother me anymore.

My messages are filled with other well-wishes, and I take the time to reply to each one. It reminds me that there *are* people who love me and care about me. People who appreciate what I'm doing and want me to succeed. And I'm grateful for them all.

Finally, I open my group message with my photography friends. They still haven't said anything yet.

I'm about to type a message to them, finally saying something along the lines of, "Hey, I won, but you guys are awesome and I wish we could have all been winners," when a text alert pops on the top of my screen.

From Jacob.

The first words I've heard from him in two months.

I tap it quickly, opening the message.

*I saw you won the competition. Congratulations, Emma. I'm really happy for you. And I hope with all my heart that you're happy, too.*

I read the words once, twice, three times. I can hear his voice saying the words. I can see his green eyes, their sparkling intensity as he looks at me. I can see his lips saying the words, and I can still feel them moving on mine.

How does he even know that I won?

The words blur as the tears form and start to fall. Here's the one and only person from my real life congratulating me on my win.

And he's the person I pushed the furthest away.

What do I even say to him? I *want* to tell him I'm sorry and that I need him.

But that would be selfish. I can't tell him I want him back now that everyone has abandoned me. Not after I pushed him away.

I can't do that to him.

With shaky fingers, I type out a message and press send. I read the words one more time, and they flash before my eyes as I start my car and drive home.

*Thanks. I am.*

# Chapter 23

After that one night of weakness, I refuse to wallow in my misery anymore. I'm an award-winning photographer, dang it! I am Exceptional Emma, and no one can get me down. Not trolls on the Internet, not the people who knew me before. Not my family.

No one.

I throw myself into my photography and Photogram. Even though I don't have any clients on Sunday, I head to the beach and practice taking pictures of the people and the scenery. The lighting is terrible, but it's good for me to practice. I try to catch a few pictures of the surfers and realize that I need to work on my action shots, just like I thought I did after Rose's session. So after I get home that day, I spend the rest of the afternoon researching action shots and how to improve with that.

The next week, I'm busy with clients and photo sessions. I research lighting setups. Even though I specialize in natural light, I want to know everything I can about this hobby. Because it's not enough to win one competition. Now I have something to prove.

And I'm not the only one who thinks so.

My follower count has shot up in the two weeks since I won the competition. It's been overwhelming, to be honest. I didn't consider this effect. Every morning, I wake up to hundreds of new people who know my name and want to see my pictures. At this point, it's getting hard to keep up with all the comments and messages being sent to me. It's become a job of its own. I kind of miss the days when I was just trying out hobbies and could have conversations with the people I met online.

But I don't let myself dwell on that thought. Because back then, I didn't know what it was like to be exceptional.

Apparently, being exceptional comes with a bit of baggage, too. Not all followers are here for the right reasons.

Some are sugar daddies. Those are easy to spot, with their many selfies and claims to be doctors and lawyers. I usually just remove them, unless they send me a creepy message saying they want to send me a "weekly allowance" for the "pleasure of my company, nothing sexual." Uh-huh, sure dude. *Blocked.*

Other accounts are companies looking for followers. Doesn't matter who or what I am, they just hope that I'll follow them back. They leave on their own, so I don't worry about them.

But then, there are the ones that are interested in photography...but not necessarily interested in me. The ones with a lot of opinions and feelings about my posts. Some of them have gone back to the beginning of my journey and leave...not very kind comments on there.

*Wow, beginner much?* Uh, yeah. I was a beginner at the time.

*Is this supposed to be in focus?* Yes...it is. But I pause and take a second look...it *is* in focus, right?

*Is she lifestyle photography or sports? Because clearly she can't do either. Stick to your own lane!*

I wish I could say those comments didn't hurt.

But they do.

I try to brush them off and move on. I remind myself that I won a competition. First place! But little doubts keep needling their way into my mind.

*Maybe you only won because you have so many followers.*

*Maybe you* do *suck at photography.*

*Maybe they only voted for you because of your personality, not because of your pictures.*

*Maybe you're not exceptional, after all.*

So I find new ways to convince myself that I am, in actuality, exceptional. I'm going to win more competitions. I'm going to do better. I'm going to improve until there's nothing left to prove.

But when I lie awake at night, I wonder if that's even possible.

Two weeks later, I'm on my phone, responding to a message in the group chat with my friends. They claimed they hadn't seen the announcement about my win that first night, which is why they hadn't responded. Jenessa had a wedding, and Jonah had a family emergency. The next day, they wrote me their congratulations, and I felt better.

But I've noticed that there haven't been any more huge gaps in communication since then. Even if they have a wedding or emer-gency...they're usually back on within an hour or two.

So why didn't they respond that day?

I don't bring it up. I don't want to cause drama with the only friends I have left, so we don't talk about my win or any other competitions. I'm pretty sure we're all eyeing the Shutter Society's new competition, Adventures in Aperture, but we don't talk about it anymore.

My phone starts buzzing a minute later, and Cynthia's name flashes across my screen. Why is she calling? I sent her the gallery from Rose's photoshoot a few weeks ago, and she was thrilled. Curious, I answer the phone.

"Hey, Cynthia," I say.

"Hey, Exceptional Emma! How are you doing?"

"I'm all right."

"I saw you won that competition with my picture," she says.

Oh, shoot. Did I ever ask her permission? My nerves jump out of control. "I'm so sorry. Is that why you're calling? Are you upset that I used a picture of you?"

"No, no!" She laughs loudly, and I have to pull the phone away from my ear. "I'm so happy for you! That was a magnificent picture. You deserved the win."

"Thanks." I'm glad she thinks so. Not that she knows anything about photography, but I appreciate the sentiment.

"Listen, I'm calling because I wanted to see if you'd come and do another session for me."

"Oh? What did you have in mind?"

"I was hoping to get a family photo session in. Some with Calvin, Rose, and me."

I grimace. I'm not sure I want to see her right now. It's just another reminder of the past and how much things have changed over the last few months. So I use the first excuse I can come up with. "I don't really do posed family photos. I just like to capture moments in time."

"That's what I'm looking for. I don't want any of those fussy pictures of the family at the beach in white shirts and jeans."

I laugh out loud. She knows exactly what the trends are in this area.

"I just want you to come to my house and take some photos of what's going on here. Nothing fancy. I think you have the eye to capture what I'm looking for."

I put her on speakerphone and pull out my calendar. I don't think I can get rid of her now. "How does Thursday sound? Maybe around two?"

"Perfect." I can hear the smile in her voice, and I feel a tiny twinge of joy. Maybe I do have one in-person friend left. "I'll see you then, Exceptional Emma."

"Bye, Cynthia." I mark her name and the time down in my calendar and smile.

Everything is going just fine.

Chapter 24

I pull up to Cynthia and Calvin's house at 1:55 on Thursday. It looks similar to what I would have expected from her. The front yard is full of wildflowers of all colors and sizes, nothing like the perfectly curated rose bushes at my parents' house. I can imagine Cynthia out here on the weekends, getting dirty with Calvin and happily planting her flowers in the sunshine.

I try to let the cheery colors improve my mood, but I'm a little messed up this morning. After that grumpy client emailed me about a month ago with complaints about their session, I asked Mona for her advice. She looked over my pictures and agreed that the photos I provided were in line with my portfolio, the lighting issues were not my fault, and that I didn't owe them anything else. With her help, I wrote a professional but firm email stating my stance.

Apparently that wasn't good enough, because the client wrote a very nasty email back saying she was going to discourage anyone she knew from using my services.

And then this morning, she posted scathing one-star reviews on my Yelp and Facebook pages.

So, needless to say, my feelings are pretty raw right now. But the show must go on, especially on Photogram. The obligation to respond and interact is starting to feel suffocating. But I can't stop now.

The smell of the lavender hits my nose on the cobblestone path up to the front door, and I knock, smiling at the sign at the front: WELCOME TO THE JUNGLE.

Cynthia opens the door, a small smile on her face. "Hey, Emma." She pulls me in for a hug, and I squeeze her back. But I'm a little surprised by the less-than-enthusiastic response.

"Hey, Cynthia," I say. She walks into the house and gestures for me to follow. The house itself is a wonder. Bright fuchsia couches, orange throw rugs, and wooden knick-knacks sprinkle the room. Tall green plants live in each corner. Now the sign makes even more sense than before—it really is a jungle.

"Your house is amazing," I comment.

"Oh, thank you. Calvin and I have collected quite a few things over the last few years." She looks around and sighs. "We have a lot of good memories."

"Hey, Mom!" Rose's voice calls from down the hall. "Can you bring me a snack?"

I'm a little surprised to hear a grown woman asking her mom for a snack. I half-expect Cynthia to tell her to get it herself, but instead she calls down the hallway, "Sure thing, hon!"

Cynthia scurries to the kitchen and has me follow. We squeeze down the narrow hallway and into the kitchen, where Cynthia busies herself opening the fridge, and I take a seat at one of the barstools by the counter.

"I haven't told you everything," Cynthia confesses, turning around with an apple. She pulls out a cutting board and starts slicing the apple, and I wait patiently for her to explain herself.

"You're not here to take pictures of the family," she says. "Rose has…had an accident."

"Oh?" I look down the hallway, as if I'll get some kind of answer. Obviously not, since I can't see Rose anywhere.

"She's injured. Her ankle…" Cynthia aggressively slices the apple, and I worry for a moment that she's going to cut herself. She takes a deep breath and sets down the knife, probably realizing the same thing. Looking me in the eye, she says, "She tore her Achilles tendon."

I hiss in sympathy. "Is she in a lot of pain?"

Cynthia nods, tears forming in her eyes. "We hoped we could avoid surgery, but it doesn't look like it's healing well enough on its own. So she's staying off of it and resting as much as she can right now." She turns away from me and rummages in the cupboard for something.

Injured. A professional ice-skater, years and years spent practicing and rehearsing, to all lead to this. Going from being exceptional to laid up in bed and unable to do the thing she loves.

My heart pulls for her. "Is she okay with me taking pictures of her?"

"Oh, sure," Cynthia says, pulling the jar of peanut butter down and opening the lid. "Apples and peanut butter," she explains. "It was Rose's favorite snack when she came home from school every day."

I nod. "I'm sure she still loves it."

"She does." She scoops a big spoonful of peanut butter into the bowl. "I've taken quite a few pictures of Rose and my other kids over the years." She gestures at the wall behind me, which is a full collage of framed black and white photos. I get out of my seat and head over to the wall, in awe at the artistic photographs in front of me.

Not just the photographs, but the memories within them.

"These are incredible," I breathe. "You did these?"

"Mm-hmm," she hums. "I dabbled in photography for a while there, myself. I know how important it is to get those moments saved forever."

I study a few pictures in more detail. There's Rose, an adorable little girl, playing in the park with her two brothers. Another of Rose on the ice. Some more of the boys building a sandcastle at the beach.

"They're beautiful memories," I say.

"They are. And I'm so thankful I have them frozen in time. It's like I can relive those days every time I see them." She joins me over at the wall, and we look at them together. "But even in these beautiful moments are the not-so-beautiful parts of the memories, too. You know?"

I shake my head. "What do you mean?"

She points at the picture of the boys at the beach. "That day, my ex-husband and I were arguing. He didn't want to take the kids to the beach. He said it was too messy, and he wasn't in the mood. But I had promised to take them. So the kids and I went on our own. We had a great day, but I remember being so angry on the drive over, wishing we could have all gone together as a family." She points at the picture of Rose on the ice. "That day, I found out my mother had cancer. She died six months later." Then she points at the picture of Rose's high school graduation. "And that's the day my husband told me he wanted a divorce."

"Those are awful memories." I can't help the words before they come out of my mouth, and I instantly feel guilty for saying it.

"You're right. They are awful." She smiles at me. "But that's not what I choose to remember from those days." She puts an arm around my shoulder. "That's the beauty of photography, right? You take something that's ordinary, or sometimes even downright awful, and you make it beautiful. It's a gift, Emma. To take these moments and freeze the beauty in them. It's all in the perspective."

There's that word again. Perspective.

She points again at the picture of Rose's graduation. "So yes, that day was awful. And it could have been the worst day of my life. But that's also the day that Rose got her first professional ice-skating job. And that's what I choose to remember about that day." She squeezes my shoulders and walks back to the kitchen.

I feel a swell of emotion, almost a sense of pride in what I'm doing as a photographer. I love photography and capturing these memories. But lately it's become...a burden.

"Do you still take pictures?" I ask.

"I do," she says. "I like to capture everyday moments. Like you. But when I'm too close to the moments, sometimes I like to hire someone else." She smiles at me and picks up the bowl, then nods her head toward the hallway. "Let's go see Rose, and you can take some pictures of her."

I feel so inconsequential and unimportant. I shouldn't be here. This feels so private, so intimate, and I feel *wrong* being part of this emotional moment. But I follow Cynthia down the hall to Rose's room.

"Hey hon, here's your apples and peanut butter," Cynthia says.

"Thanks, Mom." Rose scoots herself up in her bed, watching an episode of Seinfeld. Her hair is piled up in a messy bun, her face free of makeup. She smiles at me. "Hey, Emma. Good to see you."

"You, too. I'm so sorry about your ankle."

She just nods. "My mom said you're coming to 'capture this pivotal moment in time.'"

I smile, but as she's about to take the bowl from her mom, I realize I'm missing my opportunities to take pictures. I'm so caught up in what's happening that I'm forgetting the real reason I'm here. I pull out my camera and start snapping pictures of her mom handing her the bowl and smoothing down her hair as Rose looks up at her.

I take a few pictures of the two of them talking, then set the camera down and look around the room. "I'm not...really sure what you want me to do."

Cynthia shrugs. "Whatever you think will help us remember this moment."

"Do you want to? I thought that's what all the pictures in the kitchen were about. Remembering the good moments instead of the bad."

Cynthia and Rose exchange a glance. Rose clears her throat. "I wouldn't call my current situation 'good.'"

"No. Definitely not." Cynthia agrees.

Rose smiles at her mom and takes a deep breath. "But sometimes...sometimes we need these moments to remember what's most important."

Her words trigger a memory, but I can't put my finger on it. I take a couple pictures of her talking, because the love and affection and, yes, adoration between the two of them is palpable. "Explain that," I say. "What do you mean by what's most important?"

Rose twists her lips to the side. "I've been so focused on skating. I got my first job right after I graduated high school, and I let it pull me away from my family."

"You were going through a hard time," Cynthia reassures her. "After the divorce, I didn't want to be here either."

"No, I know. But I let myself get sucked into skating, and I didn't remember what was keeping me grounded." She turns back to me. "I love skating. It's part of my soul. So this," she gestures at her ankle, "is killing me inside. And the uncertainty of what will happen in the future...it's eating me up. But at the same time," she squeezes her mom's hand and looks up at her with pure love, "I'm so grateful that I have this opportunity to rest and remember that life isn't about *what* you do, but *who* you do it with."

My heart pounds at her words. I hide behind my camera, taking picture after picture of Rose and her mom, the bond that the two of them have that I can almost taste in the air, and my chest squeezes tighter and tighter. And finally, I remember the moment that Rose's words reminded me of: the drive to the campsite, where I told Cami that the sad things help us appreciate the good.

And after I said that, Jacob held my hand for the first time.

But now, I've pushed away every person who's important to me.

Every.

Single.

One.

"Well, I'll let you take some more pictures," Cynthia says. I wonder if she knows exactly how Rose's words affected me. I wonder if that's why she brought me here in the first place. She leaves the room, and I keep my eye on the camera, not acknowledging that she's gone.

Rose doesn't say anything for a few minutes, just eats her snack and watches the tv.

I finally get the courage to talk to her again. "Are you used to this? Someone randomly taking pictures of you all the time?"

"I guess." She laughs. "It was annoying when I was a kid, but I'm glad we have that wall of memories."

I finally pull my face away from the camera and scroll through the pictures I've taken. They're pretty incredible, if I do say so myself. The room has a window across from Rose's bed, and the lighting is beautiful. But more than that, the raw emotion between Rose and her mother jumps off the screen and into my heart.

"Can I see?" she asks, interrupting my thoughts.

"Sure." I head over to the bed, and she scoots over, patting a space for me to sit. I hesitate a moment, then sit and hand her the camera.

"Wow. These are great." She scrolls through the shots, eyes wide, and I feel another swell of pride.

"Thanks."

"You must really love it, huh?" She keeps her face down, scrolling from one picture to the next.

I don't say anything.

She looks up at me again. "Don't you?"

"Love...what?"

"Photography." She says it like it's so obvious.

My heart pounds in my chest, and the tears well up in my eyes before I realize what's happening. "I don't know," I whisper.

Rose tilts her head at me and sets the camera down. She takes my hand in hers and squeezes it tight, and the tears start to fall.

"I don't know anymore," I say between sobs.

She doesn't say anything, just lets me cry. I wipe my cheeks with my free hand, despair over the last few months washing over me.

Have I made the worst decision of my life?

Did I push everyone away...for nothing?

And for a moment in time, I feel the loss of everything that was once important to me—my job, my family, my friends—and I don't know what to do.

Chapter 25

After an embarrassing crying session, I pull myself together and take a few more shots of Rose. Calvin comes home while I am in her room, and I get a couple of cute shots of him and Cynthia in the kitchen before I leave. Now I'm sitting in my car, preparing myself to go home and get a better look at these pictures.

But I haven't done an update on my stories in a while, and the obligation pulls at my conscience. I almost feel sick thinking about putting a fake version of myself online, but I should just get it over with. I flip down the visor and check my reflection in the mirror. My eyes are a little red and my face is puffy, but the filter should hide that. I turn on the camera, paste on a huge, fake smile, and start talking.

"Hey, everyone! Sorry I haven't done an update yet. Today has been crazy! Just finished up a beautiful session at someone's home. I can't wait to show you how these pictures turn out! Thanks for being here!" I blow a kiss at the camera and rewatch as I add the captions.

I watch the girl in the video, smiling and laughing, and wonder how on earth I'm able to pull her out of me when I feel so sad. I can tell I've been crying just by looking at my eyes, but will anyone else?

No. Because they don't actually know me. They know Exceptional Emma.

I sure don't feel exceptional right now.

And when I get to the part where I say I can't wait to share the pictures, I realize what a lie that is. These pictures are personal. Intimate. I don't *want* those moments shared. They were beautiful, heart-wrenching moments shared between a mother and daughter, and now it feels wrong to share those with random strangers on the internet.

But I can't say that to my followers. They would hate that.

So I post the video and start my car. The surrounding silence is deafening. I remember the days I would call Sharleen on my drive home from work, and we would talk about nothing. Even if I didn't get to see her that often, I loved knowing what she was doing and how school was going. We haven't talked in months.

I miss talking to Garen. Sometimes he'd call me in-between games to tell me about his latest tournament or to complain about how they updated the game and now all the characters were unbalanced. I didn't know what he was talking about, but I'd give anything to hear him complain right now.

My mom has called a couple times, but I ignored them. I still have so much anger built up toward her. Now I feel like that was a mistake. Before, she would call me and talk about her students, and I'd give her advice on dealing with this "new generation" who didn't know basic algebra and expected to pass her advanced calculus courses. I'd talk to her about my engineering work, and how I was using the math she was teaching in her classes. I'd vent about the people at work, and she'd listen and give me advice on how to deal with other adults.

My dad would call, just to say hi really quick. He'd ask about work and give me his fatherly advice on how to handle difficult coworkers.

And Jacob.

Oh, I miss Jacob.

His smile, his piercing green eyes, the way he was so patient and taught me everything, the memories I have of our childhood together and the new memories we made. The way he made me feel special, even if just to him. That what mattered more was the person I was inside, and not what I did and how accomplished I was.

The tears start falling again, fast and hard, and I can't see the road. I make a turn into a neighborhood and park down the street, hoping no one in the house will come out and see a hysterical woman having a quarter-life crisis in her car.

But I can't drive right now. I can barely breathe.

I've lost everyone and everything important to me, and for what? A hundred thousand followers and a first-place photo in a competition?

*What have I done?*

I cry and cry, gasping for breath, until my body literally cannot make any more tears. I'm all dried up inside. My phone buzzes with notifications, and I know it's people sending me messages from the story I just posted. With a shaky hand, I grab the phone and check.

Message after message:

*Can't wait to see the pictures!*

*Sounds amazing, Emma!*

*Great to see your face! You look gorgeous!*

Hah. There it is. Confirmation that these people don't really know me. Because I *don't* look gorgeous; I have puffy eyes and my cheeks are raw from crying.

They're well-meaning. All of them. And I'm so grateful for the people who have been following me this whole time and support me. But here's evidence that they don't know me at all. Because all the people I just thought of—Sharleen, my family, Jacob—would have instantly known I was crying.

But they're not watching me.

Because I pushed them all away.

I open a message and start to tap out my usual reply: *Thanks so much!* with a couple of hearts.

But I can't do this anymore.

I can't be fake.

Because I'm *not* Exceptional Emma.

I'm not exceptional, after all.

I close out the message and go to my profile page. I scroll through the pictures, seeing the likes and comments, mostly good, some bad, and I feel like I'm looking at someone else's life.

*What am I doing?*

I keep hearing the words over and over in my mind: I can't do this anymore. I can't be *this* anymore.

With a shaky hand, I click the settings button on the top and navigate until I find the button I'm looking for:

Delete Account.

I don't know who I am anymore, but I'm not Exceptional Emma.

# Chapter 26

There are only so many episodes of Planet Earth I can watch in twenty-four hours. My stomach hurts from all the Ben & Jerry's I ate, and the next morning, I decide to put on reruns of The Office to mix things up. Part of me just wants to hear the sounds of a workplace. I didn't realize how much I missed working in an office until I just sat and listened to Michael calling dumb meetings and Jim messing with Dwight.

I alternate episodes of The Office with bouts of crying and feeling sorry for myself. I have no friends, no family, and no passion. I don't *want* to do anything, and I don't know how to fix that.

I'm lost.

At noon on Friday, one day after my session with Rose and deleting my Photogram account, I hear a little squeal at my door.

*"I want to knock!"*

I freeze. I don't want anyone to see me like this. And who the heck would be here at noon on a Friday? With a little kid?

The knocks echo through my apartment, and I turn down the sound on the TV so they won't know I'm home. But curiosity gets the better of me, and I peer through the peephole.

And then I can't *not* open the door.

I unlock the latch, pull the door open, and whisper his name.

"Jacob."

There he is, standing in front of me. Without a second thought, I throw my arms around his neck and start sobbing. I can't believe he's here. I can't believe I'm feeling his arms around me, and I'm crying because I'm so lonely and sad, but also because he came.

He *came*.

For *me*.

He pulls back from me, sympathy filling his eyes.

"What are you doing here?" I ask incredulously.

He opens his mouth to answer, but gets cut off.

"Emma?" The tiny voice sounds again, and I realize that the tiny voice belongs to Jacob's niece, Cami. What is she doing here?

"Hey, Cami," I say with a shaky voice. I pull away from Jacob and wipe the tears from my eyes, finally feeling embarrassed.

"Are you okay?" Her eyes are wide. I'm probably going to give her nightmares.

"Um..." I don't really know how to answer that question, so I change the subject. "Hey, do you want to come inside? I think I can find some episodes of Bluey for you to watch."

"Really?!" She looks up at Jacob. "Tío, is that okay? Can I watch TV?"

"Absolutely." He gives her his heart-melting grin, and I open the door to my apartment and let them in.

Jacob looks around, taking in my place. "Cute apartment," he comments.

"I didn't realize you hadn't been here before," I say.

"You didn't really let me in." He looks over at me, clearly conveying the double meaning, and another pang hits my heart.

I move the tissues and mugs of tea from my coffee table and find some Bluey episodes for Cami. She bounces on the couch and grins from ear to ear.

"We should come here more often, Tío," she says.

He smiles at her. "Maybe we will."

I hope he does.

I lead him over to the kitchen table. "Want anything to drink?"

He shakes his head and pulls the chair out for me. "Sit. You look like you need a drink yourself."

"It's been...a rough couple of days."

He waits for me to sit down in the chair he pulled out, then sits in the seat next to me. Taking my hand in his, his piercing green eyes look deep into mine. "Tell me about it."

I inhale a shaky breath and start to describe the last few weeks to him. The picture of Cynthia and Rose that got me thinking about being adored. Winning the competition. The troll comments. Disappointing my family. The burden of constantly posting and comparing myself with other people. And finally, about going to Cynthia's house yesterday, and the moment it all fell apart.

"And for what? Just so a bunch of people online can tell me I'm good at something? Today they think I'm great, tomorrow they won't care about me anymore. There's always someone better, something new. I don't matter. Not to them, not to anyone."

"That's not true," he finally says. "You *do* matter. To me. To Sharleen. And Garen. And Mariam."

"Mariam!" I laugh. "How would you know that?"

"I saw her today."

My heart rate picks up. He saw her? Is he *seeing* her? I wouldn't be surprised. She's beautiful, kind, talented... Everything I'm not.

"Oh." My voice comes out as a whisper, and I look down at our joined hands. It must be a friendly gesture. "How is she?"

"Emma."

I snap my eyes up to his.

"She's Cami's preschool teacher. I didn't know that until today when I went to pick Cami up from school."

"Oh." *Oh.* Okay, that's a relief.

His lips tease up in a smile. "Did you think...that I was dating Mariam?"

I shrug. "Or...maybe Laurie?"

"Laurie?" He looks genuinely shocked, his eyes wide.

"I saw her in your YouTube videos," I admit.

He smirks, taking a moment to answer. "You watched my YouTube channel?"

Whoops. "Uh...yes."

"What did you think?"

I exhale. "That you're incredible. I was so proud of you."

"Thank you." He pauses a moment, taking a deep breath. "I started it right after we broke up. In a way, you were right. I needed to use my talents. But I figured out a way to do that without sacrificing the most important piece of my life—Sara and Cami."

I nod. "I understand that now. I'm so sorry I pushed you to go back on tour and listen to your dad."

He smiles softly. "Thank you."

I gaze at him, amazed at this incredible man. But he still hasn't answered whether he's dating Laurie. I look down at my hands on the table, unable to meet his eyes, and speak quickly to get the words out. "But I wondered if you were dating Laurie, since she was all into you at the studio, and we weren't together anymore, and she was in your videos."

"Emma." He puts his hand gently under my chin, lifting my gaze to him. "I'm not dating anyone else. I've been following you this whole time."

I furrow my brow. "What do you mean?"

"I made a fake Photogram account. My username was pho-to_luver. I needed to see you. To know that you were all right." He strokes my cheek with his thumb, and the tenderness brings another set of tears to my eyes. "I'm glad I did. That's how I knew to come see you today."

"What do you mean?"

"I saw your last story yesterday, and I could see that something was wrong. And then ten minutes later, your account was gone. I've been sick, trying to figure out whether I should reach out to you or if you'd be angry with me."

"Why did you do all of that? Especially after the way I treated you?" I ask, keeping my eyes shut to hold in the tears. My treacherous heart leaps, and I pray I'm not reading this wrong.

"Because I'm still in love with you, Emma."

My eyes spring open, and the tears fall down my cheeks.

"Don't cry," he says with a smile, wiping the tears away.

"You don't understand. I don't deserve to be loved."

"You do." He brings my chin up again. "You *do*."

And he leans toward me. I suck in a breath. This is happening. His lips are nearly on mine, just a breath between us, and then—

"Are you going to *kiss*?" Cami's little voice squeaks from the couch.

We jump apart, and I breathe a sigh of relief. Because kissing Jacob right now would probably have been a terrible idea.

I have a lot of healing to do.

Jacob stands and heads into my kitchen. "I'm going to...get a glass of water."

I need a distraction for a moment, so I get up from the table and sit next to Cami, whose attention has been captured again by the little family of dogs.

"What's this episode about?" I ask her.

"They're camping. The boy doggy at the next campsite doesn't speak English, but they still play together every day. And then he leaves, and she doesn't know, and she's sad."

"Oh. That *is* sad." I watch the little blue dog asking her mom where her friend went.

"It's okay. They're going to meet again when they grow up."

"Oh, really?"

"Yeah, it's at the end of the episode."

We sit together and watch the next few minutes. I smile at the end, where grown Bluey is sitting under the tree they planted as children, and her old friend says hello. I feel a stirring, a sense of companionship with Bluey and being reunited with a childhood friend.

"I like that episode," I say.

"So does Mamá. She cries when we watch that one."

"I think I can see why."

We sit in silence for a moment.

"You cry a lot, too," Cami says.

I snort a laugh. "Today I do."

"Why are you crying so much?"

I look down at this little, tiny, wise soul, considering how to put my feelings into words. "I tried to change things in my life, and I made some bad choices. I made my friends and family very sad, and I feel bad about that."

"What were you trying to change?" She blinks her giant brown eyes at me.

I sigh. "I wanted to be really good at something. I'm always so...average."

"Oh, average. Right." She nods knowingly, like she's trying to be a grownup having a conversation with another adult.

I smile down at her. "Do you know what 'average' means?"

"Uh huh. It means...pretty high up there, right?"

"Not really." She's so adorable, I feel bad bursting her bubble. "Average means...not bad, and not good. Just right in the middle."

"Oh." She thinks for a moment. "So it means...enough."

"No, it..." I begin to correct her again, but I can't finish that statement.

She waits patiently for me to tell her she's wrong, and to explain how being average *isn't* enough. How average is boring, that it's not what I want, and that being extraordinary is worth striving for.

But...maybe *I'm* the one who's wrong.

Maybe being average really *is* enough.

"Oh, no. Are you crying again?" Cami asks.

I sniff loudly. "I guess so. Sorry, Cami."

"It's okay." She pats my leg, then looks up at me. "Do you need a hug?"

I nod. "I would really like that."

She wraps her tiny arms around me, and her mass of brown curls tickles my chin. But this has to be one of the top five hugs I've ever gotten in my life.

"What did I miss?" Jacob asks. "Everything okay?"

I pull away from Cami with a smile. "I think so."

He holds up his cup of water. "You should really put your glasses somewhere more obvious. It took me forever to find this."

I smirk, and he sits down on the couch right next to me, stretching his arm up and over my shoulders. I settle into the curve of his upper body, and for the first time in six months, just...be.

⚜ ⚜

"...Yes, I'm here with her now... Cami's good. She's just watching Bluey... No, I don't know if that would be a good idea..."

I blearily open my eyes, my neck stiff from sleeping on Jacob's shoulder. I don't know how long I was out for, but it feels like it's been at least an hour. He's on the phone with someone, and I look over at my other side to see Cami happily watching yet another episode of Bluey.

Jacob squeezes me close to him. "Hey, lemme call you back." He hangs up the phone and rubs my arm. "How was your nap?"

"Good. I have a crick in my neck, but it's okay." I sit up straighter. "Was that Sara?"

He moves his hand up to my neck and starts kneading the knots. I close my eyes and relax. "Yep. She wanted to know where we were. And she wanted me to say hi to you."

I smile. "Hi back to Sara." I sit up and look at his unfairly handsome face, the green eyes that have haunted my dreams for the last few months. "What have you been doing while I was sleeping?"

"Thinking." He gives me a sad smile. "Just wondering where I went wrong and how I could have helped you more."

"Jacob, no," I insist.

"Shh!" Cami says.

"Sorry, *princesa*," Jacob says, then grabs my hand and pulls me off the couch and over to the kitchen table again. He pulls out my chair and I sit down for another conversation. Jacob doesn't sit, he goes straight to the cabinet where I keep my glasses (right above the fridge, which is pretty obvious if you ask me) and gets me a glass of water.

"You think you're all fancy now that you know where I keep my glasses, huh?"

He smirks. "I've always been fancy." He sets the water down in front of me and sits with me at the table.

I take a sip of water. "I don't want you to feel any guilt about this."

He shakes his head slightly, almost imperceptible. "I knew where you were heading. And I watched you this whole time. I should have come back sooner."

"No." I lay a hand on his forearm. "This was *my* journey. I needed to experience all of this to understand." I pause. "I don't know that I still *do* understand. Not completely. There's a lot I need to sort out."

"But maybe if I'd been here, by your side the whole time—"

"No." I put my hand up to his beautiful mouth and cover it. I can feel him smile under my fingers, his eyes crinkling at the sides. "This had nothing to do with you. I needed to do this for myself. But you came at the perfect time." I try to lower my hand down, but he grabs it and kisses my fingers, lighting my nerve endings on fire. "Thank you for coming back."

"You're welcome." He smiles with a twinkle in his eyes, knowing exactly what he does to me. But he doesn't try anything else, just holds my hand and sets it back on the table. "So, what now?"

"I don't know. I feel like I need to take it easy and back away from anything that was part of my 'Exceptional Emma' journey." I cringe as I say the words. I don't ever want to hear someone use that nickname again.

"So we should do fun things that make you feel alive again."

"We?"

He smiles. "We."

My chest fills with warmth, and my eyes fill with tears *again*, knowing that I'm not alone. Cami was right. I do cry a lot.

"Let me ask you a question," he says. "When was the last time you felt truly alive and free?"

Alive and free. I look out the window of my kitchen, taking a few moments to think. Have I ever felt that way?

I look down at our joined hands, and a memory strikes me. Yes. That was definitely when I felt alive and free.

"Dancing with you and your friends. When we were camping at the beach."

He blinks a few times, like he wasn't expecting that answer. "Really?"

"Yep. I know I wasn't good at it, but...I was happy."

A huge grin spreads across his face. "Well, that works out perfectly."

# Chapter 27

Jacob wasn't kidding when he said it was perfect timing.

Because tonight, Ricardo is throwing a huge bonfire at the beach, complete with dancing and friends playing the guitar.

And s'mores. Lots of s'mores.

Soon after our conversation, Jacob took Cami back home so they could get her ready for the babysitter. He promised that he and Sara would come pick me up on the way to the bonfire.

I won't lie. There were quite a few times I was tempted to pick up my phone and check my Photogram notifications. But the second I remembered I had deleted my account, I felt a freedom, like a weight disappearing from my chest. I wasn't accountable to anyone anymore. I could just be *me*. I could live my life, in real time, without anyone knowing what I was doing and judging it.

I wasn't exceptional, and that was fine.

The shower was probably one of the best I'd ever had in my life. I brought my Bluetooth speaker into the bathroom and blasted "Despacito," remembering the first night I went dancing with Jacob. I did my hair and makeup, got dressed, then watched a few more episodes of Bluey while I waited for them to pick me up. This show feels like it's almost more for the adults than the kids. I had to force myself not to cry so I wouldn't ruin my makeup.

The knock sounds at my door right at four, and I jump up to open it. Jacob stands there, looking like a Hollywood star, and I have to suck in a breath so I don't start drooling.

Thankfully, he looks at me with wide eyes, too, then a big grin emerges on his face. "You look amazing," he says.

"So do you." I pull a hoodie from the coat rack and hop out of the door. He holds his hand out to me, and I put mine in it.

"You seem a lot better," he says.

"I feel better." There aren't many steps to the truck, so I want to get this out before we see Sara. "I don't know what I would have done with myself if you hadn't come by."

He stops in his tracks and turns to me. His green eyes are searching mine, and I'm captured by his gaze. "You are a strong woman, Emma. But I'm so glad I was here for you when you needed someone to help you up."

The moment is charged and intense. I don't want to look away, I just want to be here in this moment with him forever.

But Sara has other ideas.

The horn on the truck sounds loudly. "Come on, guys!" she yells. "We're gonna miss the sunset!"

Jacob rolls his eyes but smiles, and we head to the truck. We're back in our usual spots—Jacob driving, me in the passenger seat, and Sara in the back. She says she wants to stretch out and relax since Cami isn't here tonight.

On the drive to the beach, I settle back into my seat and look out the window. No thoughts of taking pictures, perspectives, whether or not I should post something from tonight. Right now, at this moment, I'm living.

And that's enough.

We park at the beach and head over to the crowd. There are about twenty people around the bonfire, all watching the sun slowly disappear over the horizon.

Out of the corner of my eye, I spot something familiar: a playground. It's a cold January evening, so no one has brought their kids here tonight and it's completely empty. A huge smile fills my face, and I grab Jacob's hand, pulling him over.

"Remember this place?" I ask him.

He smiles and nods. "I remember playing hide and seek with you over here. You loved hiding under the slide, and you thought you were so smart."

"I was! You never found me!"

He chuckles. "I knew where you were. I was just pretending to look for you."

I gasp in mock outrage. "I'm insulted."

Still holding hands, we head over to the swings and each take one.

"I haven't been on a swing set in...probably eighteen years," Jacob says.

Eighteen years. Meaning he hasn't been on a swing set since he moved away. "I think tonight is the perfect time for a reintroduction."

We swing gently together, watching the sky painted in pinks and oranges just for us. The sounds of the waves crashing and the salty air fill my soul, and I'm not sure I can imagine a more perfect evening.

I look over at Jacob, and he's not looking at the ocean. He's looking at me.

"What?" I ask.

He shakes his head. "I'm just grateful to be here with you."

I slow my swing to a stop, rocking back and forth so we can have a conversation. "I'm grateful to be here with you, too. I haven't known what I've needed for a long time."

He opens his mouth to say something, then looks past me, over my shoulder, and smiles. "Well, it's a good thing I have an idea what you need."

"Huh?" I look over my shoulder and see someone I didn't expect at all, walking across the sand toward us.

Sharleen.

I cover my mouth in surprise. I'm not sure what her reaction will be, but she's here, right? So that must mean something.

I jump out of the swing and run to her. She mirrors my action and runs toward me, then squeezes me in a huge hug and tackles me down to the sand.

"Hey!" I squeal. "You're getting sand all in my pants!"

"Good! You deserve it!" She rolls us around in the sand for good measure, like a WWE wrestler.

I finally break apart from her, and she's panting, but her eyes are bright with laughter. I smile at her. "You're a punk."

She pushes my shoulder lightly. "So are you."

I nod. "You're right. I have been a punk."

She sits next to me and squeezes me tightly. "And I've missed you."

I rest my head on her shoulder and squeeze her back. "I've missed you, too," I say softly. "I'm so, so sorry."

"I forgive you." She pulls away and looks me in the eye. "It's not okay. What you did, and the way you acted, were not okay. But I forgive you."

I blink away the tears that are forming in my eyes, because I've cried enough today and I don't need to ruin my makeup. "Thank you."

I have sand all over my hair and my clothes, but I don't care. Because I'm with my best friend, and I know everything will be okay.

Just then, someone turns up the music on the speaker system, and everyone cheers. We're the only group on the beach tonight, but we're about to all warm up with some dancing and s'mores by the fire.

Jacob appears in front of me, holding out a hand. "Shall we dance?"

I look over at Sharleen, wanting to ask if she minds if I dance with Jacob and leave her, and she pushes me away. "Girl, you know I can handle myself. I'll just dance with..." She takes a moment to glance around the crowd. "Him." She stands up, wipes the sand off her body, and marches over to the eligible bachelor.

Jacob pulls me to standing, and I end up right against his chest. He smiles down at me. "That's a little closer than I was thinking."

I smirk up at him. "Then you shouldn't have pulled me so hard."

He laughs out loud and leads me over to the dance area with an arm around my waist. "Do you remember the steps?"

"I think so." I take a moment to listen to the beat, watch Jacob's steps, then try to imitate them. Even though I took a nap on him today, it's hard to concentrate when he's dancing so close to me. But after a few missteps, I get back into the groove and find the rhythm.

I look up at Jacob, and he's smiling down at me. "You're doing great," he says.

I shake my head. "I'm pretty bad at this."

He stops dead in his tracks, ignoring the people around us, and tips my chin up to face him. "You're doing great," he says slowly. "You're having fun, you're with your friends, and you're alive and free."

I blink a few times, letting his words hit my heart. And then I nod. "Thank you."

He leans in and kisses my forehead softly. But then he pulls back and gets into a dance position, and with a lightness I haven't felt in months, we dance.

Jacob dropped me off after midnight. We spent the night laughing with friends, eating s'mores, dancing, and even putting our feet in the frigid water. We still haven't kissed yet, but I think that's for the best. I still have some things I want to figure out before I let myself get carried away in him.

But it's late, and I can't sleep from all the adrenaline running through my body. I look over at my nightstand, and buried beneath the photography books is my journal. I slide it out from the bottom of the stack, feeling comforted already by just holding it in my hands. How long has it been since I've written in it? I flip through the pages, smiling at the pictures I drew of me in hip hop class, playing beer hockey, surfing with Jacob. All the energy I used to write for myself had been channeled into Photogram, and I realize I've been sharing so much of myself with complete strangers.

No wonder I'm an emotional wreck.

My fingers itch with the desire to draw and write again. So I pick up a pen and start sketching me, Jacob, and Sharleen at the bonfire.

But in my stomach, I know there's still one more person I really *need* to talk to right now.

I dial his number, knowing that he's still awake at this time of night. He might be in the middle of a game, though, so I'm not sure if he'll pick up.

Or he won't want to take my call.

But after two rings, I hear my baby brother's familiar voice. "Emma? Is everything okay?"

"Hey, Garen. Everything is fine."

"Why are you calling so late?"

Just hearing his voice is enough to make me cry again.

"Emma?" He sounds alarmed. "Do I need to come get you?"

"No, no!" I sniff once. "I just needed to tell you I'm sorry!"

"Oh, Em." I hear a few faint clicks of his mouse and keyboard, and then they stop. "You didn't have to do this right now."

"No, I really did." I wipe my runny nose, thankful he can't see me right now. "A lot has happened over the last few days, and I've been realizing how awful I let things become. And you're so important to me, and I'm so sorry for the way I've been treating you, and—"

"Okay, okay, okay," he says, and while his words sound irritated, I know it's just my little brother trying to keep himself from getting too emotional. "I get it. You're sorry. And I forgive you."

"I don't deserve for you to be so awesome."

"You're right. I am awesome. But you *do* deserve me. Because you're awesome, too. You just made a few mistakes."

"I did. And I promise I'm going to do better."

"I believe you." He pauses for a moment. "I already talked to Mariam."

"Mariam?"

"Jacob called her today. After he was with you. He kind of let her know what was going on, because she was so worried about you, too."

"Oh." I feel a little embarrassed that everyone knows all my business. But I guess it means I have people who care.

I sigh. "I have a lot of apologies to make."

"You do."

"Jeez, you could be a little more empathetic," I say.

"Nah, you need this. You were kind of a jerk to everyone."

The words sting, but they're true. "Yeah, you're right. I'm still trying to figure out how to make everything better with Mom."

"I might have an idea."

# Chapter 28

One week later, I pull up to my family's house, giant rolls of paper in tow. I take a moment to wonder if I should go through the garage like I usually do, or if I should ring the front doorbell. I haven't felt like a stranger in their home for years, but that's exactly how I feel now. Ringing the front doorbell will set Sparky off, though, so I decide to just go through the garage like I usually do.

Even so, the second I step in the door to the house from the garage, Sparky comes rushing over to bark at me. He stops when he realizes who I am and happily sniffs my legs, wagging his tail.

"At least *you* don't hate me," I say to him.

"Emma?" My mom's voice comes from the kitchen, and she emerges from the living room, wiping her hands on a towel. "What are you doing here?"

"Is everyone home?" I know they are. I made sure with Garen before I came over.

"Yes, they're all in the kitchen eating lunch." She looks at the roll of paper in my hands, but doesn't say anything.

"Perfect. I wanted to talk to everyone." I follow her into the kitchen, and I don't blame her for being a little cold. I didn't end things well, and I've been ignoring her calls. But hopefully they'll feel better about me in a few minutes.

My dad, Garen, and Mariam are sitting around the table, eating sandwiches. Garen greets me with a big grin, Mariam gives me a timid smile, and my dad just raises his hand to say hello.

"Hey, everyone. I wanted to come by...and apologize."

No one says anything, but I have their attention. So I continue.

"I'm not proud of the way I've been acting for the last few months. I've been selfish and self-absorbed...and obsessed with being better than everyone else. But things have changed for me in the last week, and I wanted to prove that to you before asking for your forgiveness." I take the rubber bands off the roll of papers and lay them out on the kitchen counter. My family peers over at the papers, curious.

I stand to the side, holding my arms out with a big flourish. "Here are the plans for your new deck."

My mom takes a couple of steps toward the counter and peers over the papers. I know she probably doesn't understand most of what she's looking at, but the smile on her face says everything I need to know. "You designed the deck for us?"

"I did. Actually, I made a few different designs." I flip through a couple pages and point. "This one has stairs that come down to the backyard." I flip through a few more pages. "And this one has a slide that goes into a pool."

"We don't have a pool," Mom says.

"But you could!"

She laughs, and there is moisture in her eyes. "I thought you didn't have time to do this."

"I made the time. It's important to me, because it's important to you."

The joy in her eyes fills my heart. She wraps me up in a huge hug. "Thank you, Emma."

"You're welcome, Mama. You deserve it."

Mariam and Garen beam happily at the table, but my dad eyes me carefully. That makes me a little nervous.

"Sit, Emma," my mom says. "I'll make you a sandwich."

"Oh, I'm okay, I just ate."

"No, no, no."

There's no point in arguing with her, because food is her love language. So I let her make the sandwich as I sit at the table.

"Mariam, how's work?" I ask.

Her eyes open wide in surprise, but she pulls it back to neutral. "It's going really well. I'm putting together a play for the kids, and they're having so much fun."

"That's right. Cami told me about that."

Mariam smiles. "She's playing the wicked witch. I think she has a flair for the dramatic."

"And what about you, Garen? How's gaming?"

"Good. I have a tournament next week, and I think Aaron and I have it in the bag."

"That's awesome." I rub my dad's arm. "How's work?"

"Good." He looks me in the eye, and I see a bit of skepticism there.

He stands, his chair scraping the floor. "Emma, come join me in my office."

My stomach drops all the way to the soles of my feet. "What?"

He pulls out my chair, not saying another word. Mariam and Garen just shake their heads at me, wide-eyed.

This isn't good.

I follow my dad to his office, the place I've only been a handful of times in my life. I remember the first time he called me in here, when I'd gotten into a fight with Mariam over her constant crying, and he told me I needed to be kind to her. The room hasn't changed much in twenty years—bookshelves line the walls, and the mahogany desk sits in the center. He sits behind the desk and gestures for me to take the seat across from him. After we're seated, he reaches into the bottom drawer and pulls out a bottle of whiskey.

"Oh, Dad, no thank you."

"That's not for you." He reaches into the drawer again and pulls out a bottle of red wine. "Don't tell Jacob I had other options. I wanted to see him squirm."

I snort a laugh as he pours us drinks. If he's joking, this can't be *so* bad.

He hands me my cup, and we take a sip. He places his hands on the table and looks me square in the eye. "I'm not sure I can fully believe that you've learned your lesson."

"What do you mean?" My heart picks up speed. Dad is the one person who has seen me for who I am my entire life. Even if he wasn't able to encourage me, he knows what makes me tick.

"I believe that you've gone through a tough time. And I believe you want to change." He pauses. "But it's hard to know that you won't just refocus your efforts on something new and lose sight of what's important again."

I blink at him, processing his words. And in a way, he's right. I've transitioned from school to engineering to my journey to photography and social media...and now what? He's not wrong; I always have some kind of focus that drives my thoughts and actions.

"I don't know how to convince you that you're wrong," I say slowly. "But I think I want to prove it to you by my actions."

He nods slowly. "All I ask is that you listen to us, Emma-jan. We love you so much and want what's best for you."

"I know." I sigh. "I don't know that you really understood what it was like, all these years, being...average."

He smiles sadly at me, takes a sip of his whiskey, and sits back in his seat. "Then explain it to me."

After a beautiful conversation with my dad (along with quite a few tears), we head back to the living room and watch some funny videos Garen insisted on showing us (I think they're funny, Mom and Dad—not so much). I'm about to head back home when my mom stops me and pulls me into the music room.

"I never got to see the picture you used for the competition," she says.

I'm surprised she's bringing it up now. "Oh. Did you want to see it?"

She nods. I pull my phone out of my purse and scroll back a few weeks until I get to the picture of Cynthia watching Rose at the rink.

"I used a picture from a session I did a few weeks ago. Do you remember Cynthia? From the beer hockey league?"

"Beer hockey?" my mom repeats.

I clear my throat. I can't remember how much she really knew about all of my original adventures on the path to photography. At the time, I didn't think they really approved of my journey to finding my *thing*, and now doesn't seem like the right time to go into all the details of my quest.

"Yeah, it was just one time. Anyway, her daughter is a professional ice-skater, and Cynthia asked me to take pictures of her rehearsing. I got a great shot of them at the rink."

I show the picture to my mom, curious about what her reaction will be. I never really shared much of my photography with them. When I first started taking pictures, I tried showing them my work, and they would smile and nod, but they weren't really impressed. I figured it wasn't something they were interested in, and it ended up turning awkward. So, instead, I kept it mostly to myself.

My mom looks at the picture, her expression difficult to read. This isn't like the normal times when she would look at my pictures. She's studying it, analyzing. My heart beats a little more quickly, wondering what she's thinking.

"What did you call it?" she asks softly.

"'Adoration,'" I reply.

She smiles at that. "Like Garen and Mariam's piece." Her smile falls, and she looks up at me, like she's seeing me for the first time. "This is what you wanted to feel. Adored."

I nod slowly, uncomfortable. "I just wanted to feel like people admired *me* for once, you know?"

Her expression is free from judgment, and she places a gentle hand on my forearm. "Did I never make you feel that way?"

"I...I don't think you did." It hurts to admit it to her, and I don't want to hurt her feelings, but I also need to be honest. "I felt like I always did what you expected me to do, you know? So even when I was good at math, it wasn't worth celebrating. I got a job, and that's what I was supposed to do, so no one cared. But with Garen and Mariam…"

"They got to do everything special." She brushes my hair back and runs a thumb over my cheek. "I'm sorry I didn't show you how special you are to me. You're my firstborn, and I wished I could give you the world. But we had you so young, and we didn't have the money to let you explore your talents—"

"I don't blame you, Mom," I say, cutting her off. I don't want her to think I'm accusing her of doing anything to hurt me. "You gave me the most important thing you could—a stable family and loving parents." Compared to Jacob, and everything he went through with his dad, I've realized lately just how blessed I am to have the family I do. I want her to know that.

"I'm glad you feel that way." She drops her hand to mine and squeezes it tight. "So, what are you doing now? Going to keep doing your photography?"

"I'm not sure." Glancing down at the picture, I realize I *do* miss taking pictures and capturing these beautiful memories. "I have a couple more galleries I need to edit and send to clients, but I've shut down my Photogram account and haven't gotten any new commissions." I look back up at my mom. "But when I worked on the plans for the deck, I realized that I actually miss engineering."

"Really?" My mom's eyes light up, but she tries to hide it. "I mean, if that's what you want to do."

I laugh. "I think so. But I don't want to get caught up in the rat race of corporate life again. I might try to see if there's some middle ground I can find."

"I think you will." She smiles at me with a teasing glint in her eye. "You could always go into teaching, you know."

"Maybe." I just say it to placate her, but I don't think that's what I want to do. "I have some research to do this week."

"No matter what you decide, I want you to know that we love you and you have our support."

"I do know." I lean in and give her a hug, and slowly, piece by piece, I feel my life coming back together.

# Chapter 29

After making up with my family, I sleep better than I have in months. I finally feel a peace within my heart, a peace that doesn't come from any kind of accomplishment or accolades. Just peace from being myself, and having a strong, healthy relationship with the people I care about the most.

Jacob and I are constantly in communication, and I've gone over to his apartment a few times to have dinner with them. We hug and cuddle, but he's cautious, waiting for me to decide to let him back in. I'm getting there, but I have a lot of healing to do.

This morning, I emailed Samuel, asking if they really did still have an opening for a part-time consultant. While I don't love the idea of going back to the same firm, maybe it will be a good way to get my foot in the door.

But now it's time to get through Cynthia's pictures of Rose at home, along with the other sessions I had done that week. It's nearing the two-week mark, and I need to act like a professional, even if I don't know what my future holds with photography.

I open up my laptop and take a deep breath before double-clicking the folder of my photography sessions. My heart races, and I feel the familiar sense of excitement and nerves at analyzing the pictures I had taken.

I start with the easy ones, pictures of a family session at the beach. The lighting that day was perfect, and the pictures were done well, so the edits are minor. I create the gallery and send them to the family. I get into a groove and knock out a few more sessions within the next few hours.

Then, finally, it's time to do Rose's pictures. I suck in a breath, nervous to see them on my screen. I hadn't even loaded them on my computer yet, because I was so upset after the session. In fact, I haven't touched my camera since I came home that day. So first I have to dig the card out of my camera and download the pictures to my computer. I bite my nails, anxiously waiting to see them on my screen, and worried about the feelings they're going to dredge up.

The folder pops up on my computer, and I'm slightly relieved that there are only one hundred pictures. I guess I spent more time sitting and crying with Rose than taking pictures. But the ones I got are beautiful. The first few are of Cynthia and Rose, the light from her window illuminating the two of them in an almost ethereal glow. There are a few more of Rose watching TV, a small smile on her face despite the wrapping on her ankle.

I touch up the pictures here and there, but they don't need that much editing. I put her gallery together and send it off to Cynthia with a personal message:

*Dear Cynthia,*

*I'm happy to send over the pictures of Rose. I hope they bring you joy and help you remember the beauty of these moments. I also want to thank you both for that afternoon. Witnessing the bond between you two, along with our conversation about what's really important, has led to some changes in my life (again). I guess it's been a big year of growing up, and I have you and Rose to thank for a lot of that.*

*So thank you for always being there for me, even as I work on figuring myself out. I hope to see you again soon. Maybe I'll stop by beer hockey league in the future.*

*Love,*

*Emma*

I send the email and realize I'm all done with my photography work. Relief mixed with disappointment washes over me, and I slump back in my chair.

I get an alert on my personal email and pull it up on another browser tab. It's from Samuel.

*Hey Emma,*

*Good to hear from you. Sorry to say that the consultant position has been taken, but I'll let you know if anything else opens up in the future.*

Dang it. My heart sinks. Even though I wasn't thrilled with the idea of going back there, it was my only option. Now what? I guess I'm completely back to the drawing board.

I scour engineering firm websites, searching for any kind of opening, when another notification comes in. This time it's a text from my sister. *Hey Em. Wanna grab lunch?*

I don't think Mariam and I have ever had lunch, just the two of us. But considering that I don't have anything else to do or anywhere to be, I figure it's worth seeing what she wants.

*Sounds good. Text me where and I'll meet you.*

The young server fills Mariam's glass with water, and she smiles at him with her princess face. "Thank you so much."

He beams, like he's been granted a wish from a fairy, and turns away, nearly knocking another server down with a tray full of food.

"Oh, you're too much," I say, taking a sip of my water.

"What?" She looks over her shoulder at the server, then back at me. "I was just saying thank you."

I shake my head. She's too cute for her own good. "How's work going?"

"Good. We're off today, so I figured I'd catch up with you." She takes a sip of her water, then grabs a piece of bread and starts breaking it into pieces on her plate. "I feel like we never really get a chance to talk."

I study her and realize that she's nervous. "I guess you're right," I say gently, hoping to put her at ease.

"Why is that?" She looks up at me, pausing her task. "You're so close with Garen, and I thought that having a sister would mean...you know, girl time. Getting to be good friends."

I wish I knew how to answer that without hurting her feelings. She's so *good*, so kind and sweet, but that's part of the problem. "I feel like I don't understand you."

She lets out a laugh. "What do you mean?"

"You're a walking contradiction," I say. "You're a genius, the most brilliant person I know. You could have been a literal *rocket scientist* at JPL. And not only that, you're so sweet and beautiful. You have so much potential. And instead...you're a preschool teacher." I grimace, thinking I'm going to hurt her feelings with that last statement.

But she doesn't look upset. Instead, she looks thoughtful. She picks up a piece of bread and finally pops it in her mouth, chews, and swallows. "You still don't know."

I shake my head slightly. "Don't know what?"

"What happened at the end of my last semester."

I blink at her. Something happened? "No. I don't know anything."

She clasps her hands together and sets them on the table, looking me in the eye. "You had just moved out, so it explains why you didn't realize how much was going on. But I had quite a few doctor's appointments that last semester of college." She looks down at her clasped hands, fiddling with her fingers for a moment. When she looks back up at me, her eyes shine with tears. "I'm infertile, Emma. I can't have children."

It takes a moment for my brain to catch up to my ears. My little sister—sweet, maternal Mariam—can't have children. The little girl who played Mommy with her dolls growing up. The little girl who said in kindergarten that her life goal was to become a mother.

She can't have children.

"Mariam," I murmur, reaching my hand across the table.

She smiles softly, squeezing my hand when it reaches hers. "I've come to terms with it now. Mostly. But I think you can imagine how..." She clears her throat. "How crushing it was to receive that news."

I can only nod.

She clears her throat. "So after wallowing for a little bit, I decided to make the most of my life. Maybe I can't have my own children, but I can still fill that piece of my heart."

"And that's why you teach preschool."

"And that's why I teach preschool." Her eyes light up. "I love the kids. I love spending time with them, making crafts, and watching them learn." She wiggles in her seat and straightens up a little more, the light in her eyes returning. "I love that I can teach them all about rockets in a way that makes sense to them. And because *I'm* excited, *they're* excited." She smiles widely at me, her eyes still full of tears, the emotion pouring out of her. "I love what I do. I wake up every morning, excited to spend time with these beautiful kids. And if I had taken that job at JPL, I would have felt so...empty. But now, I have something that makes me happy every day. Something that gives me purpose."

I feel like I'm seeing my baby sister for the first time. I ache for her, knowing the loss she feels, and I'm not sure how she's so strong. I wish I had taken more time to get to know her sooner. She's wiser than I gave her credit for. "I'm so sorry Mariam. I wish I knew."

She shrugs. "I didn't tell you."

"But I didn't make it easy for you."

She squeezes my hand. "I think we can change that now."

I squeeze her hand back and pull mine away, exhaling a deep breath.

She wipes her eyes, then looks at me with new determination. "So. What are you going to do from here?"

I sigh, adjusting to the change in conversation. "I know I don't want to do photography full time. While I love it, I can't tie my entire self-worth to people's perceptions of me online and how many clients I'm getting. And it's difficult doing it full time while not looking for that praise."

"I can understand that." She nods thoughtfully. "What about going back to engineering?"

"I considered that. I don't want to do that full time either, because I don't want to get caught up in the competition of promotions and bonuses and raises. So I asked Samuel about working part-time as a consultant, and he said they don't have any openings."

"Well, that's not the only firm in the area! I'm sure there are other options."

"Maybe. It's just another world I have to explore."

She tilts her head, studying me like a painting. "But you don't really want to work at a firm."

"I don't?"

She shakes her head. "Nope. You weren't happy there. I think you're happier being your own boss."

"I am?" I don't disagree; in fact, her words are speaking to my heart. But I hadn't really considered this side.

"You are," she says decisively. "You should do projects like the deck you designed for Mom and Dad's house. I bet there's a million home remodel projects happening in this area."

She's not wrong. It sounds exactly like something I'd love to do. And with all my experience now doing photography and marketing myself, it feels...right. A few butterflies start fluttering in my stomach, my mind starting to think through the possibilities of making this work.

"But that's not all," she adds.

I furrow my brow. "What do you mean?"

"There was something about sharing your life that you enjoy. But if there was some way for you to do it without all the negativity and the pressure to do it for the likes…I think you'd be happier."

I smirk. "I don't think that's possible, or even exists."

"I bet it does. I'll keep thinking about it." Mariam sits back in her seat, satisfied. "I know I can figure it out."

"How?"

She squeezes my hand. "Because I'm your sister. And no matter what happens, we're all here cheering you on."

*Chapter 30*

A week later, my mom officially starts construction on their deck. I'm a little bummed that she didn't choose the option with the slide into a pool, but it's pretty fulfilling to know that my designs are going to be used again.

So I take Mariam's suggestion and start searching for ways to get my name out there as an independent structural engineer. Without the SE license, I can still design most buildings on my own. Amazingly, I've found a couple of other home remodels that I can do, and the pay is incredible. Not being under a firm means I earn the entire cost of the job, which still leaves me enough to cover health insurance.

I get to be my own boss, feeling satisfied with doing work that I love, without the pressure of an office environment and competing with my coworkers. I feel free.

But now, I'm curling my hair in my bathroom, freshly cut thanks to Sharleen, and I get an email alert on my phone. Normally I wouldn't worry about checking, but it's from Cynthia, and I've been curious about her response to the gallery. It's taken so long for her to get back to me, and I've wondered why.

I open her message and read.

*Hey Exceptional Emma,*

*I hope you don't mind me calling you that. I know you shut down your account, but I mean it. You are exceptional.*

*I've been a little worried about you since you left our home, but I'm glad to hear that you're doing better now.*

*The pictures of Rose are beautiful. Thank you so much for taking them. Maybe I could have taken them myself, but as you get older, you realize how important it is to be in the pictures, too. I want to make sure I leave memories for my kids of our time together.*

*But I hope you don't mind this picture I'm sending. This is why I've hesitated to respond to you, unsure if I crossed a boundary. I felt a little guilty spying on you and Rose, but it was a beautiful moment that I thought you might want captured. If nothing else, just keep it for yourself and remember that there is beauty, even in our lowest times.*

*I know you shut down your account, but I also think you have a special platform that you can use for good. You may want to consider sharing the things you've learned over the past few weeks. I think a lot of people are wondering what happened to you, and being real with them could lead to a lot of interesting conversations.*

*But, of course, that's entirely up to you. Your mental health is more important, and I respect whatever decision you make.*

*I'm always here for you. And please bring that handsome dancer friend of yours to beer hockey. I think we'd have fun with him.*

*Love,*

*Cynthia*

I read the message once more, then scroll down to find the picture she referenced. I gasp out loud when I see it. It's Rose and me, sitting in her bed, and holding hands as I cry. The window behind us makes it so that you can just see our silhouettes, and the beams of light coming through give it an almost ethereal feel. As painful as that moment was, I can't stop looking at it. My eyes fill with tears as I look at the picture, so I close out of the app and put my phone away.

But the idea is in my head now. Should I restart Exceptional Emma? Is it worth the potential damage to my mental health to be back on there? I finish getting ready, the pros and cons weighing on me the whole time.

I shove the idea to the furthest corner of my mind while I grab all my supplies and head over to the dance studio. Sharleen is waiting for me outside.

"Laurie is *not* happy about this. I think she wants Jacob for herself." Sharleen opens the door for me and leads me into the studio where we reserved Jacob for a thirty-minute private lesson. He thinks he has a new student coming to train with him, but instead...it's me.

And no, we won't be dancing. At least, not until later.

But first, we have a setup to...set up. I teach Sharleen the basics, which isn't saying much, because it was one of my worst attempts as "exceptional Emma." We spend the next half hour getting the room ready for him. I don't miss Laurie peeking in through the window now and then, a scowl on her face. *Sorry, girl. He's mine.*

I look over our creations, giggling at the ridiculousness of it all, then push Sharleen out of the room.

"I don't even get to see his face?" she protests.

"Fine. You can spy from the window. But don't let him see you when he comes in."

She pumps her fist in the air and rushes around the corner to hide. I stand in the middle of our creations, and at one on the dot, Jacob walks into the room.

His eyes are wide as he takes in his colorful surroundings. "What...what is this?"

I gesture at my balloon animal display. "I wanted to do something special for you. Since I'm so supremely talented at them."

"If by 'supremely talented,' you mean you make them look deformed, then yes, I agree." He's next to me now, and he slips an arm around my waist, sending shivers down my spine.

"Well, yes. But I made you your own ocean animal collection, so you can feel like you're scuba diving."

He walks through the ocean of puffer fish, octopuses, and seahorses. He pauses near the dog and raises a brow at me, and I just shrug. Finally, he stops in front of the starfish, which has two legs shorter than the others. He picks it up with an evil glint in his eye. "I like this one the best."

"Oh, yeah? Why's that?"

"Because it reminds me of you. Always falling on your back." He pulls me into a hug. "But you keep picking yourself back up. And this starfish will eventually grow its legs back, too."

"I wouldn't be so sure," I murmur, and his chest rumbles with laughter.

I tilt my head back to look up at him. "I wanted to say thank you, in my own weird way, for everything you've done for me the last few weeks. Actually, the last few months. You've supported me and stayed by my side, even when I didn't deserve it. And..." My throat gets thick with emotion, but I will myself to continue. "You've shown me I'm good enough the way I am."

"Do you believe it?" he asks earnestly. "Because that's what's most important."

"I think so." I rest my head on his chest, listening to the pounding of his heart. "Thank you."

He wraps his arms more tightly around me, as if he can't get close enough. "Thank you for being you."

I look back up at him. "What do you mean?"

"When I came home, I didn't know what to expect. I was so upset about my mom, and Sara and Cami needed me, but I hadn't thought much about making my own place here. But I found it with them." He kisses the top of my forehead. "And with you."

My heart stirs at his words and their meaning. "I think we make a good team," I say.

"The best." He gently places his fingers under my chin, tilting my head up to him. He searches my eyes for permission, and when he sees what he needs there, he gently brings his lips to mine.

His kiss is warm, soft, and gentle, as we have our first truly intimate moment in months. I've ached for him, and this kiss is like the oasis I need in the dry savanna. I feel cherished and loved, deeply admired, and, yes, adored. I could kiss him forever. This moment, right here and now, is the final piece of my soul that was missing.

But even kisses have to end, and we finally break apart, smiles lighting both of our faces. And I look him in the eyes, and say the three words I never said before.

"I love you."

The smile he had before is nothing compared to the pure elation on his face. He kisses me again, then picks me up and spins me around while I squeal.

I haven't felt this happy in a long, long time.

"Oh, you two are just the *cutest!*" Sharleen cries, entering the room.

Jacob sets me down and looks over at her, then back at me. "Did she help you with this?"

I nod.

"That explains why some of them look halfway normal," he murmurs.

I gasp in fake outrage, but he's right. Sharleen's balloon animals look way better than mine.

"I hope you don't mind," she says. "I got some really cute pictures of you guys. Maybe I should find out how to become a member of the paparazzi."

"Don't you dare," Jacob says.

Sharleen holds her phone out to me, and I smile when I see the pictures of Jacob's face and the few moments of pure love we just shared.

"Too bad you don't have your Exceptional Emma account anymore," she says. "These would have been great to post."

I shake my head. "These are just for us. We don't need to share them with anyone."

Jacob lifts the side of his mouth into a grin and pulls me tightly to him.

"But I do want to talk to you guys about that," I say.

"What is it?" he asks.

I press my lips together, preparing to say the words out loud. "I'm considering reopening my Exceptional Emma account." I peek up at his face to gauge his reaction. While we made the balloon animals, I wondered if he or Sharleen would be disappointed if I did.

But Jacob just looks curious. "What would you want to do with it?"

"I'm not entirely sure." I peek over at Sharleen, who looks a little more unsure. I dig my phone out of my purse and find the picture Cynthia sent me, showing it first to Sharleen, then handing the phone over to him.

His face is solemn as he takes in the moment. "Was this at Cynthia's house?"

I nod. "It was kind of the turning point for everything. And Cynthia suggested...that maybe I should post it with an explanation of what I've been going through."

"You don't owe anyone anything," Sharleen says.

"You're right. I don't." I take the phone back from Jacob and put it in my bag. "I know that. Just because someone follows me online doesn't mean they're entitled to know everything about me. But I think...that maybe it would be a good opportunity to share the things I've learned over the last few weeks."

Jacob and Sharleen exchange a glance, and he shrugs. "I think that could really help a lot of people. But I don't want you to do it at the expense of your own mental health."

"I agree. That's why I'm talking to you about it." I take his hand in mine, then grab Sharleen's. "Both of you. If I do this, I want us to be a team. Not against each other. That way, you can help me if things get out of control."

Sharleen squeezes my hand. "You got it."

And Jacob then lifts my other hand to his lips for a kiss. "I'm there for you. No matter what."

# Chapter 31

Hi everyone. It's been a while. And as you can see from this picture, I've been through a lot.

About eight months ago, I started this account with the goal of finding what made me special. The closest people in my life told me I already was, but I didn't believe them. I needed praise and admiration—at least, I thought I did.

After trying ice-skating, video games, balloon animals, calligraphy, pottery, and surfing, I finally stumbled on the thing you know me for—photography. But being extraordinary at something wasn't everything I expected it to be.

As I got sucked further down the rabbit hole, everything started piling up: expectations from clients, followers, fellow photographers. I painted a happy face and posted in my stories and acted like this was the best life ever. But it wasn't. I was selfish, lonely, and sad.

It took a serious reset, including deleting this account, for me to realize that being exceptional isn't what I thought it would be. It's not about being the best of the best, because there's always someone better. Besides, in this world of social media, you're only seeing everyone's best moments. I didn't show you my terrible pictures, only the good ones. And it affected me, too.

*All I'm trying to say is that I want to live an exceptional life, and that doesn't mean being an exceptional person—at least not in the way I thought it meant. I want to feel alive and passionate. I want to be excited about the work I do, and to know that I'm making a difference in other people's lives. After all, isn't that really what it means to be exceptional?*

*So, will I keep doing photography? Yes. But only because I want to, and not because I want to act like I'm better than everyone else.*

*Because everyone is exceptional in their own way. You just need to know what you're looking for.*

# Chapter 32

## One Year Later

"**E**ven though I won first place, emptiness still surged inside of me. I had achieved exactly what I set out to do, but it still wasn't enough." I click the remote in my shaky hand, and Cynthia's photograph of me and Rose projects on the giant screen. This is the part where I have to fight not to get choked up. One year later, the photo brings up a lot of emotions.

I look out at the audience of one hundred people and find Jacob, who winks at me and gives me an encouraging nod. He already gave me a kiss for bravery before I began. This is the part where he's witnessed my many tears rehearsing this TEDx talk. So I do exactly what he told me: I take a moment to breathe deeply, calm my nerves, and continue on.

"And twenty minutes after this picture was taken, I deleted my entire account. I had one hundred thousand people following my journey and cheering me on, but I had lost the six people who meant the world to me." Next to Jacob sit the other five people: my mom, dad, Mariam, Garen, and Sharleen. Sara and Cami are there, too, along with Cynthia, Calvin, and Rose. "But it took me hitting rock bottom to realize that being exceptional doesn't mean excelling at something."

I click the remote again, and a picture of my family rolling dolma fills the screen. "The word exceptional has a couple of meanings. One is the way I always thought of it: 'unusually excellent,' or 'superior.' All I wanted was for someone to look at me and say, 'Wow. Emma is incredible. Look at her.'" I shake my head. "I didn't realize that the other meaning of the word was more fulfilling."

I take a couple of steps to the other side of the stage, my brand new Louboutins clicking under me. "The other definition, which is actually the primary definition, is 'unusual, not typical.' It's the *exception* to the rule. So I started thinking about what made me truly exceptional, or different, from others. I'm a woman in STEM, who loves engineering. I come from an Armenian-American family with an insane dog that I adore." The audience chuckles a little at that. "I love fancy shoes, but I also love watching nature documentaries with a pint of Ben & Jerry's."

I click the remote to the picture of me flat on my back in the ice-skating class. "And when I try something new, I try with all my might. I might end up as a starfish, flat on my back, but it's always worth it in the end. Because you never know what friends you might find."

Cynthia whoops from the audience, and I smile a little wider.

"Being incredible at something wasn't the solution I was looking for. At the end of the day, I wanted to *live*. And what does that come from? Passion. Love. Family and friends who support me. Likes and follows mean nothing to my value as a person. Do I have people who are there for me, reminding me when I'm being an idiot and cheering me on when I'm doing my best? I didn't have that when I was playing the part of Exceptional Emma." I switch to a slide of my current Photogram profile for Exceptional Emma. "This is what the

Exceptional Emma account looks like today. Instead of showcasing myself and my talents, I use photography to showcase what makes other people unique and special. Some of those things might seem ordinary." I switch to a slide of a veterinarian working with a dog, then to a grocery store worker, then to an elderly couple dancing in the moonlight at a wedding I recently attended. "But I hope that by highlighting the parts of ordinary people's lives that are actually extraordinary, we can start to believe that everyone is exceptional in their own way."

I take a deep breath and switch the screen to my last slide, a recent picture taken of Jacob and me salsa dancing together. Jacob is smiling, my head is thrown back in laughter, and my hair looks wild, but the love and life is leaping off the screen. "I propose we redefine what it means to be exceptional. In a world filled with competition and scrutiny, what makes your life the exception instead of the rule? Passion. Kindness. Compassion. And, at the end of the day, love." I click the remote and the screen turns black. I end my speech with Jacob's words to me on the beach that morning of our first kiss. "Please remember: in every way that truly matters, *you* are absolutely exceptional."

The audience erupts in applause, and I smile widely. I did it. It wasn't perfect. I'm not a natural-born public speaker. But I practiced my butt off for weeks, and I delivered the best speech I possibly could.

I give an awkward little curtsy, then exit the stage. Other presenters shake my hand and give me congratulations, but I wait anxiously for the person who matters most. The one who believed I was exceptional all along.

My Jakey.

It feels like an eternity, but I finally see him. And the smile on his face fills my heart with joy. We rush toward each other, and he squeezes me in a tight hug. "I am so, so proud of you," he whispers in my ear, then kisses the side of my head.

I'm so happy, I could burst. This last year has been filled with many ups and downs, but Jacob has been there for me through it all. In fact, we've been there for each other. His YouTube channel took off, which has been incredible for financially supporting Sara and Cami, but he's had to deal with his own difficulties of being in the limelight again. Together, we keep each other balanced, scheduling specific time to deal with social media and spending the rest of our days enjoying the world and people around us.

My family and friends all arrive after that, and I'm swarmed by hugs and congratulations. It's a little overwhelming, but I remember that this was what I craved for so long.

"Are we going out to dinner? We want to celebrate our girl!" Cynthia says.

I shake my head. "I have plans tonight. But we'll see you for beer hockey next week."

Cynthia huffs, but it's all in good fun. "Fine. We'll see you next week." She gives me a hug and whispers in my ear, "Proud of you, kiddo."

Tears well up in my eyes. "Thank you for everything."

She squeezes me one more time, then leaves with Calvin and Rose. Garen squeezes me in a side hug, Mariam's eyes are brimming with tears as she tells me she knew I could do this, and my parents each hug me, their eyes filled with pride. Cami hugs me next and leaves with my parents, ready to spend the evening making balloon animals with Mariam. Turns out Mariam is a natural balloon artist, which isn't surprising at this point. But it doesn't make me feel inferior, either.

So now it's just me, Jacob, Sara, and Sharleen. "Ready to go?" he asks us. We nod eagerly and follow him to the car.

The drive is full of loud music, car dancing, and singing. We arrive at the same warehouse where Jacob invited me for the "booty call," and I feel the tingling of excitement running through my veins. Because even though I'm not the best dancer, dancing with Jacob is one of my *favorite* things to do.

As soon as we enter, Sharleen finds a dance partner, and Sara gets swept into a dance with Ricardo. They've finally stopped dancing around their feelings for each other. Jacob is trying to play the role of protective little brother, but I know he's thrilled for her.

"Despacito" comes on the stereo, and I look up at Jacob with delight. "It's the first song we danced to!"

"What are the chances?" he says, a mischievous glint in his eyes. I don't know what he's up to, but he pulls me into his arms and distracts me with the nearness of his body. My feet find the rhythm, and even though I can't move my hips like Sara, I can hold my own on the dance floor.

"You've gotten so good," Jacob comments, as he pulls me back in from a turn.

"Why, thank you," I say. "I might not be amazing at it, but you know I love it."

"And I love you," he says. I thought I'd get sick of hearing those three words a year later, but I never do.

"I love you, too," I say.

He stops in his tracks, ignoring the music and the people around us. The hand around my waist pulls me in even tighter, and his other hand gently grasps the back of my head and pulls me in for a deep kiss. I forget about where we are and who's watching, because this man loves *me*. He believed in me when I didn't believe in myself, and there's no one in this world I'd rather be with.

He breaks away suddenly, then tugs on my hand. "Let's go outside."

"Now? It's pretty cold out there."

He tilts his head toward the exit. "I'll keep you warm."

I smile, then follow him outside. The air is chilly, just like I expected, but he wraps me up and warms me immediately.

"Do you remember the first time we had a conversation out here?" he asks.

I pull back and look up at him. "Unfortunately, yes."

He chuckles. "I do, too. But I don't think it was unfortunate. It was my first chance to connect with you, to see you as the woman you've become. And while you thought you were average, I thought I'd never seen anyone more beautiful." He leans down and whispers in my ear. "I love you, Emma. And I think I did when we were kids, in my own childish way."

I smile. "I think I loved you then, too."

"I don't want to spend another day without you."

"I don't think we have," I laugh. "We've been together pretty much every day."

"But I don't want to be apart at the end of the night."

I suck in a breath, because I think I know what he means.

"Emma, you are perfect for me. Even when you didn't know it, you were the most extraordinary person I'd ever known. I promise I will love you for the rest of my life, if you'll let me." He gets down on one knee, and I immediately miss his warmth. But the gesture means more than anything else. He pulls a velvet box out of his jacket and shows me the gorgeous, simple diamond ring. "Will you marry me?"

"Yes! Yes!" I grab his arms and pull him to standing, needing his lips on mine more than I need oxygen. He wraps his arms around me, kissing me senseless, until I realize I want that ring on my finger. We break apart and he slips it on. A perfect fit.

"I love it," I whisper.

"I'm glad," he says. "I can't wait to spend forever with you."

I look up at him, his eyes full of adoration, and I can feel his love down to the tips of my toes. Instead of answering him, I lean in and kiss his lips.

And that kiss is truly exceptional.

THE END

# Acknowledgements

This book has truly taken a village. I am so grateful for every single person involved!

First and most importantly, thank you to my incredible husband, Caleb. I'll never forget the morning we spent on the beach a year ago talking about this story and brainstorming things Emma could try. Thank you for helping me think through the story and giving me all your perspectives. You're the most wonderful support, and I'm so grateful to have you as my best friend. I love you.

My kiddos: thank you for always being patient with Mommy and her writing, and thank you for inspiring me to write feisty, insightful conversations with kids. Nova, thank you for telling me that being average is enough. (For anyone reading this, Emma's conversation with Cami is almost word-for-word a conversation I had with my daughter.)

My incredible cover designer, Melody Jeffries. Not only are you talented, you're an incredible person and I'm thankful to have you as a friend. Can't wait to keep designing books with you!

Chelsea! I will always and forever be grateful for our plotting conversations. You gave me all the inspiration for Jacob and his dancing, and you made the photography connection! You know I'll need you forever. You're the best.

My beta readers. Oh, goodness. I don't know what I'd do without you. Christina, Haley, Lola, Tiarra, and Sarah. Each of you added something incredibly important to the story, and I'm so thankful. Sarah, I'll always be grateful for your reminder that I need to go back to the story I set out to write.

My editor, Jennifer. You are AMAZING. Thank you for working with me on each book and knowing exactly what I need. You're the best!

The author friends I've made, thank you for keeping me grounded and pushing through the tough times. Monique, thank you for listening to all my rants and encouraging me to keep going!

And my readers: I never thought I'd have people say they were excited to read my next book. It feels like a dream. Thank you for reading, sharing, reviewing, and supporting my writing.

## *Also by Marie Soleil*

**Canyon Cove Love Stories**
Speak Your Truth
Feel the Rhythm
Let Love In
Nights Beneath the Stars
Take a Chance


**Once Upon a RomCom**
Cookies & Kisses
Cinder Luna (coming December 2023)

# About the Author

Marie writes heart-warming, sweet and clean romantic stories with big life lessons and character growth. She won the Swoony Award in 2022 for Best Debut Author. When she's not writing, she can be found watching The Office, playing the piano, sewing a dress, or reading a book (while consuming copious amounts of chocolate). She lives in sunny Southern California with her husband of 15 years, three children, and seven chickens.